Set in the 1850s and spanning time and place, this intriguing contemporary yet historical novel weaves a tale that immediately pulls readers into the story and engages them with both characters and plot. With a very special quilt being the tie that binds together two women from different centuries, *The Fabric of Hope* by Susan G. Mathis is a delightful read. —KATHI MACIAS, best-selling author of more than fifty books

A family legacy is woven together in an inspiring story, like the threads of the quilt that bind the two main characters together. Susan G. Mathis crafts a masterful tale, rich in human struggle and triumph. —AMBER STOCKTON, author of over twenty novels, including *A Grand Design*.

Travel with Margaret in the 1850s, and Maggie in contemporary times, and receive a sweet reminder that even when we face difficult circumstances, there is always hope in Him. In *The Fabric of Hope*, Susan Mathis stitches together a encouraging story of women from two generations and the heirloom quilt that ties their lives together. —MICHELLE COX, bestselling author of God Glimpses from the Jewelry Box, and God Glimpses from the Toolbox.

The Fabric of Hope weaves a compelling story out of the lives of two women joined by blood, yet living one hundred and fifty years apart. Both face daunting challenges and heart-trembling fears, both cherish the Irish crazy quilt that displays their heritage. Excellent dialogue and meticulously researched historical detail make *The Fabric of Hope* an enjoyable read. —Award-winning author LINDA J. WHITE

Brew yourself a cuppa Irish tea and settle in to read, *The Fabric of Hope*. Have you ever questioned God's plans? Susan G. Mathis masterfully draws her readers into her two heroines' lives. You will be inspired to persevere in your own challenges and reminded that God will work all things to the good for those who love Him. —LORI WILDENBERG, author of *Messy Journey: How Grace and Truth Offer the Prodigal a Way Home.*

Some family stories beg to be told—*The Fabric of Hope* is one such story in which Susan Mathis creates a compelling and heartwarming tale of faith, hope, and forgiveness, steeped in family history and linked to the present by an heirloom quilt. —JAYME H MANSFIELD, award-winning author of *Chasing the Butterfly*

Hope finds the smallest ways to change us. Susan G Mathis stitches an amazing tale of two women finding hope where there seemed to be none. This will touch your life.—VIRELLE KIDDER, a happy wife, nana, and author of six books

The Fabric of Hope is an endearing story where past and present meet in search for an Irish family heirloom. Maggie discovers her quilt is stitched with strong ties that bind family and faith together with certain hope for her future. Highly recommended! —APRIL MCGOWAN, author of *Jasmine* and *Macy*

Susan G. Mathis's *The Fabric of Hope*, invites us to follow elements of the rich history of her Irish immigrant family and her characters' connection to the present through a simple handmade "crazy" quilt which transforms over time into a beloved heirloom, emblematic of faith, family and friends, both old and new. A truly enjoyable read! —LINDA KOZAR, author of Cozy Mysteries and more

Susan G. Mathis takes readers on a compelling journey of hope and redemption that spans time and continents. This touching story of faith, family, and a mysterious missing Irish quilt is a wonderful read for those who enjoy historical or contemporary fiction. —JACKIE M. JOHNSON, author of *Praying with Power When Life Gets Tough*

THE FABRIC OF HOPE

An Irish Family Legacy

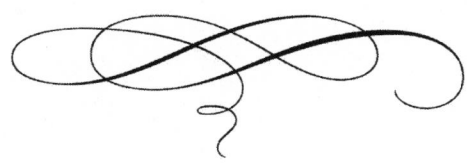

SUSAN G MATHIS

Published by smWordworks

www.SusanGMathis.com

Printed in the United States of America

ISBN: 1542890861

ISBN-13: 978-1542890861

tadderle@twcny.rr.com

Eileen

Banking that's right at your fingertips.

Online | Mobile | Telephone

- Instant account access 24/7
- Check balances
- Review transactions
- Transfer funds
- Make loan payments
- FREE eStatements
- FREE online bill pay
- FREE mobile deposit

www.cbna.com
1-800-991-4280

G-710
Rev. 12/2017

DEDICATION

TO DALE, whose love and encouragement made this dream a reality. Thanks for always believing in me, loving me, and cheering me on.

TO JANELLE AND SEAN for all your love and support.

TO MARY, my wonderful mom, who has been my lifelong cheerleader.

TO GRANDMA GRAHAM, and to all my Irish ancestors who gave me a legacy of hope.

TO MY EDITOR, BETA READERS, AND FRIENDS who have journeyed with me in my writing, thank you.

AND TO YOU, MY READERS. Much of what you'll read has historical truth, threads of truth, and patches of truth, all woven into a story of redemption. May you always find hope in your story.

SUSAN G MATHIS

CHAPTER 1
MARGARET

September 1850
Hilltown, Northern Ireland

"NO! I CANNOT TAKE ME family on a coffin ship!" Margaret Hawkins shook her head as she spoke her thoughts aloud to her eight-month-old baby. The drooling baby girl sat on the dirt floor, playing with a wooden spoon, unconcerned with her mum's words. Margaret stabbed her needle into the quilt on her lap. "How could Father even suggest such a thing? Half the poor Irish people don't even survive the trip to the New World. No!"

Margaret glanced down at baby Meg and tried to dismiss the unpleasant thoughts racing through her head. She felt much older than her thirty-two years and weary of all the troubles.

She resumed her work, holding up the partially finished quilt to survey the stitching before setting it back on her lap. She took off her spectacles and rubbed her aching eyes, but she was grateful to finally have a few moments to add a piece of her mum's favorite dress to the quilt. Maybe she would get one of Father's old shirts to add to it, too.

By the dim morning light of the calfskin-covered window, she sewed. From where she sat, she turned her ear toward the sounds of four of her six children, squealing and playing tag outside in the yard. She chuckled as she heard Susan, her eldest daughter, bossing the others around, as usual.

What a brood they be. Growing up too fast, that they are. I shall add a patch of cloth for each of them, and one day this quilt will tell our family history. Before it be done, it will be filled with fabrics from many of our dear family members who are now here, already in heaven, and one day, heaven bound.

Determined to sew as much as she could while her children played, Margaret hummed an Irish melody while her fingers worked. Though she felt a little guilty for neglecting her job of sewing a quilt for the English baroness who had a summer home nearby, work that would bring needed funds to their home, she had to work on her own quilt. For a little while.

The door to their tiny Irish cottage suddenly banged open. Thirteen-year-old Michael bolted through it, breathless and red-faced. "It's Grandfather, Mum. Dead in his bed!"

Her hands froze. Margaret held her breath at the pain in her eldest son's eyes. Yet she could not move or speak or console the lad as her own eyes filled with unbidden tears.

He had to be wrong!

Margaret's husband, James, quietly stepped in behind their son and shushed him. Then James gently touched her shoulders. "Did you hear him, lamb? Your father be found this morning when Sara called him to breakfast. We must go presently and tend to his wake."

Her hands began to shake and Margaret dropped the needle in her lap. She let out a piercing wail, covered her face with her hands, and crumpled in the chair.

It cannot be true. It must not be true!

"Ah, lamb. I know…" James bent down and embraced her. His strong muscles held her tightly and stroked her hair.

"Who brought these bad tidings?" she cried.

"Grandfather's neighbor boy, Conor, came on horseback." Michael's voice cracked. "He met Father and meself in the field. 'Twas a good deed he did presently, don't you think?"

Margaret nodded to her eldest and clung to her husband as she wiped a river of tears from her cheeks.

"We must go," James said and shook her tenderly. "'Tis important to lay him out before nightfall. 'Tis only fittin' for a man like your father."

Her kind husband brushed a wisp of her hair back into place as she trembled in his arms. He rubbed her back, trying to soothe her. "Ah, lamb. I know. I know…but we must go."

The cry of wee Meg brought her back to her motherly concerns. Margaret shook herself, took a gulp of air, and left her husband's arms, turning her attention to the child. She wiped her eyes and nose on the sleeve of her dress as she picked up the babe and held her close.

"Michael, take the wee one outside," James said. Michael obeyed and took Meg. At the sight of her son's sad face, Margaret whimpered and plunked down on the chair.

"He…he can't be gone," she sobbed. "Father be healthy and well. He was going to take us to the New World. Now we cannot go. We can't leave him here…alone."

"There, there, lamb. The good Lord musta wanted him in heaven with your mum. We must take heart and be on our way."

Margaret furrowed her brow and stared at her husband. His kind, dark eyes somehow gave her the strength to prepare to go. She stood and began her unwanted task.

James joined her as she silently gathered a few things they needed for burial, along with a handful of cooked potatoes for a meal on the journey, and changes of clothes for each of them. Like a corpse, she plodded through.

Margaret wiped down the already clean, hand-hewn table James had made. She glanced at the three beds—one for herself, James, and the babe, one for the laddies, and one for the lassies—which stood like silent soldiers on the far end of the one-room cottage. As she went over to the lads' bed and fidgeted with the quilt, she heard the eldest nearly shouting outside the window.

"Grandfather be dead I tell you!" Michael shouted as he spread the news to his younger sisters and brothers outside their thatched cottage.

Margaret froze at the sound of Michael's announcement. She looked at James, imploring him to do something, anything, to stop this terrible day. The sounds of her children's whimpering broke her heart. James walked over to her, touched her cheek, and left to gather their children to help ready the wagon.

"Me poor babes. How they loved their grandfather. As I did." she whispered as she picked up the basket of goods. "How can we bear it?"

With the heavy farm wagon loaded and ready, each of them climbed in for the nearly two-hour journey to Father's house in the town of Newry. The mid-morning sky was filled with billowy clouds that seemed to threaten a spring storm. Margaret took a whiff and couldn't smell any rain. It didn't matter now.

As the horse began his gait, she settled beside her husband and held the baby in her arms, fighting the emotions that threatened to overwhelm her again and again. The other children huddled uncommonly still in the back of the wagon. But not Susan.

"What shall we do without Grandfather?" nine-year-old Susan asked, sniffling back tears. "He be our North Star. Least that's what you call him, Mum."

James answered before Margaret could. "He be with Jesus now, child, so hush."

They stopped at the nearest neighbor's home to confer the news and request help with the farm while they were gone. That done, they resumed the journey to Newry.

They jostled along the rough, dusty road as they passed the endless rolling, green pastureland. Herds of sheep and a few cattle speckled most of the green hills, while vast fields of ryegrass sprung up on others. Margaret's heart tightened as she considered her father's request to leave this beautiful land she loved.

Baby Meg nursed while Margaret listened to the rest of her brood, all too quiet for her comfort. She shifted on the bench and glanced over her shoulder to see her frail, little two-year-old John staring at the sheep and cattle on the hillside. He seemed unaware of the heartache and sadness that surrounded them, and she was grateful. And though shy Mary, barely four, and energetic Ned, barely six, appeared to know something was wrong, she surmised that neither fully understood.

But her eldest two, Michael and Susan, did. She could hear it in their voices as she strained to listen to their conversation.

"Grandfather should not have stayed alone in that house after Granna died." Michael's dark, teary eyes blazed with grief turned to anger. "'Twas a stubborn man, Grandfather."

"You're just like him." Margaret watched Susan toss her thick, unruly braids and wipe her face. Susan's dark brown eyes glared at him to make her point. "He was a good man, Michael, and we'd best not talk bad about him. We should be thankful he's with Jesus and Granna. That's what I think."

"But he was going to teach me more ciphering." Michael's voice cracked.

Margaret pursed her lips and shook her head as she glanced at her daughter. Susan's eyes were almost too big for her face. Combined with the constellation of freckles dancing over her nose and cheeks, she appeared young and childish. But Susan always spoke her mind, even as a wee thing.

Margaret heard them, but she couldn't find the words to end the unwelcome conversation. She knew Susan's tender heart had always smoothed things over with her brother before, so she waited and listened.

"You can learn to more ciphering in hedge school, Michael," Susan insisted, placing her hand on Michael's forearm.

SUSAN G MATHIS

Margaret squinted as a ray of sunshine burst through a bank of clouds and lit up Michael's curly red hair until it almost appeared to be on fire. Hot tempered he was, yet the tears in his eyes said he was sad and in no mood for smoothing over.

"It won't be the same." Michael scowled at his sister, shaking her hand off his arm.

"No, it won't," Susan agreed, ending the conversation with another round of quiet sniffs.

Margaret's throat constricted and she turned back to face the road. Susan had made amends. Good. She patted the baby's back as they passed the tiny hamlet of Hilltown, where friends and acquaintances waved greetings. Then they plodded on through the larger village of Mayobridge.

As the wagon neared Derry Lake, James pulled under a tree, stretch their legs, and eat their potatoes. Margaret handed the baby to Susan and left the family to walk along the shore alone. She needed time to think before she got to Father's house. Before she saw his lifeless body.

Dear God, I'm all that's left of me father. He loved me always, even when I married me James, a poor sheep farmer. He depended on us. How can he be gone?

After a moment, Margaret turned and gazed on the man she married, the father of her brood. She looked at her gentle James from afar, even as he made his way toward her. She admired him. Loved him. Still handsome after all these years—short and stocky, with jet-black hair graying nicely at the temples even though he was only a year older than she. Strong as an ox, but his heart was as tender as the lambs he raised.

"Shall we move on?" James asked as they met.

"We must. We have much work to do before nightfall."

* * *

By early afternoon, the grieving family entered the bustling town of Newry, the place of Margaret's birth, her father's home, and his soon-to-be resting place. Margaret kept her eyes straight ahead as they rounded the corner to his neighborhood, purposely avoiding the gaze of anyone who looked their way. By now the neighbors surely knew the sadness that had befallen them. Margaret was keenly aware that by sunset, friends and neighbors would come to say goodbye to Edward Caulfield, this good and wise man, this rock of the Newry community.

When the family arrived at the five-room, whitewashed, thatched home that was Father's, James clucked his tongue and tugged on the reins as the creaking wagon rolled to a stop. Wordlessly, Margaret passed Meg to her husband before climbing down to the ground. She dusted her heavy skirt and stared in silence at the house, then put one foot in front of the other, forcing herself to face whatever came next. She left James outside with the children and went to her father's room, alone, to bid him a private farewell, to be with him one last time.

There he lay in his bed, still in his nightclothes, as if he were sleeping. But he wasn't sleeping. He was white and lifeless and…gone! She sucked in her breath as the reality of his passing filled her heart. She perched on the edge of his bed and touched his hand as a barrage of memories flooded her mind. She remembered the warmth of his love for her, and she began to wail. While Margaret didn't want her cries to frighten the children, she knew her grievous wails permeated the walls, yet she desperately needed to let out the depth of her pain.

Before she came out of her father's room, Margaret steeled herself for what had to be done. She had to be strong. She had to do her duty.

She squared her shoulders and determined to carry on as her father's only child. She turned into the kitchen, nodded to her brood, and silently waited as James took the children to say their goodbyes too.

When the children returned, Margaret shooed them all out of the house to play in the yard, save Susan. She bid Susan to wash the dishes and tidy the kitchen while she took to a flurry of work, preparing the body for the wake. With the help of Sara, the plump, elderly housekeeper, Margaret lovingly washed her father's body and dressed him in his best Sunday suit. Then Sara helped her lay the body upon the dining room table, as was the custom. Finally, Margaret adjusted the pennies on his eyelids, tenderly brushed his gray hair off his forehead, and bent down to kiss his ashen, wrinkled cheek as Susan came out of the kitchen and silently watched her mum.

"'Tis a handsome job, me lady," Sara said. "Such a kind man, he was. Such a grievous day."

Susan stood timidly against the wall, her big eyes staring at her lifeless grandfather. Margaret knew her daughter well; Susan needed to be busy at such a terrible time as this. She kissed her daughter's forehead, gave her a cloth, and bid her to dust. Susan scurried to the living room and began to furiously wipe down the furniture.

As they worked, several times Margaret noticed that Susan sneaked glimpses of her grandfather through the wide doorway. When she came in to dust the dining room, Margaret heard her mumbling to herself.

"Can't be touching no dead body," Susan whispered as she dusted the table legs. "Even Grandfather. Gray and cold he looks, like he's needing a hug." Tears rolled down Susan's cheeks, but she brushed them away, trying not to let her mum see her.

But Margaret did see. "Come here, sweet child, and put these cups on the drain board." She pointed to the cups as she touched Susan's shoulder, and the poor lassie fell into her arms.

"Oh, Mum, 'tis such a tragic day." Susan pressed against her mother's body, her shoulders shaking.

"'Tis true, sweet lassie, but we've no time for this." Margaret smoothed her daughter's hair and hugged her. "People will be here afore long."

* * *

8

By and by the first neighbors and friends came through the door. Margaret took in a deep breath, smoothed her skirt, and prepared for a long evening of greeting guests, enduring neighborhood gossip, and hosting an event she wished had never come.

The house soon filled with familiar faces, including the minister, and the evening slowly wore on, with many prayers and people and promises of heaven. The shrill wails of the keening and drone of the Gaelic prayers sounded like fingernails on a butter churn to her ears, and she shuddered. But surely, she could pay no mind to it nor think about her own deep heartache, at least for the moment. The mourners kept on coming; the long queue stepped through the door into the crowded room to say their goodbyes.

Neighbors and fellow churchgoers waited patiently to give their hugs and condolences. Several brought food and drink that Sara gracefully tended to and even accepted help from her closest friends. A few men sang hymns of hope.

In between the waves of people, Margaret walked around, numb, listening to conversations while she tried to keep an eye on the children—all six of them. The children stayed quiet, and she was glad of it. Even baby Meg barely cooed as Margaret passed her to James. Michael sat in the dining room, stiffly staring at his grandfather, while Susan bustled about the crowd, trying to serve and do anything she could, as if she was trying to make the night pass quickly.

Those two be like night and day! But I be blessed to have them all.

Margaret scanned the room for the others. Ned and John had chosen a far corner to quietly play with a handful of pebbles, while Mary sat on the lap of one of the grannies, sucking her thumb and absorbing all the love she could. She caught Mary's eye and nodded, pleased she was content.

For more than two hours, neighbors, friends, and strangers continued to file past her to see her beloved father. She tried to smile and be grateful for their love and concern, but it took all the strength she could muster.

I'd rather be in the corner with Ned and John.

A gruff, deep rumble of a man's voice interrupted her thoughts. "Excuse me, lass. Today be a grievous day to be telling you this, but your father be owing a mighty lot of death tax." Margaret turned to see a rotund, white-haired man staring at her.

"Pardon me, sir?"

"The tax will be taking it all." He shook his head and waved his arm to indicate everything in the house. Without another word, he moved into the dining room to view her father's body.

Realizing the implications, panic coursed through Margaret. She scanned the room for James and his comforting strength, but when she didn't see him, she felt the room spin, let out a deep groan, and fell into the nearest seat.

* * *

When the last mourner had left, Margaret slumped down on a dining room chair. James kissed her, brushed his hand over her thin hair, and left her to nurse the baby. Meanwhile, James gathered the children and readied them for bed, creating makeshift pallets for the older children on the living room floor and putting Mary and John foot-to-foot on the sofa. No one wanted to sleep in Father's room. No one would.

Tears flowed as Margaret bid the children goodnight and shuffled back to the tiny guest room. *Too quiet. Deadly quiet. In the morning I will see me father, me precious father, put in the cold, hard ground. How will I ever bear it?* She lovingly burped Meg, kissed her, and laid her down to sleep on a bed she made of a quilt. The windowless room and deep darkness closed in on Margaret, so she opened the door and found James in the hallway.

James entered the room and the two donned their nightclothes. Margaret told him about the tax man. "He said Father would owe a lot of tax. James, what will we do?"

"The Lord knows, lamb. We shall trust Him." James took her in his arms and held her close. She had stayed strong all evening, but now she had to mourn.

* * *

The morning dawned with a cold, misty fog. Margaret put on her spectacles and steeled herself for the day ahead. Today she refused to cry.

Not today. Father would not want it.

Margaret hugged each of the children as they awakened and bid them to don their Sunday best she brought from home. She gave each of them a hearty bowl of porridge and tried to cast an air of strength so the children would follow her lead. Even when James entered the kitchen, Margaret smiled and gave him a reassuring nod.

All day long she bravely held true to her determination. She stayed strong, unwavering—all through the eulogy and even when they lowered her father into the musty, wet ground. Her silence and strength were the last gifts she could give to him.

After the last mourner keened her sorrow, Margaret still refused to shed a tear, didn't whimper or moan or wail. Yet she knew her eyes betrayed the fear that had taken hold of her no matter how hard she tried to hide it. Emigrating to the New World without her father's leadership? How could she leave him behind and move on? And what about the tax man? A terrible many unanswered questions filled her mind even as the pain of her loss filled her heart.

* * *

The next morning, Margaret awoke to the rare smell of bacon. Where was she? What had happened? Finally her mind became aware of her reality, and she began to cry uncontrollably.

James entered the room, hurried to her side, and took her

in his arms. "'Twill be all right, one day. Can you smell the gift from the O'Brian family? Let us enjoy the bounty, if only for a day."

Margaret found strength and peace in her husband's arms. She took several deep breaths, blew her nose, and rose to dress for the day. After she gathered her composure, James handed her a sealed envelope with her name on it, written in her father's hand.

"This, me love, be from your father. His solicitor delivered it just now."

James kissed her, patted her shoulder, and left the room. When the door closed, she slowly put on her spectacles and began to read.

Dearest Margaret,

You have been the joy of me life, the sunshine of me days. Your sweet family has filled me quiver to the full. If you are reading this, you have laid me to rest. I am with Jesus and your mum, and I am content. Do not mourn, daughter. We will meet again one day.

I must ask you to do something very brave. Our homeland, our beloved Ireland, has not been good to us these many years, and I fear it will continue to betray its people with even more sorrow.

You must go on to the Promised Land without me. Your husband's Uncle John has invited you to join him in Canada. I plead with you to take your sweet lads and lassies and make a new life there. Our great Ireland be no longer a good place for our family. It be a cursed land that will take your children from you if you stay.

Go, dearest daughter. Flee this place! Flee the hardship, the hatred, the hunger, the cruel landlords, the British rule. Find a new world that will allow you to worship God and grow food aplenty.

No doubt the journey will not be easy. But determine to start anew. Move to the new land that awaits you. Be strong for your father, for your husband, for your children, and for all the generations to come who will find a new life in that new land.

Your mum and I will look down from heaven, urging you on, praying for you and your children, your grandchildren, your great-grandchildren to come. They will know what a strong and brave woman you are, and they will be thankful.

I am proud of you, daughter. Godspeed!
Your most affectionate Father

Margaret sat for a long time, holding the letter to her breast. *How can I leave me homeland, me precious Ireland? How can I be strong when me heart is filled with fear and hopelessness? How can I be brave and obey me father's last request?*

CHAPTER 2
MAGGIE

July 2010
Colorado, USA

MAGGIE DOLAN GAZED OUT the open window at the view of Pikes Peak and the Rocky Mountain Front Range. In the distance, storm clouds gathered quickly along the mountains. Music, a little too loud, drifted down the hallway from her teenage daughter's bedroom. Maggie's grip on the phone tightened as she waited for Bill to pick up.

"Hello." The voice on the other end of the line sounded thick with sleep.

"Where is it, Bill?" She fidgeted and tried to control the tremble in her words, but it was no use. Her ex-husband's presence—even the sound of his voice—always made her feel shaky. "Where. Is. It?"

"Maggie." Bill yawned into the phone.

"It's gone! It's not in my hope chest where I always kept it. I spent the entire morning searching through the few belongings you 'kindly' left me. I looked in every closet, every box. Even in the Christmas stuff. Mom entrusted it to me to give to Bree someday. *Where* is my family's heirloom quilt, Bill?" With her free hand, she tucked her unruly hair behind her ear and then slammed the window shut.

"Get a life. You're crazy. I don't know what you're talking about."

"Oh, yes, you do! I want it back." Her eyes burned with tears and her face flushed at his nonchalant attitude. When the line went dead, Maggie turned around and threw her smartphone at the sofa. It bounced onto the floor and broke apart.

Great. Just great! She looked at the scattered pieces with little emotion. *Like my life.* Hot tears threatened to spill down her cheeks.

How could he?

There were no answers. It had been an ugly divorce. The injustice of losing so much left her exhausted and overwhelmed. Anger and frustration surged through her, not for the first time. And now this…he'd actually taken her heirloom quilt and wouldn't fess up? The betrayal was nearly more than she could bear.

"I gave him sixteen years of my life, and he tells me to get a life? Ahhh!"

Sheets of rain began to patter against the window. After a few moments, Maggie knelt down and gathered her phone, the battery, and the cover. Her eyes brimmed with tears as she tried to put the pieces back together. They refused to hold back all the feelings of betrayal and sadness. She gave in to her despair and dropped down on the living room floor, shaking with quiet sobs, not wanting to alarm her daughter, Briana.

When the tears subsided, Maggie hugged her long, thin legs. She rested her chin on her knees and bit her lip. With a weary sigh, she pulled herself up and sat on the sofa and looked out at the stormy summer day. Clouds flew past her window and the wind howled. She grabbed a tissue and blew her nose as hopelessness washed over her.

The storm out there feels like the storm inside me. I can't take this, Lord! How am I going to keep us afloat with my pittance of a salary—when Bill is living free and easy?

I know he took our family heirloom, my crazy quilt! How will I tell my mother? Our family's only link to Ireland. Why did he have to take that? Where could it be?

Her emotional exhaustion muddied her mind and weakened her resolve. All the losses piled on her, higher and higher, their weight crushing her. She had tried to be strong—for her daughter, for herself, for God. But this? Feeling like a caged bird, Maggie got up and stood by the sliding glass door, wishing she could be free.

"That quilt's little more than a keepsake I've kept hidden in my hope chest all these years," she reasoned aloud to her reflection. She tried to calm herself and make sense of it all. "It's old and not the prettiest—a hodgepodge of fabrics and buttons and embroidery. I know that. It's worn and old, even faded in a few places. But…it belonged to *me*."

Reasoning didn't help. Her desperation grew and grew and became as fierce as the storm that raged outside.

It's probably sitting on a shelf somewhere, in some dirty, creepy pawnshop, or in a dusty antique shop, or passed on to a grubby second-hand store that doesn't care a flip about the sentimental value of it. Or sold on eBay to the highest bidder or posted on Craigslist for a song. Or, God forbid, trashed!

She cringed. Shuddered. Wrapped her arms around herself to stave off the dampening chill she felt. Fresh anger rose in her again and her spine straightened. She had to do something, anything, to at least try to find her family's quilt.

"Hey, Mom." Seventeen-year-old Briana walked into the room, yanking Maggie away from her thoughts. "Madison's mom's picking me up in a few. We're gonna make the final plans for our missions trip with the team, and then we're having a girls' slumber party. You know, manicures and pedicures and facials and everything! It'll be a lot of fun. And I'll be home after church tomorrow…"

Bree paused when she turned to face her mother. "Are

you okay?"

"Fine, honey." Maggie pasted a quivering smile on her face. "Just having a stormy day."

Briana looked out at the weather and nodded, but her dark green eyes spoke volumes as she crossed the room and hugged her. "I love you, Mom."

Maggie sighed. *Bree hurts, too. But what can I do? And what am I going to do without her when she leaves? Or goes to college in a few years?*

"I love you, too, Bree." Maggie embraced her daughter, holding her tight.

Before long, Madison's mom pulled up and gave the horn a quick blast.

"You'll be all right, won't you, Mom? I...I can stay, if you'd like."

"Don't worry about me, honey. I'll be fine. You go and have a good time. And be sure to grab an umbrella. It's nasty out there."

Briana let go of her mom and headed toward the door. But then she spun around, her short, sandy brown bob swishing around her petite face. She paused and blew Maggie a kiss, just like she always did as a little girl. Then, with a wave, Bree walked out the door.

Yes, I'll be fine. Just as long as I keep breathing in and out and having kisses blown to me from my girl—who's too quickly becoming a woman.

Lord, I know she's being brave, but I can see's hurt and embarrassed. Divorce. Such a nasty word. Help us both through all this mess.

The prayer steadied her somewhat, and Maggie went to the kitchen to make a cup of tea. She turned on the electric kettle and then went to her china cabinet to choose just the right teacup—the green-and-white Irish one with lots of tiny shamrocks would be perfect to brighten the bleak day. Tea, her comfort drink of choice, would surely calm her nerves.

She poured the boiling water into the teapot and added her favorite Five Roses teabag, a smooth black tea from

South Africa. After waiting for it to steep, she poured a cup and sat down at the table with her delicate ivory Beleek teacup and admired its tiny green shamrocks. Then she aimlessly stirred to dissolve the sugar that had long been absorbed, as her mind pondered the past few months.

After Bill filed for divorce and moved to the other side of the country, Maggie discovered that he left her with several thousand dollars' worth of unpaid bills she thought were paid. She found herself in a desperate situation. Her phone was nearly cut off and the electricity disconnected, and an eviction notice was days away. Thanks to mom, she caught up on her bills and avoided eviction.

For now.

A lightning flash and the loud thunderclap brought her back to the present.

Maggie looked around and sucked in her breath. How could she ever keep this house? She only rented it, and though it was a great price and in an ideal location, she could barely afford it.

She thought about how much she enjoyed her job as a front-desk receptionist for a small corporation—she especially loved the people she worked with—but the salary didn't cover her bills and living expenses. And move? She wasn't about to move away and tear Briana from the school she enjoyed, the friends she loved, and the home she knew. Somehow she needed to find a way to keep this place, if only for Bree's sake.

Maybe find a new job or take on a second job? Guess I'll have to add that to my to-do list.

As Maggie's thoughts drifted back to the quilt, sadness threatened to overwhelm her again. She took a sip of her tea, but it was cold. She went to the sink and poured it out.

"Why did he have to take my quilt? I know he took it, and he didn't care less about how I'd feel. He probably thought he could get a good price for it, since the quilt's an antique and a handmade one at that!" Even as Maggie heard herself voice these words out loud, something deep in her heart told her that she should forgive Bill and move on, but that didn't seem possible at the moment. Both her hands came down hard on the kitchen counter. She went back to the living room and plunked down on the sofa, trying to redirect her thoughts. She turned the TV on, then off. Nothing seemed to comfort her this day.

"Forgive me, Lord," Maggie finally whispered. "I know it's just a quilt, but it feels like the straw that's breaking my back! I'm tired. Sick of fighting. I need peace, somehow.

"Maybe if I could find the quilt? Maybe I could find it before it's sold again—from wherever it is. Will You help me, please?"

As her prayer ended, Maggie glanced at the antique rocker in the corner of the room and felt a purpose rise up within her.

"Antique stores," she mumbled.

She knew what she needed to do. Besides looking for work and healing her heart and helping her daughter, she needed to find that quilt!

She looked at the clock and saw that she still had time to visit at least one of the antique shops in town. She and Bill had enjoyed perusing antique stores—before it all fell apart. She'd start there.

Maggie went to the bathroom, splashed some water on her face, washed off the mascara that stained her cheeks, and looked in the mirror. She shook her head at seeing the red lines threading around her chocolate-brown eyes and applied eye drops into each, hoping to hide her teary morning. Then she pulled her hazelnut-colored hair into a thick ponytail. Once she felt more put together, she grabbed her keys, purse, and the phone—it still worked, thank heaven—and left, hoping beyond hope to find her quilt and the peace that might come with it.

The sky began to clear and the summer sun peeked through the clouds, heating up the Colorado afternoon like a sauna and sending the storm on its way. Relaxing a bit, Maggie flipped on her sunglasses and drove toward her first stop. As the sun broke through, Maggie smiled. *This is a good sign.*

Her smile faded. *Oh, Mom, please don't be disappointed with me.*

She tried to suppress the guilt that battered her heart and mind over losing the quilt. She'd assumed the quilt would be safe in her hope chest, just as her mother had kept it safe in her big, old Lane cedar chest all those years. And just as her grandmother and great-grandmother and great-great-grandmother had also kept it safe in the old wooden steamer trunk that came over from Ireland.

Maggie flipped on her blinker and changed lanes as she recalled when her mother had shown it to her for the first time, when she was a little girl. Her mom had opened that musty old trunk and ceremoniously unfolded the quilt. She could almost smell the musty trunk even now. That was the first time her mother had shared the story of their family emigrating from Ireland, and it captivated her imagination. Maggie couldn't imagine the sacrifice it must have taken to make such a move, and she had never forgotten that story.

Her memory took her back to her great-great grandparents, James and Margaret Hawkins, poor farmers in Northern Ireland when the great potato famine had struck the nation. Sometime just before the Civil War—she couldn't remember the exact year—they had decided to emigrate with their six young children from Belfast, Ireland, to Wolfe Island, Canada, just twenty miles from the town where Maggie grew up in upstate New York.

She stopped at a light and turned right as she remembered her mom telling her that the Hawkins couldn't bring much with them across the ocean on the jam-packed immigrant ship, and they were forced to leave most of their belongings behind. But her great-great-grandmother, Margaret, had made sure that she brought the quilt, made of mix-matched scraps of cloth and clothing, with her as a way of remembering their Irish family heritage.

I'm not overreacting! The quilt's more than an old blanket!

Maggie put on her blinker as she merged on the freeway,

frustration mounting again.

The quilt was a priceless heirloom.

Which was why it had been tucked safely away in her hope chest and in her ancestors' trunk for the past 150 years.

As she turned off the highway, she struggled to picture exactly what the quilt looked like. She wanted to recognize it when—not if—she found it. How she wished she at least had a photo of the quilt! But she'd never thought to take a picture of something she kept stored in her hope chest. Something that was, by all rights, supposed to stay there.

"Argh!" Maggie felt a catch in her voice and shook it away to return to her memories.

The quilt had a heavy, maroon-colored wool backing. That made sense since it was from Ireland—sheep country. Maggie smiled at the memory of her deep roots, her Irishness. Growing up in her home, it had been *all* things Irish. Her thoughts wandered to the rich Irish upbringing she'd had— the Celtic music and the comforting Irish food, the lavish celebrations on St. Patrick's Day, and all the green—green walls, green living room furniture, green placemats, green clothes, especially in March. When her father was alive, he'd don a silly leprechaun hat and sing "Danny Boy" at the top of his lungs. Those were fun times. Maggie sighed.

Sheesh! What a family!

She turned toward Old Colorado City and felt the summer sun pound down on her and turned up the car's air conditioning and returned to her memories of the quilt. The front of the quilt had lots of colors and textures and different fabrics, all seemingly haphazardly placed. There was all kinds of fabric, from soft baby patterns to rough work clothes to many others—all "pieces of important and memorable fabrics from household cloth or everyday clothes they had worn," as her mother had told her. It was a practical, useful item—not one to be admired. Maggie remembered the embroidery and the ties of yarn at various places. Her memories came clear and vivid, as if the quilt were here with her. Her excitement grew as it became real in her mind's eye.

What color was the yarn?

As her heart raced, she tried to remember more, but her emotions took over and Maggie's fingers clenched around the steering wheel. She had to take time to search for something that should never have left her hope chest! Now she needed to ask strangers if they had *her* quilt. And if she did find it, how on earth could she afford to buy it back? She grumbled as she turned onto Pikes Peak Avenue.

"The ties were Kelly green!"

Some of the anger seeped away and Maggie smiled at the memory of such a detail. She found a parking spot right in front of The Treasure Shoppe, and went inside, sure she'd find her family's special quilt. Little did she know the journey on which she was about to embark.

CHAPTER 3
MARGARET

THE DAY AFTER the funeral, James met with the solicitor. Upon returning to Father's house, Margaret could see the worry on his face.

James shook his head as he sat down at the kitchen table. "Father left it all to us, but there are many debts to be paid. And then there is the death tax."

"Why, James?" Margaret asked. "What more can we bear?"

The children played quietly in the yard while Margaret and James discussed her father's estate and his letter over cups of tea.

James held her hand as she spilled out her heart.

"The very idea of emigrating makes me cringe with fear, husband. I understand why father wants us to leave and I know you agree, but I abhor it." Margaret lay her head on the table, embarrassed by her words.

She wanted to cling to all that she knew, all that made her feel safe and secure. Every nook and cranny of her childhood home held memories of love and family, remembrances of hardship and pain and loss, and hopes of better times.

Wherever she looked, her father's things evoked memories—the candlesticks she and James had used at their wedding, just as her parents had first used them decades earlier. The quilts and pillows and doilies her mum skillfully made, and even the lamp Margaret had broken as a child that sat there on the sideboard and still reminded her of her stubborn nature.

She lifted her head and smiled weakly at James. "We both know how I hate change. I just remembered the time when I first realized how much it bothered me."

"Tell me," James said, patting her hand.

"I was but five, and my cousin Charles had come to stay with us. When father asked me to give up my seat nearest him and move to the far end of the table, I wrapped my little legs around the chair legs and refused to budge! It was my place, and I was comfortable there. I didn't want to move or give it to my cousin."

Margaret felt her face grow warm with embarrassment, but James just chuckled and kissed her hand.

How vexed me parents must have been with me! I never wanted anything to change! Not me bedroom. Not me friends. Not anything! I…I still don't.

"That be a tale that tells me a lot, wife," James said, still choking back a laugh.

"But things do change, as the paperwork father left testifies." Margaret's lips tightened and she swallowed hard. "Me family had much land that was all lost—to pay the exorbitant taxes the Church of England imposed on them for their faith. It be wrong, James. So wrong."

"I know, lamb." Though James knew all this, he let her vent anyway.

Margaret got up and took the tiny portrait of the Earl James Caulfield, her grandfather, in her hands and returned to the table. "He once owned thousands of acres only to see it stripped away by government confiscation and the unfair land laws."

James nodded and followed her gaze as she looked at the small painting of the beautiful Mourne Mountains, the mountains she loved. "It will all be stripped away from our world forever if we emigrate."

James had no response. He simply kissed her hand again and again.

* * *

For Margaret, the emotional days of closing up her father's home became a blur. Meetings with the pastor, the legal authorities, and others produced more and more questions, problems, and decisions to be made.

During the next two days Margaret and her family packed things to keep, said goodbye to neighbors and friends, and sold what could be sold.

James did his best to settle the estate by searching for someone to buy the house and paying off debts with anything he could. After putting the children to bed, James and Margaret sat at the table reviewing their progress.

"The cow paid off Father's debts at the general store," James reported. "The dining room furniture will go to Dr. O'Donnell, and the bedroom set to the undertaker."

"I miss father more," Margaret said, choking back a sob.

James nodded, appearing so exhausted and anxious that Margaret stopped, took his hand, and said, "Thank you for all you do. I be glad I have you, James."

Margaret was weary of it, too. Besides caring for the children, she had to say farewell to her many memories. And if, indeed, they were bound for the New World, she knew they would be leaving it all behind—all their friends, belongings, everything. Hardest of all, they'd be saying goodbye forever to their dear Ireland and to her father and mum, God rest their souls.

By the end of the week, Margaret sat at the worn kitchen table in her father's house, a cup of tea before her. She realized how grateful she was to have the wee ones napping and the older ones playing outside at the same time. She needed to rest. But as she rubbed her weak eyes and lay her head on the table, James came in and sat down across from her, his face serious. He folded his hands on the table.

"'Tisn't good news, me love. They are taking the house for the death tax. We must leave tomorrow and go home."

Young Michael walked into the kitchen just then, hearing his father's news. He disagreed emphatically. "They cannot take Grandfather's house! I am nearly a man. I will stay here and tend it!"

Margaret looked at her eldest blankly. Neither James or she said a word before Michael continued.

"I will keep Grandfather's house and what little is left, and I will become the richest man in Newry!" Michael declared. His eyes flashed, adamant but not defiant. Margaret knew he was grasping for anything to stop this from happening.

"We are leaving for the New World in the spring, son," James said firmly.

"Leave? Ireland? Our homeland?" Michael asked, a hint of disbelief passing across his face. "Leave Grandfather's house and Newry? Leave our land and sheep and cattle? Leave Buddy?" As if the thought of saying goodbye to his precious dog and companion was too much, Michael began to sob. "We cannot. I will not!" He covered his face with his hands.

James rose and went to him, placing a steady but loving hand on the boy's heaving shoulder. "We are family. You must come with us."

Then James returned to his wife's side while Michael quietly shuffled out of the room. Margaret understood her son's feelings well. "Don't be vexed with him, James," she begged. "He does not like change, but he will come around. He's like Father. Like me."

She squeezed her husband's hand, then turned and went to her father's bedroom wardrobe to face the one, last task—her father's clothes. As she opened the doors, the musky smell of her father's scent brought a flood of memories.

She lovingly ran her fingers across her father's things. She whispered, as if talking to him. "The shirt you wore for Mum's funeral. The topcoat you had made especially for my wedding day a dozen years ago. Oh, Father! The nightshirt you had on when you passed on to the hand of God."

She held back a moan as she considered her quilt. She took all three of the articles of clothing, determined to take pieces of each and add them to the family quilt, the fabric of her memories. Though they were sellable items, they would be even more valued as memories in her quilt.

Margaret took the sheers from the top drawer of Father's nightstand, and one by one, she cut pieces of the items as her tears flowed freely.

"Why, Father? It was too soon," she whispered. "I will miss you terribly, as I miss Mum. But with God's help, I will do as you ask. Somehow. Some way. We will find our future and a better day. We will go, and I will take these pieces of your things, of our heritage, with us.

"The Caulfield heritage, Father. A strong and proud heritage that be now all but gone. When I was but a child, you told me that we once had a vast estate from County Armagh to Derry Lake. A baron, me great-grandfather, he was. And me grandfather, an Earl who had such a love of art. I will remember, Father. I will not forget. These pieces of your clothing will remind me to tell the story of the Caulfields. Mum's patches will too. I will not forget. I promise."

Just then baby Meg stirred from her nap, crying for her midday milk. Margaret kissed the cloth, dried her tears, and went to care for her wee one. Her anger had subsided, but the fear of such a journey, of such change, remained.

As she settled down to nurse her baby, she could hear the other children in the yard squealing and playing. *I mustn't neglect a one of them for me sorrow, for me fear. Please help me, Lord.*

After a few quiet moments, Susan knocked on the open door. "May I come in, Mum? What can I do to help, please? I cannot play my days away."

"My child, you are all me hope and me future!" Margaret said, smiling wide for the first time in days. "Can you take the babe out for some sunshine, please?"

Susan nodded, tucked a bothersome strand of her hair behind her tiny ear, and hugged her mum tight. "We'll be all right, won't we, Mum? Michael says we must keep Grandfather's house and stay here in Ireland. But I want to leave. I want a new life, far from all this sadness."

"You be a wise child, daughter," Margaret said. "Michael will join us in heart soon enough, you just mind that. We must be patient."

"When can we leave?" Susan implored.

"We have much to do, lassie, and besides, we must wait until the cold winds leave our shores and the winter storms pass from the grand Atlantic before we make such a passage."

"I want to leave this sorrow behind now," Susan insisted.

"We may leave it behind, but we must never forget our family, your grandfather and granna and the others," Margaret said. She picked up the pieces of her father's clothing and handed them to Susan. "These will be added to our family quilt and we will never forget. Would you like to help me and learn how to sew them onto the quilt after I finish the quilt I'm making for the baroness?"

"Oh, that would be grand, Mum! I am ready to learn." Susan's eyes lit up.

"Now go, and take heed what I said about Michael," Margaret warned. "We are family and we must journey these sorrows together."

Susan took her wiggling sister outside. Margaret turned back to her duties but wondered how the other children would weather the many changes to come. Would they remember Ireland at all?

* * *

As Susan settled under a tree with baby Meg, Ned—for that was what Edward was called—joined them. His big brown eyes and freckles always made her smile. *He's such a funny little fellow,* Susan thought.

Before long little John saw the gathering and broke away

from Michael's grasp, running to sit under the tree with them. Michael disappeared around the corner of the house. Susan took charge of them all.

"What's Mum doing?" Ned asked, wiggling his newly loose tooth.

"I want Mum!" John whined. Susan looked at him and beckoned him close. *Poor wee John. So small and weak and such a tiny bit of sandy brown hair and those slight grey eyes. Makes you look ill—for two and a half. May the good Lord watch o'er ye, me wee brother.*

Just then, Mary rounded the corner with a handful of flowers. She reminded Susan of a porcelain doll she'd seen in the Newry Mercantile, with her pale complexion, dark thin hair, and dark eyes. Mary had full rosebud lips and a solemn face, but, at nearly four years old, she was a kind, quiet, and sweet-spirited little girl.

"Where's Mum?" Mary asked.

"Settle down, both of you," Susan said gently. "Mum be busy with Grandfather's affairs, you just mind that. Leave her be. She needs peace in such a time."

"I want Mum!" John whined louder. His tiny body began shaking with emotion.

"Will we leave Ireland?" Ned asked. "Michael says we cannot, but I want to sail on a big ship!"

"I want Mum!" John howled until Ned rolled his eyes and took him by the hand to lead him into the house.

"The ocean be scary," Mary said to no one in particular, popping her thumb in her mouth for comfort.

"It be big," Susan consoled. "But the sailors know what to do and will take us to Uncle John in the New World. There will be food enough and land to have and people who are good. Uncle says so in his letters. And no one will scold us for our faith, and we will go to a real school, and we will be safe again."

Mary cuddled up to Susan and began to play with little Meg's bare toes. Susan patted her head and smoothed her hair. Then Michael walked up—with his Uncle Robert!

"Hallo, little lassies," said Uncle Robert cheerfully. "I hear you be talking about sailing the high seas. Might you mind if I join you on the journey?"

Michael grinned. Susan's eyes widened and she nodded her head vigorously, surprised to see her uncle. Mary popped her thumb out of her mouth and clapped.

James's brother, Robert, was Susan's favorite uncle, and she was thrilled to see he had come.

Uncle Robert bent low to speak to the girls. "When I heard about me sister-in-law's loss, I left me fishing in Kilkeel to be with you. Though your grandfather is not me blood, we are family all the same."

Uncle Robert sat and continued. "When I arrived just now and heard Michael's tale of woe about leaving Ireland, I knew in an instant where me destiny lies—in the New World with you, me family! It barely took me a moment before I had made up me mind to join you all on the voyage and begin a new life on Wolfe Island, me lassies."

"Oh Uncle, 'tis a blessing for all of us, not just for Michael," Susan said. She shot a glance at Michael, who stood with his back against the tree, listening and grinning wide.

"I had also been invited by Uncle John to join him on Wolfe Island," Uncle Robert went on, "but I had been reluctant to journey that far alone. This be me chance, and I will gladly take it! I'm a carefree bachelor, but I am your uncle first and foremost, and I will help with the wee ones on the journey. Then I will work hard in the New World, find a wife there, and buy land instead of being a poor Irish hired hand. I will say farewell to me beloved homeland with the rest of you, and I will make a new start for meself."

Susan laughed with joy and watched as Mary threw her arms around her uncle's neck and squeezed him as hard as her little arms could.

Yes, we all love him so. And such a handsome man he be, with a full head of dark hair and those mischievous amber eyes. I believe any lass would love to be his wife—even though he be old—twenty-one years old! Best of all, he loves us all.

"Might you teach me the whistle, Uncle?" Susan begged. "The Sailing will be terribly long, and I will learn well."

"Me, too!" said Mary.

Robert smiled and patted Mary on the head. Then winked and nodded affirmatively to Susan.

He stood and threw his arm around Michael's shoulder. "Come, lad, let's tell your mum and father the news and see how we can aid in the work." As they walked into the house, Susan noticed that Michael's attitude was starting to change even then.

"Thank you, good Lord, for working on Michael's heart," Susan whispered. "We are family, and we will journey together."

* * *

Margaret turned the corner as Michael and Robert entered the house. Michael proudly announced his uncle's arrival. Margaret wiped her hands on her apron and smiled.

"Welcome, Robert! And such long a way you have come!" Margaret hugged her brother-in-law.

"Aye, and for many sorrows I have come," Robert said, grasping Margaret's hands. "Your loss cuts me heart, 'tis true, sister."

"Thank you, brother," Margaret said. "'Tis a sad time under this roof, to be sure."

Robert heard wee John calling for his mum and excused himself to go and surprise his nephew.

A moment later, James returned from yet another meeting. Margaret smelled alcohol on his breath as he entered the tiny kitchen. *Not again. He partakes of that demon liquor far too often these days!*

Margaret turned her eyes to the dining room as Robert came through the doorway, John right at his heels.

"Robert!" James exclaimed. "'Tis a blessing from heaven you came, and such a sacrifice you have made to come from afar."

The brothers gave each other a big hug and patted one another firmly on the back, laughing with joy at their reunion. John tugged on Uncle Robert's trousers. He picked up the little lad and plopped him on his shoulders, being careful to not hit his tiny head on the low ceiling. "You'll be reaching the rooftop, me laddie, 'tis so big you be getting!" Little John reached up and banged the ceiling with his hand. Everyone laughed, including John.

By then the entire family had entered the small kitchen to be with Robert and James. "Your arrival be a reason for celebration." James said. "Let us rejoice with a bit of bread and honey and a cool sup of water."

As the family gathered around the small table, Margaret set a tea towel on the floor as a makeshift picnic cloth for the wee ones. Before long, all of them were munching on the heavy Irish soda bread, licking the sweet honey, and slurping the cool water. They sat silently, listening to Robert tell the story of his long journey to Newry, his overnight stay along the Carlingford Lough and catching fish for his breakfast, and his ride on a pig wagon from the lake to Newry.

Then Mary spoke up. "Uncle Robert be going to sail with us, Father!"

"Will thee now?" James said with a chuckle in his voice. "That be a gift to us all, brother, that it be! Please do, and with our blessing!"

Everyone cheered and clapped and smiled. It was the grandest news they had had in a long time.

Family, Margaret thought. *'Tis a gift from heaven.*

CHAPTER 4
MAGGIE

MAGGIE'S FIRST ATTEMPT at finding the quilt was unsuccessful. She returned home, worried about what she should do next. The house seemed all too quiet and lonely with Bree gone, even for just this one evening. And the idea of her daughter being overseas for nearly six weeks—all the way across the world in Zimbabwe? It was more than she wanted to think about just then. She donned her tennis shoes and went for a power walk, hoping to rid herself of the incessant ponderings of her mind. Unfortunately, her thoughts traveled with her, an unwelcome walking partner.

For the past seventeen years, Bree had given Maggie a reason to set aside her pain and find the strength to go on, even through the hardest days of her marriage and subsequent divorce. She had shielded her daughter from her husband's drinking, carousing, drugs, but now Bree was aware of them. Yet, Bree motivated her to wake up each morning, put on a smile, and trust God to do His work in both of them.

Maggie turned the corner and gulped the fresh mountain air as she thought about how she had trusted God ever since she'd become a believer in college, even through the difficult days and years of her spouse's addictions, even when she felt alone and abandoned. Her faith held her fast, but her faith sometimes faltered when it came to Bree.

As the sun began to set, Maggie waited for the light to turn so she could cross the road and return to her house. She shook her head. "How can I not worry about her? And our finances?"

Almost tripping on an unlevel piece of cement, Maggie thought about her daughter going to Africa. Bree's freckles, smile, and big, green eyes often gave others the impression that she was strong enough to tackle anything, despite her petite frame. She rejected the worry that tried to take over.

She can do it. I just hope she's safe in such a place!

Maggie returned home, took off her sneakers, and went to her computer. She turned her attention to something she might be able to fix—her finances. She determined to find a better paying job and then continue her search for the crazy quilt. She took a sip from her water bottle, sat down, and scoured the Internet for local job openings that might fit her, but she found nothing.

"Nothing? Such a lousy time to be searching for a job in this economy," Maggie said aloud, trying to fill the quiet of the house with her voice. She flipped on her iTunes to keep her company.

Panic tightened her chest. Though she was thankful for her job, she needed more. She jotted down some notes about where to look next week, and then turned her attention to the matter of the quilt.

Maggie checked out Craigslist and eBay, searching the ads for anything that might lead her to the quilt. She found a few leads online and decided to create a list of calls to make the following week. Then she did a Google search for pawnshops, antique shops, quilt stores, and she made more lists. It was nearing midnight when she closed her computer and went to bed.

* * *

Briana returned from her overnight stay late the next day. After a quick dinner of tomato basil soup and grilled cheese sandwiches, Maggie helped Bree finish packing for her trip.

"I can't believe you're leaving in a few days, and that you will be gone most of the summer." Maggie groaned.

"I know, Mom. You know I'm going to miss you, too," Bree said. "It's really hard to believe I'll be on the other side of the world in just a few days. But I think this will be a great trip, Mom!" Briana placed a T-shirt in the suitcase. "Our team had a great meeting last night. We'll be teaching children and building an addition on the church and then there will be a place for a children's church. I can't wait to go out to the rural villages and help those needy people."

"I'm happy for you, Bree. You really are an amazing young woman."

Maggie blinked back tears as pride for her daughter welled up in her heart. Yet while she tried her best to put on a good face and help her daughter feel secure, guilt and anxiety pulsed through her. Maggie barely had any cash to send with Bree on her trip across the globe. Supporting the two of them on her salary was difficult enough, add to that the stress of the expenses of a mission trip and she couldn't help feeling overwhelmed. Bree had done her best to raise money for the trip, but Maggie had needed to help make up the difference. Anger at Bill's refusal to help his daughter groped at her heart.

A little child support sure would've helped.

Maggie pressed her lips together and tried to focus on rolling pairs of shorts to save room in Bree's suitcase. The wide smile on her girl's face told Maggie she was excited and ready. She didn't want her own anger to dampen her daughter's happiness. So she composed herself and listened to Bree chatter on about the trip, as her thoughts drifted to their relationship.

Though their mother-daughter spats had become more

frequent lately—Maggie assumed that was normal as Bree was getting older—the two still loved one another deeply and held one another together emotionally. Maggie wanted to show her precious girl as much love and support as she could muster, especially since Bill didn't seem to care.

"What'll you do while I'm gone?" Bree asked, pulling her away from her thoughts.

"Oh, work…and try to find the quilt. I might even try to line up a second job, you know, to earn a bit more money," Maggie admitted. She had told Briana about her discovery of the missing quilt, but she had tried hard not to incriminate Briana's dad.

"I'll pray you find both," Bree said with a hint of sadness in her voice. "I sure will miss you, Mom."

The phone rang, and Maggie bit her tongue. She winked at her daughter, left Bree to chat with her friend, went to her own room, and sank down on the bed.

* * *

Two days later, the early-morning ride to the airport and their final goodbyes were tearful. Maggie prayed with Briana, and they hugged.

"Mom, you're the best!" Bree's eyes glistened with tears. "Thanks for all you've done to support me in this. I know it's not easy."

"I love you, Bree. You'll do great, I just know it." Maggie refused to cry though she felt her eyes burn.

As Briana walked down the jet way, waving goodbye, Maggie steeled herself for the weeks ahead. She stayed at the gate, watching the airplane ascend and then pass through the clouds.

"Godspeed, dear daughter!" she whispered to the clouds.

Maggie glanced heavenward, pulled her car keys from her purse, and drove to work…alone.

Yet Maggie was grateful that her work provida a welcome distraction from Bree's absence—and from the matter of the quilt. But many times throughout the day, her thoughts, and then her prayers, turned to her daughter, flying across the globe.

She imagined her girl bumping along the dangerous roads of Zimbabwe and then along the dusty rutted paths in the rural jungle. Bree would soon be living in a mud hut, helping people living in primitive circumstances, among wild lions and other dangers. Maggie had to periodically and consciously choose to trust the One who had called her daughter to serve in such a way.

Throughout the day, Maggie stayed busy answering phones, welcoming visitors, and fulfilling staff needs, large and small. She loved the variety; she loved the people. She found comfort in the security of knowing what needed to be done, working with colleagues she could trust, and doing a job well.

If only it paid more!

Over the next several days, each evening, and even during some of her lunch breaks, Maggie stayed busy. Especially since she was alone, she needed to feel productive. She went through her list of calls and checked new job openings almost daily for anything that paid better. But the search yielded nothing. Nada. Nothing.

During her lunch hour and after work she had called eight pawnshops she'd found online, asking if any had bought old quilts in the past six months. Three admitted they had; two said the quilts had since been sold to antique shops. When she'd asked for the names of the shops where the quilts had been sold, she'd been informed that neither place kept those kinds of records. At least she had a place to begin.

* * *

That weekend, Maggie called her mom to bounce some thoughts off her. "I think I should stay at my current job for now. I like my colleagues and the consistency, and at least I'll have insurance and a strong employment history."

"That's wise, Megs," her mother agreed. "So I guess you should concentrate your efforts on finding a second part-time job to work evenings or weekends."

"Thanks, Mom. It's always great to glean from your wisdom." Maggie and her mother chatted for awhile longer before they finally hung up.

Later she spent hours online searching and found two job openings that might fit her schedule. She sent in her applications. Now she'd have to wait, definitely not one of her favorite pastimes.

That weekend, Maggie also called several antique shops, but that posed an even greater quandary. Six of them had quilts, but none admitted to buying them from pawnshops. She'd have to go and see for herself, but she'd also have to wait until the following weekend.

Waiting. Worrying. Wondering. Maggie despised all of them.

Most evenings Maggie found herself frustrated by all the time, energy, and emotion that the quilt search caused, and she often plopped down on her bed at night and cried herself to sleep. On Thursday evening, Maggie called her mom. They talked about the weather, Briana's trip, and Maggie's work. Then, Maggie's mother, Elizabeth, turned to the topic of her great-grandparents.

Uh, oh! What am I going to say to her about the quilt if she asks?

"I was cleaning out the closet today, and guess what I found?" Elizabeth asked. Without waiting for Maggie to ask, she continued. "A picture of your great-grandmother Susan! I totally forgot I had it. I'll copy it and send you one. Susan's mother, Margaret, was the one who made that quilt you have. You're named after her, remember?"

"Oh, I'd love to see the picture, Mom," Maggie said, praying she wouldn't ask about the quilt again. "Do you have a picture of Margaret?"

"No," Elizabeth said. "Back in those days, it was often too expensive to take pictures, and they were poor immigrants, remember? Even after they settled on Wolfe Island, I imagine it wasn't easy to raise twelve children on a farmer's income, and I'm sure they didn't have money for pictures."

"Too bad," Maggie said. "I thought they had six children when they immigrated? Didn't you tell me that Margaret used to sew quilts for other people as well as her family?"

"Yes and yes," Elizabeth responded. "They had six children and then had six more on Wolfe Island. As for quilts, back then, quilts were really important. Women didn't write their family story on paper; they sewed it. Mothers and grandmothers taught their girls how to cook and sew and keep house. That was their education instead of book learning."

Elizabeth continued. "Margaret made lots of quilts for other people. She often quilted with the Irish Chain pattern. She was known all over County Down, Ireland, for her fine work. A couple of the wealthy English gentry women, who came to their country estates in the summer, often hired her to make quilts for them. There was only one Irish Chain she had time to make for her own family, and she didn't even make that until she immigrated to Canada. Grandma had it for a while, but then one of the cousins got that quilt when she died. The only Irish quilt we received was the one you have."

"Margaret sounded like a special lady," Maggie said, hoping to redirect the conversation before the fact that the quilt was missing might be revealed. "I've got to go, but I'd love to hear more someday. I love you, Mom. Thanks for sharing."

Yes, I'd love to hear more after the quilt's safely back in my hope chest!

"I love you, too, Megs," said her mom.

Maggie's pent up anxiety—mixed with a bit of shame for evading the conversation—threatened to overwhelm her. She got on her treadmill and ran a few miles. Once she was good and tired, she plopped into bed, prayed for wisdom, and eventually fell asleep.

When the weekend finally came, Maggie determined to

visit as many of the antique stores as she could. She prickled at the tedious and troubling, time-consuming and expensive journey she was on. But on her drive from store to store, Maggie's resentment softened a little with thoughts of a better tomorrow. She remembered how her mother, her grandmother, and all the others had gone through tough times.

"If they could do it, so can I!" Maggie said aloud.

Maggie pulled into yet another parking lot, refreshed by the warm thoughts of her grandmother, the family quilt, and her heritage, Maggie discovered that her family's strength could somehow keep those negative feelings in check. She would simply keep searching until she found that quilt. She had to.

CHAPTER 5
MARGARET

MARGARET AND JAMES'S FARM was larger than most, nearly ten acres of rolling hills at the foot of the beautiful Mourne Mountains. Unlike other families who had eight or ten boys among whom the land had to be subdivided, the Hawkins farm fared better since there were just the two brothers, James and Robert, and Robert chose not to farm. Robert had always longed for more than farming, and the ocean seaport of Kilkeel seemed to call his name, calling him to a life of fishing rather than farming.

The farm, the home they had always known since the day she and James had wed, lay straight ahead. Though the menfolk had made a few trips back to the farm since Father's funeral, Margaret and the wee ones had lingered at Grandfather's since that terrible day. They had done all they could to sell Father's belongings and clear his accounts, but they had little left to show for all the work, all the memories, all the years her father had lived.

"Oh how I've longed to be home, James!" Margaret slid her arm into her husband's arm as they drew closer to home. "We have all tasted the bitterness of being homesick."

Margaret looked back into the wagon and smiled at her children. Their faces glowed with anticipation and excitement as they sat on and around the few things Margaret had kept from the estate sales. She'd saved her parents' most sturdy clothing to refashion into the family wardrobe, as well as anything she thought they might need on a ship, just in case they really did cross the ocean. She also kept a few family photos and mementos. That was all. Everything else they sold or gave away.

Margaret turned back to enjoy the final miles of the journey home, but pondered the many conversations she and her family had regarding her father's challenge to sail to the New World. She wondered how they would endure an entire winter in their tiny cottage, with the knowledge of emigrating out on the horizon.

Susan's excitement about leaving Ireland spilled over in her giddy actions and chatter, yet Margaret had little patience for such "nonsense." She could understand Michael's reticence much better. Ned wouldn't stop talking about ships and sailors and the ocean, but Margaret tried to dismiss his endless jabber; life was an adventure to young Ned. Mary and John seemed unaware of the changes to come, and Margaret was glad of that. And this wee babe in her lap? She would remember none of it.

For Margaret, though, the thought of turning their world upside down, leaving their cherished homeland, launching out into the unknown, and starting over seemed thoroughly incomprehensible. She drew in a shuttered breath and looked at the green hills nearing her home. She had never traveled more than a few dozen miles from the place of her birth, and she didn't want to! She didn't want to start over. She didn't want to say goodbye to all that was familiar.

As her husband coaxed the horse to climb a small hill, Margaret looked at her husband and thought about him. Though she worried about his occasional fall to drinking too much, James was the strong silent type—the rock on which their family stood firm. He said little, but with his gentle wisdom, he commanded respect and held the family firmly together.

Our new North Star.

"Thank you, James, for everything," Margaret said, choking back tears.

James looked at her with questioning eyes and smiled. "For what, me love?"

"All of it," Margaret said as she gave his arm a gentle squeeze. James gave her arm a squeeze as well, but turned back to driving the wagon home.

Finally, Margaret caught sight of their far pasture in the distance. Their herd of sheep sprinkled the hillside, and though rather small, it provided enough to pay the many taxes and enough for her to keep the spinning wheel busy, as well as food to fill the stew pot with a bit of mutton on a few special occasions each year. Even when the tax collectors demanded more and more and showed no mercy during the Potato Blights, her faithful James paid his dues, absorbed the stress, and kept the faith. Though his sporadic drinking and his eternal optimism infuriated her at times, Margaret knew James resolved to stay strong for them all.

"I hope the two cows, the chickens, and the three pigs be found safe and sound in our yard," she said to James. James nodded but concentrated on driving.

Margaret shifted baby Megs in her lap and rocked her gently. The animals had decreased their reproduction in the last few years, but she was thankful they reproduced at all. Two new piglets and a scrawny young calf were God's provision that year. They would fare well at the spring market, Margaret was sure of it. And the cows still gave milk and cheese for the children, the chickens produced a few eggs now and then, and the rooster—God bless 'im—kept them all in line.

Margaret smiled at the thought. Perhaps all would be well after all. She breathed in the fresh farm air and furrowed her brow.

But the garden seemed to be cursed over and over again,

and their two apple trees did, too. After the Potato Blights of 1845 and 1846 that took their entire crop of potatoes, Margaret and the family were left with only a few turnips, parsnips, onions, and a handful of apples to get them through the long, cold Irish winters. Thank God the milk and meat held them fast, but Margaret feared for the future, even though this year's spring crop had given them a small, but sufficient yield.

"I do pray our garden will fare better this year," Margaret mused aloud.

"It will, me lamb. It will. Look o'er yonder. We are nearly home now," James replied, giving her a wink.

Margaret smiled as they turned off the road and neared their cottage. Since their farm was off the road and away from the path to the city, few came their way.

For that, she was grateful. The Great Famine hadn't hit her family as badly as many of their neighbors, but she and the family still felt its pain, especially when they lost loved ones because of it. Many neighbors and friends lost their homes, and far too many died from starvation. Margaret and James had little extra to help their suffering neighbors and friends, some of whom were scattered to the four winds when they couldn't pay the ridiculous rent on the land that had betrayed their hard work.

Still, she and James had helped as much as they could. A few folks had taken refuge in their tiny barn. Others had received sustenance from them, and all who came and went from their farm had left with grateful hearts. These poor, dying Irish were the betrayed, the forgotten, the forsaken. Poor creatures.

This is why Father implored us to flee. To find a new future. A new start. But how can I embrace the changes to come?

She shifted in her seat and turned her attention to the necessities of daily life. If, indeed, they were to emigrate, the long winter ahead would be filled with much to do, much to decide, much to let go of. Yet until that time, they were nearly ready to harvest, and they would survive until the Sailing.

"There she be, my lamb!" James said, pointing to their cottage. "We be home again." He turned and planted a kiss on her cheek, and she heard the children giggle at their father's demonstration of love for her.

Margaret gazed at her tiny home. The small thatched cottage was kept tight and strong by James' persistent patching. So were the outbuildings, solid and secure—the tiny byre and the chicken coop and the two-seater outhouse. Even when the famine rains came for two years in a row, terrible rains that unceasingly drowned the crops and turned the potatoes to putrid black mush, the cottage stayed dry. James worked fiercely, relentlessly. He did everything he could to secure safety for his family, without complaining. Margaret knew he would continue to toil as long as he had breath in his body.

When the wagon pulled up to the barn, the children quickly scattered to play with their dog, greet their animals, and run off some energy they had stored up on the journey from Newry.

It appeared that all her family were glad to be back. None more than Margaret.

Margaret, James, and the baby entered their little cottage, and Margaret paused to watch James bend his head low as he always did, for the doorway was just shy of his height. Margaret smelled the familiar smells and observed her beloved surroundings.

She looked around and took it all in. The earthen floor was dry and hard, and though the two tiny windows gave little light, they still let in a few rays of sunshine now and then. The small hearth lay cold, waiting for Margaret to bring it to life again. She set the baby down for a nap and went straight to it, happy to be home.

At least home for now.

"I must tend to the animals, me lamb," James said. "I'll keep the children outside while you settle in."

"Thank you, James." Margaret turned to her duties.

Margaret looked around and smiled. The four rush chairs

around the table were too few for their family of eight. James had made four simple stools for the older children. Cups and plates and pots crowded the kitchen shelf, but Margaret happily added four more plates and cups she had brought from Father's estate. She stacked them carefully and began to consider dinner.

"I will make a special sausage stew to celebrate our return, Megs," she said, handing the wee babe a wooden spoon and bowl. She gathered onions, potatoes, and a small bit of sausage, and began to chop and cook and prepare the meal. While she did, she continued to appreciate her home.

She was thankful for the shelf that held the half-dozen books Father had given the children, books of Irish poetry, fairy tales, and history. They were treasures she hoped they would not have to leave behind.

Baby Megs put her head on the bowl, obviously ready for a nap. So Margaret picked her up, set her in her cradle, and patted her back. "What will we take with us if we sail, eh, Megs?"

The baby's eyes fluttered and closed, so Margaret turned and surveyed her belongings.

The featherbeds, lumpy but valuable and warm, would have to be sold at the spring market. And what about the quilts that covered those beds? They were old, worn, and of little value, but they would likely be needed for the long, cold journey across the ocean.

She went to the kitchen, stirred the dinner, and stoked the fire. Suddenly, Margaret began to view things with different eyes than she had just a week ago. Much would have to be left behind. Did all this no longer matter?

The cottage's white plastered walls were cracking and chipping, but if the family were to leave, there would be no reason to patch them. James had planned to build another room for their growing family, but was that no longer necessary? Was there no longer a need to make more rush chairs or another bed? No longer a reason to fix the byre or enlarge the outhouse?

Would they turn their attention to preparing for the Sailing, preparing to say goodbye to all they had ever known? Margaret shrugged her shoulders and turned to check on the food.

Susan and Mary came into the cottage, asking about dinner. "Wash up, dinner's almost ready!" Margaret said. They did as they were told and then set the table.

"Mmm. Smells like Dublin Coddle," Mary observed.

"That it be. You have a keen nose, child," Margaret said, pleased at her daughter's perception. "'Twill be ready presently. Call your brothers, please."

After James thanked God for the meal and for being home, Margaret divvied out plates. The savory sausage, onion, and potato meal seemed to be a treat for them all. Sunshine burst through the half-open door and splashed on the table. The children giggled and chattered with more energy than Margaret had seen in a week. Both she and James laughed at the sight of their family happy to be home.

"I never want to leave this place," Michael said, rolling a potato around his plate.

"But we must leave. Grandfather said," Ned responded.

As the children chatted about the changes to come, Margaret's appetite vanished. She forced herself to take a small bite of sausage.

I will not burden the others with my cares. Even if I have to be silent for a fortnight!

James saw the shadow of sadness fill his wife's eyes. "God will take care of us through all of this," James said. "He will give us a good future together."

Margaret looked at her husband, grateful for his confidence. Then she looked at Michael. He visibly shook with anger.

"God gave us this land. I will not abandon it!" Michael said, slamming his fist on the table and then running out the door. James followed close behind him.

Mary and John burst into tears. Margaret knew they were afraid to see their big brother angry. She jumped up to comfort them. Then she saw Susan and Ned roll their eyes.

"Stop it, you two!" Margaret scolded. "Can't you see how hard this be for him, for us? Have you no mercy?"

Margaret glared silently at Susan and Ned, while the two wee ones were left crying, inconsolable.

"Sorry, Mum," Susan mumbled, and Ned's apology soon followed.

"Take the wee ones outside," Margaret said to Susan and Ned. "I'll clean up in peace."

Margaret went to get baby Meg from her nap, for she, too, was crying. The children left the cottage, and Margaret nursed her baby silently. James returned and stood by the table.

"Me love. How can I help?"

"No one can help us, James," Margaret said, her tone flat and lifeless. "We are like those on the road, tossed by the winds of change. Lord knows where we will find ourselves."

James went over to the quilt on the sideboard, and he held it gently in his rough hands. He intentionally rubbed the various patterns as he spoke. "Our ancestors endured much suffering over the years, just as this work of art you be crafting testifies. Generations have suffered under the cruel hand of English hatred and the Famine times. But God wants to take us to the Promised Land like He did with the children of Israel. Your father be correct. Ireland has betrayed its people with much sorrow, and we must bid it farewell—if not for us than for our children and children's children. We will take this quilt as a testimony, our memories as our anchor, and our heritage as our foundation, as we find a new life together."

"But this be our home!" Margaret could feel her steely gray eyes fill with anger and sadness and confusion, and James didn't seem to know what to say. After several minutes of silence, he laid the quilt on the sideboard and sat next to his wife, caressing baby Meg's cheek with his forefinger.

"Home, me wife, is where we are—together as a family," James said.

CHAPTER 6
MAGGIE

CUT BACKS? Maggie's mouth fell open as she sat across from her boss, Mr. Duvall. Friday morning she'd been summoned to his office. The middle-aged man in a gray suit and striped tie cleared his throat and shifted in his chair uncomfortably.

"I'm sorry, Maggie, but the budget is tight and we need to cut hours. I know you've had a rough few months, but we have to take you down to thirty hours a week."

"But…" Maggie squeezed her hands together. She was barely surviving on forty hours a week, now this! "I've worked here five years. Does this mean I'll lose my benefits?"

"There's some time for transition. We'll have you meet with HR to look at your insurance options."

Maggie willed herself not to cry in front of him, but panic threatened to consume her.

"We really do value your work, Maggie." Mr. Duvall's tone softened. "It's hard. Every department has to make cuts."

Maggie made her way back to her desk, numb from the news. The office buzzed with the gossip of who had been laid off and who'd had their hours cut. Several of Maggie's friends stopped by her desk to check on her and offer encouragement.

Five o'clock couldn't come fast enough. When it did, she sat alone in her car, taking deep breaths and trying to ward off the despair that settled on her.

Maggie tried to look on the bright side, small as it was. *At least I didn't lose my job completely!*

After a long night of tossing and turning, Maggie still waffled between hope and despair. She hadn't heard from any of the companies where she'd submitted job applications during the past week, and it was now the weekend. She'd have to wait until Monday to check for any updates. Over breakfast, Maggie scrolled through the latest online job openings but found nothing worthwhile. Disappointed, she wondered what to do next.

Maggie felt her losses pile up again, and so did her need to grab a hold of anything that would give her some semblance of normalcy, however small.

"I'll go on a quilt-finding adventure!" Maggie heard her voice quiver with uncertainty but shook it off. She'd make the best of a bad situation. Somehow.

Maggie decided to go to an antique store that she had never visited before. As she drove into town, she remembered a time as a child when she had tossed the family crazy quilt on the attic floor and got in trouble for doing it. She felt bad that she had mistreated the heirloom then. She felt even worse that she'd mistreated it again by not keeping it in her care.

"Oh, man! I sure did some dumb stuff back then...and now." Maggie glanced at the radio and back to the road. She shifted uneasily in her seat.

Forgiving herself had never been easy for Maggie; she often held herself captive for her past mistakes. Blaming herself for other's actions had become a nasty habit as well, and shame became her prison. She even tended to blame herself for the divorce—at least at first. She'd allowed Bill to do whatever he pleased, even when she knew he was drinking, mishandling the finances, and more. Even when she suspected an affair. She was afraid then; she was afraid now.

The "if onlys" bombarded her like a hurricane, but she dared to say them aloud. "If only I'd been stronger. If only I hadn't enabled him. If only I hadn't married him in the first place! But then…I wouldn't have Bree."

Maggie countered her thoughts aloud. "I will not take the blame for all of it, and I will not regret the marriage for it gave me Briana."

She turned on the radio to distract her from her thoughts. She simply had to find her family's quilt and make it all right. She must.

Anna's Antiques was a little tricky to locate, but after a few twists and one wrong turn, Maggie turned down a one-way street and saw the little shop. She found a parking spot and entered the store, but no one seemed to be around.

"Hello?" she called out. "Are you open?"

A gray-haired woman with a big smile peeked around the corner. "Yes, dear, come on in. I'm Anna Kelley. Welcome to my shop."

The plump little elderly woman clicked her heels on the linoleum floor as she came near. She wore a bright, daisy-covered dress and sported a perfectly styled haircut. Behind half-rimmed glasses, her soft blue eyes studied Maggie. With a warm and welcoming smile, Anna Kelley radiated a peacefulness that Maggie wished she had.

"I'm Maggie Dolan, and I'm looking for a quilt." Maggie stepped closer. "But not just any quilt. An old Irish crazy quilt with maroon backing and Kelly green ties."

"Well, now, that's quite the specific request. I'm sorry, but I haven't seen one like it." Anna frowned for a moment. "Is it something that you've seen before?"

Unexpectedly, Maggie burst into tears. Her sleepless night, the stress of her work hours being cut back, and the frustration over the quilt collided within her. Embarrassed, she turned away from Anna, but Anna just wrapped her arms around Maggie and held her tightly, like a doting mother.

"There, there," Anna said, patting Maggie's back gently. "Let it all out, and cry as much as you need to. I have all the time in the world, and there's no one here but you, me, and the good Lord."

For several minutes Maggie wept, unable to hold it in. And the release of it felt good.

Anna handed her a box of tissues and guided her to a chair just a few feet away from where they'd been standing. Once Maggie found her composure, she whispered, "Thank you."

"We all have our days," Anna said with understanding. "Lord knows, I've had oodles of them. Now how about I pour us both a cup of tea and we get to know one another a bit? I was just making some when you came in."

Maggie nodded and Anna disappeared into the back. Maggie blew her nose and looked around the quaint little shop. The orderly displays held hundreds of items perfectly placed, as if everything might be a part of someone's home. From where she sat, Maggie couldn't see a single pile of random stuff nor even a speck of dust—quite unlike the other antique shops she had visited. A display of quilts hung on a tall wooden rack in the far corner of the store caught Maggie's eye.

She liked the store.

Anna returned with a beautiful silver tray. On it sat a delicately flowered china teapot and matching cups, dainty silver teaspoons, and a plate of assorted shortbread cookies. Each teacup rested on a real crocheted doily, and two embroidered linen napkins lay beside them, both held by a ceramic butterfly ring.

"How pretty!" Maggie said, smiling for the first time in days. "You needn't go to all that trouble for me."

Anna smiled at her with such kindness that Maggie nearly melted into a puddle of tears again. "You are what will make this teatime special!"

Me? I'm a stranger, a nobody! Why bother?

"Do you like chamomile? It's a soothing tea, don't you

think?" Anna handed Maggie a cup with daisies on it. "And don't you think daisies are a happy flower? I do."

Maggie nodded again, not sure what to say or how to explain her breakdown. All she could do was sip her tea and feel ashamed, like she didn't deserve such kind attention.

"I've had my share of troubles, too," Anna confessed. "My husband, Sam, and I were missionaries in Kenya when he was killed, leaving me with two young children and no means of support. I opened this little store a few years after returning to the States, but it wasn't an easy time in my life. The children are grown now, and this place gives me not only a means of support but also my very own mission field. I love meeting new people and learning about their lives, and I've found that sometimes a cup of tea and biscuits are just the things to soothe a broken soul."

"It was my family's quilt," Maggie blurted out. "My mother entrusted it to me, but now it's gone." Maggie told Anna the whole story of the missing quilt, including the part about her messy divorce. Anna listened patiently, letting Maggie pour out her heart. Several times she patted Maggie's hand or handed her a tissue. When she was done, Maggie's silent tears placed a footnote on her story, giving Anna all the information she needed.

"Tears are a good thing, Maggie," Anna said softly. "The Bible says that God will wipe away every tear, and one day there will be no more mourning or crying or pain or sorrow. Now that will be a lovely day, don't you think?"

"I just don't understand why all these troubles have come my way." Maggie wiped her eyes. "I know I've fallen short, but it seems that even though I've tried so hard, I've still failed. No matter how much I try to do things right, it falls apart. I don't know why God's punishing me."

"Do you think God's punishing you, Maggie?" Anna asked. "Oh, dearie, God's plans are much bigger than punishing His beloved. He has good plans for you, Maggie; plans to prosper you and not to harm you, plans to give you hope for your future. That's what Jeremiah 29:11 says, and I think this verse is especially for you this day!"

"I would like to believe that, but my circumstances sure don't show it." Maggie's voice cracked with emotion. "I don't even make enough to support my daughter and myself, and I don't know what I'm going to do!"

Maggie then spilled out the details of her job cutback and her financial challenges. Maggie couldn't believe she was telling a "stranger" all her hurts. But at the same time, she felt safe. Safer than she'd felt in a really long time. Maggie and Anna continued to talk for a long time—until a customer finally came through the door. At that moment, Maggie glanced at the clock on the wall, shocked at how long the two women had been talking.

"I'd better be going, Anna." Maggie stood up and grabbed her purse. "Thank you for the tea, the talk, and your kindness. You've made my day."

"Hold on to God's promises, for they are true," Anna said. Then she added, "Maggie, would you like to join me for lunch tomorrow? I know it's Sunday, but we could meet here after church, say, at noon? I'll fix something simple, and we'll visit some more. How does that sound?"

"That would be nice," Maggie said sincerely. "Really nice."

CHAPTER 7
MARGARET

THE HARVEST HAD BEEN MEAGER, but the New Year held both promise and trepidation, depending on who was looking at it. The fruit trees produced little, but Margaret was still able to can half a dozen jars, to be used on special occasions. But the vegetable garden—yielding only potatoes and onions and turnips for the long, cold winter—had been a bitter disappointment. The oats would also hold them until spring, but that was all.

For Margaret, the New Year brought forth more anxiety, apprehension, and the unwelcome reality of change. She knew Michael felt the same. But she could see that, for Susan, Ned, and James, the winter passed torturously slow. The hope of emigrating held them in its spell.

Then, on a cold, rainy Irish day in February, Uncle John's letter came, all the way from Wolfe Island, Canada.

"Good heavens!" James exclaimed, opening the envelope. "Look at the Lord's bounty!" Margaret took the contents and held the handful of Canadian dollars with awe and wonder, wondering what it could mean. James quickly read his uncle's letter, excited at the blessing they had received.

January, 1851

Dear family,

Thank you for your letter. I was glad to hear that both of my nephews are coming to Wolfe Island and that the entire family will be joining us here in this New World. I cannot wait to meet the wee ones and see how you have fared since I left Ireland these many years ago.

I must offer some counsel for your sailing, for it is a difficult journey.

Do not take the free Irish passage to America that the English Queen has offered. These are mere slave ships where passengers are treated like animals, and many die. Coffin ships they are called, for coffin ships they are.

Find a fairer ship, a newer ship, a safe ship that will not bring such death. Sail in the spring, when the seas are fairer and the storms less treacherous. Many have died from the cold and the storms, and I expect to see all nine of you here, safe and healthy, at the end of your passage.

The enclosed money will aid you in finding such a ship and provide you with second-class passage. Though steerage class passage is less costly, it is often filled with sickness, disease, and many sorrows. Pay for second-class, for you will fare better, even though the quarters are small and cramped. You will also have a measure of privacy, far from the sickness that spreads below decks.

Heed well this counsel, family, and search for a good sturdy vessel. Many weak vessels perish in the storms, and yours must not be one of these.

Stay healthy. Fatten the wee ones for the journey ahead. The passage will likely hold troubles—meager rations, little water, and cold, with the sick and dying all around you. It will not be easy, but look to the horizon. Look to the New World! I will gratefully see you on the other side.

> *Warmly,*
> *Uncle John Hawkins,*
> *Wolfe Island, Canada*

As James read the letter to her, she sat silently nursing baby Meg. She couldn't speak. She couldn't even react. She just sat there, trying to hold her tongue.

"'Tis wisdom, don't you think, me lamb?" James said. She knew that her husband wanted to hear her thoughts, but she feared what she held inside. "We ought not to share these concerns with the children, but we'll keep them in our prayers. I will send letters to those in Belfast and talk with the lads in Hilltown who travel to the city. They will keep a watchful eye out for the proper ship. Do you not think this wise, me wife?"

She could hold it in no longer. "Nae! Belfast be a dangerous city! I never want to go there. I do not want this blessing." Tears overflowed her eyes, and she lay the baby down and took off her spectacles to wipe them away.

"We will be there for only a few days," James soothed. "You must see this as Providence. Do you not?"

She stayed silent, not looking at James and not saying a word. He continued.

"Until it be time for our journey, let us fatten the wee ones with milk and cheese, and if we must, I will bleed the fair cow to give them black pudding, and since Uncle John graciously sent the money for our sailing, we can slaughter a pig for all our sustenance and partake of such a luxury."

Margaret tried to ignore him; she tried not to listen to a word he said. Instead, she stubbornly turned the topic of conversation. "My birthplace, Newry, be the grandest city I've ever known. The great Newry Canal lay next to the River Newry, right in the middle of town. I used to stand along Hill Street and watch the passing of the barges and boats, and the streetlights and night patrols that kept us safe. I was Susan's age when the cathedral of St. Patrick and St. Colman was completed. It be the most splendid place I could ever imagine, with its glowing stained glass, marble, and mosaic. I never want to leave here, James."

James looked at her, his eyes pleading for her to relent. She couldn't. She wouldn't.

Just then the children came in, wet, muddy, and chilled from doing their chores.

"Come to the fire, children, and take off those wet clothes," Margaret said, promptly ending the conversation. "Get ready for bed, and we will tell you a story."

As the children dressed for bed, she made hot tea for them all. She also cut slices of soda bread for each. She even added a dab of the honey that Michael had found only last week when he'd foraged for nuts in the fields. The children gathered around the table, excited to hear one of their father's stories, for he was masterful in the art. But it was Margaret who began.

Margaret held the quilt on her lap as she showed the children the patches of material she and Susan had added of her father's clothing after his death. "These patches were added to our family quilt to remember your grandfather, Edward Caulfield. Remember his name, remember him, and do not take this duty lightly, me children. Tell your children and your children's children. Remember that your grandfather was a good man, a man who was loved near and far for his kindness, his generosity, and his neighborliness. And your granna—remember that her name was Susan Keown Caulfield and that she was like him."

She pointed to the patchwork made from her mum's clothing that she had sewn onto the quilt just two years earlier. For a long moment she sat silent as the children munched on the bread and drank the tea and waited for her to continue.

"Your granna was a midwife who delivered many a babe in the fair city of Newry. Mary, she even helped to deliver you! Do you remember her, Ned?"

"Nae, Mum," Ned admitted, "but I remember Grandfather, and I miss him." At that, the eldest three began to cry.

"I remember Granna, Mum," Susan said through her tears. "She always smiled, even when things were bad. And she always gave me a cube of sugar when we visited her."

"Did she now?" James replied, smiling at his daughter. "She was like that, and I loved her as if she were me own mum."

"Grandfather loved the Mourne Mountains, as I do," Michael said, sounding much older than thirteen. "'Tis a splendid world of green hills sweeping down to the sea. I've not been that far yet, but one day I want to walk all the paths along the heather and moss hills, past the bilberries and cotton grass. I want to tread the Brandy Pass, the Trassey Track, and the Black Stairs. I want to climb to the Cloghmore and watch the raven and the grouse soar against the red and purple and gray sky. Then I want to journey down to the sea to Kilkeel and feast me eyes on the mighty ocean." Michael paused, as if to make his point clear. "But I do not want to sail it! Father, I do not want to leave the place where Grandfather and Granna lie in their graves!"

At that, Margaret joined her own tears with theirs, and then the wee ones cried because everyone else was crying.

"This be a fine kettle of fish," James said, almost in a whisper. He paused and picked up John and Mary and sat one on each knee. James looked at each of his hurting loved ones. Then he turned to Michael with eyes of compassion.

"We must sail together, me son. We are family, and I will not see us torn asunder as many Irish families have been. Hearts broken. Families forever split apart, never to see one another again in this life. Family heritages lost by time and space and distance. We cannot bear it, family."

James set Mary and John down and took the quilt from his wife's hands. Then he continued. "We will take Grandfather, Granna—all of those we've lost—with us, in our hearts, in our minds, in our memories, and in our family quilt. This be what your mum was saying to you."

One by one, the entire family dried their tears. Then prayers were said—prayers that begged God for peace, for patience during this time of waiting, for healing of their broken hearts, for protection and provision in making the journey. After the children were tucked in their beds and fast asleep, Margaret cuddled up to James to whisper her thoughts without waking the children.

* * *

The next morning, Susan, Michael, and Ned went to hedge school in their neighbor's barn, as they often did during the winter days.

"How I love learning!" Susan said to the sky, swinging her lunch pail. "Irish language and grammar class. Latin and reading. 'Tis a wonderful thing, to learn."

She looked at her brothers, shuffling ahead of her. Michael loved every kind of math. Ned was the youngest student, but he had passed some of the older students and was quickly promoted to the next level, thanks to playing school with him for the past two years.

Susan was proud of him. Ned loved reading all the children's chapbooks, for they held exciting stories of well-known outlaws and adventurers, and she knew that Ned was a lad of adventure. When he could, Ned enjoyed eavesdropping on the older classes as they learned about Irish history and the bardic traditions of storytelling, and he often told Susan what he had learned.

Susan ran and caught up with her brothers. She addressed Ned.

"I be ever so glad they let lassies go to the hedge school here. Many schools only allow the lads to learn, and I'd be frightfully sorrowful about that. But I get to learn and teach what I learn."

Ned grinned and nodded, but Michael raised and eyebrow and rolled his eyes. "Lassies," he mumbled.

On the way home from school, Susan was filled with excitement. She praised her younger brother. "Ned, I'm proud of you! Now I'll have to start teaching Mary so she will be ready for hedge school on Wolfe Island."

"Humph!" Michael grumped. "I'm not going to school on Wolfe Island—or anywhere but here!"

"Michael, you know what Father said," Susan snapped her head, sending her braids a blowing in the wind. "We are family and will travel together."

"I'm Irish and must remain on Irish soil!" Michael said emphatically. "Family or no, I be Irish first! And what do you know, you slip of a lassie?"

"I know that Father won't let you stay here and that you're just about the stubbornest person I know!" She felt her face redden with anger and turned away from him.

"I am nearly a man, and I will do as I please." Michael ended the conversation by running ahead of Ned and her. She rolled her eyes and stomped her foot as she watched her big brother climb over the fence into the sheep pasture.

"Why is he like that?" Ned asked.

"Michael be hurting inside, least that's what Father says," Susan replied. The two walked along in silence, holding their cloaks against the battering wind that grew colder by the minute. By the time they got home, both were chilled to the bone.

"Let me get you a sup of warm milk, children," her mum said, rubbing her hands on her apron. "Take off your things and warm yourself by the fire. Where's Michael?"

"He ran ahead of us far back, Mum," Ned replied.

"Mary, would you go out to the byre and see if Michael be with your father?" Margaret asked.

"Aye, Mum," Mary said. Susan knew Mary was always happy to be treated like a big person even though she was tiny, skinny, and frail, which made her look much younger than her four years. Mary pulled on her boots and cloak, and then Susan helped her with her hat just before she ran out the door.

A few minutes later, Mary returned. Her dark hair had been tossed around her porcelain face by the wind. She pushed the strands out of her face. "Father said Michael be fine. They're just having a man-to-man talk."

"Thank you, Mary," Margaret said with a smile. "You're getting to be such a big girl, and a good helper, too!"

"Mum's right, Mary," Susan said, holding her cup of warm milk in her hands. "In fact, how would you like to start some learnin'? Now that Ned's such a smart lad, I can turn me attention to you!"

"Oh, can I?" Mary said, jumping up and down and clapping her hands. "That will make me a really big girl!" Mary looked down at her dress, a hand-me-down that she'd almost outgrown, and Mary said, "Mum, can I have a big girl dress now, too? This be a baby dress."

"Well now," Margaret said. "We'll have to see about that, won't we?"

"And Mum," Ned interrupted, "can I please start wearing trousers instead of this, least while, before we sail?"

Susan had heard Ned complain about his clothing over and over. He hated wearing the wee dresses that Irish boys and girls often wore until they were much older.

"Let me speak to your father first," Margaret said.

"Father will agree. I just know he will," Susan said with a wink.

CHAPTER 8
MAGGIE

MAGGIE COULDN'T WAIT to see Anna again. What a breath of fresh air she had been to Maggie's withered and weary soul just the day before. Anna's openness and acceptance seemed to fill an emptiness that she didn't even know she had, and she needed that. Anna also made her feel safe, and Maggie longed for someone to speak to her deep hurts and insecurities. She was eager to again spend time with this woman.

Over breakfast, she thought about the Scripture verse that Anna had tried to encourage her with. *What was it?*

It took a word search on her iPhone Bible app, but before long she found the verse, Jeremiah 29:11. " 'For I know the plans I have for you,' declares the Lord, 'plans to prosper you and not to harm you, plans to give you hope and a future.' "

Great words, but can He really prosper me and not harm me in the middle of all this mess? And will He give me hope when I have none? It sounds like a pipe dream.

Maggie pushed away the doubts in her head and willed herself to trust God with her present as well as her future. Over a cup of tea and a slice of toast she asked God to help her not only understand it but also to believe it for herself.

She was so anxious to see Anna that she could hardly make it through church. But before long, she was on her way to Anna's Antiques. Maggie turned on to the highway as she thought again about the incident when she was young and had tossed the quilt carelessly on the attic floor. She cringed at the thought of how upset it had made her grandmother.

Grandma was mad, spitting mad! And I don't blame her.

She recalled how her grandmother had explained to her how important the quilt was, that it was the only thing she had left of her Irish heritage, the only thing she would have of her family's past one day. Grandma had also told her that the quilt was a special part of her family story, and that she was a part of that family legacy as well.

Great! And now, will my legacy be that I failed to keep it safe? Maggie changed lanes and clucked her tongue in disgust. But then, suddenly, she remembered the rest of the story.

Her grandmother had taken her hand and made her rub it over the material, feel the material, experience it. She could almost feel it, even at this moment. There was a gray wool patch from her great-great-Grandpa James's work trousers. And there was a tweed patch from her great-great-Uncle Robert's work shirt.

Maggie shifted in her seat as the vivid memory thrilled her to her toes and gave her a burst of hope that surprised her. As she continued to drive, she smiled as she remembered the many different materials she felt those many years ago, materials her grandmother had made her touch. She recalled the delicate baby material, linen, that Grandma had said was taken from baby Meg's gown, and flannel from one of the children's nightshirts.

Maybe, just maybe, I'll find the quilt.

Maggie fidgeted as expectation began to stir in her soul, and she wondered at the timing of it, especially after reading the Bible verse just a short while ago. As she waited at a stoplight, she brushed away a tear of relief as she made a left turn and continue her drive to the store.

Just as Maggie arrived at Anna's Antiques, the city clock tower struck twelve. As she opened the door, the tiny bell that hung on the door tinkled daintily. *Funny, I hadn't noticed that yesterday when I was here.*

"I'll be right there," called a familiar voice from the back. Maggie saw the rack of quilts to her right and went over to see them. There were a dozen different quilts, all appearing to be quite antique. An ornate one had a star pattern on it and was made of velvets and brocade materials, and another that looked like a brick road but was made of plaids and heavy patterned material. One quilt had a lovely diamond pattern, and another had a beautiful pattern that looked like a Celtic cross. Another looked like an intricate pinwheel kaleidoscope.

She gingerly touched a red velvet star. *What beautiful artistry! I wonder who made them and what stories they could tell.*

"It is good to see you again, dearie," Anna said as she approached her. "Aren't these lovely quilts? All handmade. I never, ever purchase machine-made ones. Quilts are pieces of art, as far as I'm concerned. Just look at those perfect stitches." Anna took hold of a corner of the pinwheel quilt and bid Maggie touch it and admire the uniform hand stitching.

Maggie smiled. "My grandmother showed me the hand stitching on the quilts that her mother and grandmother made. I was just a girl at the time, but even back then I was fascinated by such amazing handiwork. And all these beautiful patterns and fabrics and colors!"

"Quite," Anna agreed. "I've made a few quilts in my day, but I always used a machine. They never seemed quite as special as these. And I sure won't sell a one of them cheap. I'd rather do without the cash and keep these pieces of history. Ah, well, let's go and sit awhile, shall we?"

Maggie followed Anna, excited to have the opportunity to know this woman. She was grateful, too, that the store was closed and their visit wouldn't be hurried.

"I made homemade vegetable soup. It was my grandmother's recipe," Anna said as they sat at an antique table near the back. The table was set with handmade placemats and matching napkins with little pansies delicately embroidered on them. The same teapot and teacups they had used the day before sat on the table, as did a matching sugar bowl and creamer. A plate of fresh bread and perfect little pats of butter completed the setting.

"How delightful! Thanks for inviting me."

"My pleasure," Anna said sincerely. "It isn't often that I get the pleasure of making a new friend." Anna placed two lovely ceramic crocks of soup at each of their places and sat down. Taking her hand, Anna offered a prayer of thanksgiving, thanking God for not only the food but also for her new friend, finishing with "...and whatever plans You have for my dear friend, Lord, let her heart be filled with expectation. Amen."

Maggie thanked her and took a sip of her vegetable soup. "This is wonderful!"

As the two ate, Maggie shared about her family and personal journey. Anna seemed fascinated by her story, and even though she didn't often share her difficult past with others, she felt free to openly tell the good, the bad, and the ugly.

Anna sighed and took a sip of her tea. "You've not had the easiest time of it, and I'm sorry to hear that. But God always uses our past for a purpose. Nothing goes to waste."

Even my mistakes, my failures?

Anna put her hands in her lap and leaned back in her chair. "When my husband died in Kenya, I thought my life was over. I had never worked before, but I had two children to support. I had to leave all we had worked for and accumulated in Kenya, and start over. But it seemed that everything I tried to do here in the States to make a new start seemed to go wrong. For a while I was angry with God, and I felt like a failure much of the time. But then God blessed me with this little store and provided for us in such amazing ways. We never went hungry. Never went without."

"How did he die, your husband?" Maggie asked.

"He was riding his motorcycle to speak in a nearby Maasai village, and he was thrown from his bike and broke his neck, right in the middle of the Valley of the Witch Doctors! A Maasai warrior stood guard over his body all night, keeping the wild beasts away until we could be notified."

Anna continued to share about the Maasai tribe whom she loved, and about her sad and difficult decision to move back to the States. Several times she shed silent tears as she told of her feelings of deep aloneness that had haunted her days and nights.

Maggie could relate to Anna's feelings, but she had little to say. Just knowing she wasn't the only one with such dark and hopeless thoughts gave her a strange kind of comfort.

"And your daughter's now in Zimbabwe for the rest of the summer?" Anna asked.

"Yes," Maggie said, excited to share about Bree, "and I can't imagine how I'll get through these next several weeks. She and I have been through so much together this past year. Bree's an amazing young woman, and I'm proud of her. I know she'll do great, but I'm not sure about me."

"Hold on to God's promises, for her and for you," Anna said with confidence. "Where He guides, He provides. I'm sure my mother had lots of apprehension about us going to Africa, too, especially back then. But I respected her for supporting our calling."

After they finished their meal and cleared the dishes away, Anna said, "Maggie, I'd like to ask you a favor. Yesterday you told me that your employer cut back your hours, so last night I prayed and thought about it. I'm getting on in years, and this shop's a lot of work. I've been thinking about hiring someone to help me for a long, long time now, but I've never felt that it was the right time. Now it is. Would you be interested in working for me, part-time, on Fridays and Saturdays? That is, if you can arrange your hours with your employer to be Monday through Thursday. I'll pay a fair wage, it would be a great help to me, and I'd enjoy the company as well."

"Really? Oh, Anna, I would love that!" Maggie was shocked and amazed at such a gracious offer. "I'll have to talk to my boss, but thank you! Thank you, Anna!"

Maggie stayed for several hours, filling out paperwork and hoping to learn more about what Anna expected of her as an employee. As she imagined herself working in the little shop, a wide smile crossed her lips. She couldn't imagine a better second job. She'd just have to convince Mr. Duvall to agree to the Monday through Thursday plan!

This job would be more like getting paid to be in a peaceful oasis!

After saying goodbye and lavishing a bouquet of gratitude on Anna, Maggie left Anna's Antiques, perhaps her soon-to-be new place of employment.

On the way home, she thought about the past two days. *I was looking for a quilt but found a friend—and a job? Can God really be working already?*

CHAPTER 9
MARGARET

FOR MARGARET, James, and the children, the long and dreary winter's days and months plodded on in the quiet rhythm of farm life. The days were filled with milking, mucking out the byre stalls, feeding the animals, pumping water, sewing, cooking, and stubbornly struggling to survive the northern Irish winter.

Several times during those months James visited their neighbor, Ian Fallows, who was famous for making that illegal Irish whiskey called Poteen. Margaret grew more and more frustrated each time James came home smelling of "demon liquor" as she called it. Yet because she hated confrontation, Margaret stayed silent—until one cold winter's evening when James returned particularly inebriated.

The children were asleep. She angrily whispered her discontent. "James! 'Tisn't the Lord's way to drink as you do. And what kind of example is this for Michael and the others? Please, my husband, stop this before it gets ahold of you as it did your father."

James hung his head. "Forgive me, wife. I fear I forget

whilst I am with the menfolk," he admitted. "I'll not let it happen again."

Margaret hugged her husband and tried to forgive his error, but fear continued to grip her heart. She knew that James was well aware of her concerns, and he tried to keep it at bay, but she worried nonetheless. *What if he falls to the lure of the bottle as his father did and never recovered?*

The months slowly drew closer to leaving their homeland for good, but the atmosphere in the tiny stone cottage remained heavy with unspoken conflict. Margaret still held much foreboding and apprehension in her heart for the Sailing, but Michael seemed to grow more and more sullen about it by the day.

At the start of the New Year, Margaret was commissioned to make an Irish Chain quilt for the baroness whose manor house was nearby. Since Margaret was known far and wide for her skill with the needle, it was the third time she'd been asked to complete a quilt for her. Thus, much of her days were filled with working on the time-consuming project. To do her work, she sat far from the warm peat fire and close to the one sheepskin-covered window that gave her weak eyes a little light. Though it was tedious and difficult work, it would inevitably bring a fair wage.

As Margaret worked, Susan tended to the wee ones.

"'Tis a challenge to keep these wee ones quiet, Mum," Susan said as Mary and John squealed over a game they were playing. "But I'm trying."

"You're doing fine, me lassie," she said, squeezing Susan's hand in gratitude. "You've given me much time to work on the baroness's quilt, and I am grateful. And teaching the wee ones their learnin'? What a blessing!"

When the weather was fair, Susan would bundle them up and take the wee ones outside to play in the sunshine and chase the chickens or the dog, or just run in the fields. One day, Margaret stood in the doorway watching her children play, grateful that they could exercise their tiny bodies and strengthen their lungs.

The children played fetch with Buddy for a long while, tossing a stick back and forth and laughing as carefree as children should. When their energy was spent, each one of them took turns hugging their dog, scratching his ears, and snuggling their noses in his fur.

"What shall we do with Buddy?" Margaret said to baby Meg who looked up from her pot banging with an unknowing expression.

Throughout the winter, James, Michael, and Ned tended the animals and did what they needed to do for the land. Since they were to leave in May and there was relatively little to do, James and Ned concentrated their efforts on fattening and grooming the cows and the calf and the pigs, and tending to the chickens. They would all be sold at the fair that spring, as would the sheep, and they would fetch a better price if they were fine and as fat as they could make them.

"I'll take the sheep to the finest part of the pasture, Father," Michael offered.

Margaret raised an eyebrow as she watched Michael leave and spoke her mind to James. "Our lad loves caring for the sheep and enjoys his days in the hilly fields with Buddy, exploring the land he loves. But he likes being alone too much, and I fear that it be there in the fields that our son has too much time to fret about the future."

James agreed. "Michael still refuses to accept that this land will soon belong to another, and it seems his heart be growing more and more defiant. When anyone mentions emigrating, Michael leaves the conversation and disappears for a long while. How can we settle him, lamb?"

For a long while, the two discussed their eldest but neither knew the answer. In truth, Margaret knew she wavered to accept the Sailing, too, if only for Michael's sake. So they prayed, asking God to help Michael and her to find peace.

By March, James, Ned, and Susan were anxious to get on with their sailing adventure, yet they learned not to voice their excitement in the presence of Michael. Instead, they talked together quietly when the opportunity arose.

James had spent much time and effort looking for a buyer for the farm, but no one had the money. Margaret and James realized a sale was unlikely, even though they owned some of the best land in County Down.

"There be just too much abandoned land that could easily be confiscated for nothing," Margaret said one evening as they fretted about it. "I think we should reconsider our plans and stay, that's what I think."

"Nae, me love. We must follow your father's request." Deep lines of stress grew across James's brow.

Then one sunny spring day, the children sat around the table and excitedly jabbered about the bright green sprouts coming to life on their farm. The anticipation of spring seemed to bring them all a bit of hope.

Margaret busily buried potatoes in the ashes of the burning peat to cook them for dinner when a knock came on the door. Mary ran to the door and accepted a letter from the delivery boy. James had received a letter from the baron.

As she gathered baby Meg in her arms, she looked at her husband, wondering what news it would bring. A letter from the baron was no small thing. But before reading it, James piled more peat on the fire, and with the bellows, he helped to bring the coals to life. Then he sat down at the table.

Margaret set the baby to play on the floor near James and shooed the rest of the children outside. She took the kettle off the hook over the fire and made them both a cup of tea, and only then did they read the letter.

As James read the letter, the baron called the Hawkins "a respectable farm family," and after more greetings and much verbose rhetoric, he offered to buy their land. The price? A pittance. The purpose? To grow grain for export. Once he finished reading, Margaret glanced at him and then stared at the baby playing on earthen floor. For a long while, she said nothing, could say nothing. She knew James patiently waited for her to reply, and finally she found her voice.

"Our land be worth four times the baron's price!" She complained bitterly, removing her spectacles and brushing her thin hair back toward her tight bun. "It's robbery, but who else would buy it? Perhaps we should stay here in Ireland."

"Nae," James disagreed. "I find this a grievous decision as well, and it pains me to face such a loss. But we must journey to the New World for our children's sake and for those who will come after us."

She had to protest. "But will we allow our own land to betray all we've worked for, and let it feed the fat English while our Irish brethren starve? 'Tisn't right. Shan't we stay and help our own?"

"By taking the journey, me love, we will help our own," James told her. "We cannot help the helpless and hopeless, the starving and destitute who abide here. We must find our new life in the New World."

Tears of resignation streamed down her cheeks. James picked up baby Meg and held her close. She squirmed and cooed in his lap. "This wee babe be why we leave, why we turn our backs on the land we love and turn our faces toward the Western horizon. Embrace it, me lamb, once and for all, for us all." Her kind husband put one arm around her and she buried her face in his shoulder.

That evening, James told the children about the letter as they broke open their potatoes, poured in a wee bit of milk, added a pinch of salt, and ate them slowly. And while they ate, they talked of the journey to come.

"We will take all we can, family, but that won't be much," James said, "and at the Spring Fair, we will sell whatever we can and buy what we need for the Sailing."

James took out a sheet of paper and a pencil, and he carefully began a sailing list. At that moment, Margaret fully resigned herself to go. She would sail. She would emigrate. She would leave it all behind.

She decided to engage in the conversation that night, and she even asked questions and offered ideas for James's list. She worried that Michael would feel more alone than ever, and her concerns were validated as she saw him sitting, silently stewing, his eyes dark with anger.

"We must take the family quilt, though I've had little time to work on it with the baroness's quilt occupying me hands these many days," she said.

"And we must bring the spinning shuttle, and the sewing kit, the candlesticks, and Grandfather's books," Susan added decisively.

"And the portraits of Granna and Grandfather, and the Earl's portrait, too," Margaret said with a tinge of sadness. "And we must take the herbs and ointments and medical remedies for the crossing and beyond."

Ned chimed in. "I want to bring me slingshot."

"We must be careful in choosing what we bring, for we can bring little," James warned. "Each of us can bring one special item, like your slingshot, Ned. I will bring me ax head. But the rest must be clothes and necessities. Decide carefully, lads and lassies, what you might choose."

"I want to find a four-leaf clover to bring," Mary said. They all laughed at the sweet child's remark, even Michael.

Then Ned said, "We can make crates for our things and a cage for Buddy."

James looked away, and then sadness seemed to instantly permeate the tiny cottage. Ned and the wee ones didn't know why, but Michael and Susan did.

Their beloved dog and friend, Buddy, would not come with them.

"It's time for bed, children," Margaret said, quickly trying to change the subject. "Michael and Susan, please help the wee ones prepare for bed while I clean up."

* * *

The next day, while the wee ones napped and the menfolk worked outside, Margaret and Susan made a list of the clothes they might take with them. They needed to pack several layers of clothing for each of them to stay warm, for crossing the ocean was often a cold affair, even in May.

"Each of us will take two full changes for the journey," Margaret said, "though this may be a luxury for many. And if there is room in the crates, we will pack lighter clothing for summertime on Wolfe Island."

Susan smiled as she watched her mum engage so positively in the task.

Margaret continued. "We must bring cheese, salt, tea, herbs, soap, bedding, towels, and cooking and eating utensils as well."

She went on to explain that their packing had to be done carefully and wisely. Though the ship provided basic sustenance, she wanted to supplement the meager diet that would be provided with a little extra now and then.

They added to the list their most sturdy linen chemise and drawers and the two woolen dresses that Margaret had recut from Granna's dresses. Since she always wore an apron, she chose her best two for the voyage. She added her mum's heavy wool Irish hooded cloak, and a sturdy pair of brogues for her.

"I need boots, Mum," Susan said. "Me toes hurt in these. But me headscarf, shawl, and stockings are fittin' for the trip." Margaret noted Susan's things and added a "to get" list on the backside of the paper.

Then she turned to the menfolk. "James and Michael will wear knee breeches, linen shirts, and knitted wool stockings."

"You did a clever job sewing and recasting them from grandfather's clothes, Mum." Susan gave her mum a hug and Margaret stroked her daughter's braids before returning to her task.

She decided that both James and Ned had sturdy boots, but Michael would need new boots for the journey, for the soles of his old ones were beyond repair. Margaret wrinkled her brow at the bittersweet thought that James had inherited her father's tweed topcoat with the swallowtail. That would serve him well for the crossing and beyond. She forced the memory of her father away and continued with her family's needs.

Mary, John, and baby Meg wore the typical Irish infant dresses, passed down from one child to another. Margaret decided that she would somehow find time to fashion a dress or two for the wee ones from her mum's old linen and make at least one proper lassie dress for her Mary. Moreover, she would need plenty of linen for the baby's nappies. She fought back anxious feelings and added these items to the ever-lengthening list.

That evening, Margaret talked with James about Ned. "He's anxious to be a lad, James. He's wanting to wear trousers. Shall we do his breeching ceremony before we sail?"

"What a wise woman you are, wife!" James touched her cheek. "Let's do it on St. Patrick's Day and make it a grand event!"

She happily agreed, and whenever Ned was outside working with his father, she secretly refashioned two pair of Michael's old trousers to fit Ned. She was thrilled to give her son this memory—before they left their homeland.

* * *

St. Patrick's Day dawned sunny and warm. James had chosen a lamb from the herd, the first meat they'd had that new year. Margaret made a feast of roasted lamb with a dish of colcannon from the last jar of pickled cabbage and by adding a few potatoes. After their noontime dinner, they ceremoniously had Ned's breeching ceremony. Ned's hair was cut into a boyish style similar to Michael's. Then he was given the two pairs of trousers and was encouraged to choose which pair of trousers he would wear.

"Oh, thank you, Father and Mum!" Ned said, running to hug each of his family members, even baby Meg. "I be a proper lad now!"

Once Ned donned his new trousers, James and the children played hide and seek among the hedgerows and outbuildings, and they all laughed as they hadn't laughed for a long time. Margaret watched from afar, pleased with her growing family.

About a week later, James made an announcement over warm cups of milk and bites of bread. "In the morn, we will all journey together to visit Grandfather and Granna's grave for the last time. We must pay our respects and say our final goodbyes before we leave them here in our homeland."

Margaret frowned at the thought of saying goodbye. The children seemed excited to be taking the journey, but Michael remained morose and silent. She wondered about her eldest son who appeared to have grown pensive and withdrawn.

The next day as they jostled their way to Newry, the family saw a group of thin and sickly men constructing a new road and bridge. "Public works projects," James grumbled, shaking his head in disgust. "'Tis a terrible shame that they make those poor men work such long hours for such little pay, so low they can barely buy bread for their starving families." That scene, and more like it, solidified Margaret's agreement, even determination, to leave Ireland and find a new life.

Their day in Newry was one of great emotions for all of them, none more than her. The cemetery visit brought tears to them all, save John and the wee babe. And a drive by Grandfather's old house brought floods of memories for each of them, she was sure. But they kept their thoughts inside, except Mary. She sweetly waved at the house as they passed by and said, "We love you and we will ne'er forget you, Granna and Grandfather."

Before leaving Newry, James drove them by Margaret's childhood haunts. James held her hand as they drove along the great canal and the River Newry, and she knew James could feel her trembling hand in his. She tried but failed to hold back the tears that streamed down her cheeks, but she thanked James for knowing how much she wanted to see her special places one last time.

As they rounded the corner toward the great cathedral, Margaret yelled, "Stop!"

James barely had the buggy still before she handed Meg to Susan and then raced inside the cathedral to say prayers. The rest of the family quickly joined her inside, and together they asked God for safety and health, provision and peace, for the journey ahead. As they lifted their heads from prayer, Margaret looked around and her heart filled with foreboding.

"Where's Michael?" she asked.

"I haven't seen him in a fair bit," Susan replied.

"Nor I," Ned said. "But he was heading around the outside of the church as we went in."

James looked at her with the same concern and quickly stepped into action, searching and calling for his eldest, but to no avail. For more than an hour they all searched around the cathedral, and then James and Ned took the buggy to retrace their trip through town. But that yielded nothing as well.

By the time James and Ned returned to the church, she was frantic. "Where be our son, James? What has become of him?"

Susan voiced it, almost to herself. "He has run away. I'm sure of it."

James looked at her as if they had all heard a prophecy. They knew it was true.

CHAPTER 10
MAGGIE

THE SOUND OF HER CELL PHONE shook Maggie from a deep sleep. "Hello," she yawned.

"Hi, Mom! It's me, Bree! How are you?"

She bolted upright as adrenaline streamed through her body. "Hi, honey! Are you okay?"

"Great, Mom! Just had the opportunity to call so I grabbed it. Sorry if I woke you."

"I'm glad you did, Bree." She sucked in a breath. "Tell me about your trip."

"I only have a few minutes, but it's been great! At the church we're working with, we're helping to feed lots of hungry people with all that peanut butter we brought. And every day we work with these sweet little kids who have absolutely nothing. We feed them and play with them and teach them about God. And I am learning a lot about being content with what I have after seeing their faith. It's simply amazing, Mom. What about you?"

"That's awesome, Bree," she replied. "I'm good. Lots happening here. My hours got cut at work, but then I got a part-time job at an antique store after I met this wonderful lady. She used to be a missionary in Africa, and she hired me! You'll love her."

"Way cool, Mom! Did you find the quilt?" Briana asked.

"Not yet. Still looking," she admitted, trying to keep the disappointment out of her tone. "Are you healthy, Bree? I know there's a lot of sickness there, and I worry about you."

"Don't worry, Mom. I'm fine," Briana said. "I'm sorry, but I've got to go. There's a whole line of kids who need to connect with their parents, and they're waiting to use this phone. I miss you, Mom, and I love you tons."

"You too, babe. Stay healthy and safe, okay? Thanks for calling!" She didn't want to hang up.

"I will. Bye, Mom." As the phone line went dead, she threw back the covers and jumped out of bed.

Well, that made my day. What a great way to start my mini vacation!

Maggie hopped in the shower, anticipating a great day. Both she and her friend Brigit Flanagan had taken a vacation day that Wednesday, just to get away and spend much-deserved time together. They had been friends since their girls were little, and then they'd been there for each other through each other's rough divorces. It had been far too long since they'd had some girl time.

After Maggie showered, put on her favorite jeans and T-shirt, and enjoyed a quick bowl of oatmeal, Maggie pulled her long, thick hair into a ponytail and headed out the door to pick up her friend.

On the way, she pondered her surprise conversation with Bree and thanked God for the wonders of technology. *My girl's halfway around the globe, and we get to connect like she's around the corner. It sure wasn't that simple when Anna lived in Africa.*

Her thoughts about Bree, her friend, and the quilt all melded together as she drove to Brigit's house. She prayed for her daughter, for the day, and for the new job she'd start in just a few days. She thanked God for her boss who had allowed her to work Monday through Thursday—and even give her a Wednesday off. She was grateful, but her heart still ached about all her other current challenges as she turned into Brigit's driveway.

"It's awesome to see you, my friend!" Brigit said, slipping into the passenger seat and giving her a hug. She was a large, tall Swede, and her dirty blonde shag and soft blue eyes made her look younger than Maggie was, when in fact Brigit was several years older. Only the deep crow's feet around her eyes gave away her age and the stresses in her life.

"It's great to see you, too!" Maggie patted her friend's hand. "We're gassed up and ready to go."

They had already decided to drive through the mountains, stop for lunch, and head home whenever their hearts' desired. No kids. No phones. No distractions. An entire day to visit and enjoy nature at its summertime best.

The two women chatted as Maggie drove through town to the freeway. Conversation flowed easily as they caught up on their lives—her cutbacks and her new job, Briana's trip and the early morning phone call. She heard about Brigit's grown children and her ever-stress-filled work in human resources. Once they were on their way toward the mountains, she remembered something.

"Hey, Brigit, you used to sell antiques, right?" She glanced over at her friend. "I'd like to hear your thoughts about a problem I have." She told Brigit all about what had happened with her family's crazy quilt and her desire to find it.

"I had a few quilts when I sold antiques." Brigit combed her hands through her wild blonde hair. "I'd love to help. I just can't believe Bill would take a family heirloom. How cruel!"

"Don't get me started. Please," Maggie said, her brow furrowing. "I can't think about that. I just need to find the quilt."

She knew that Brigit understood the pain behind betrayal. She'd been there, too. Though her ex hadn't taken Brigit's belongings, he'd been unfaithful and hurt her deeply.

"You probably already know a lot about crazy quilts. Stop me if I'm being a bore," Brigit said.

"Frankly, I haven't had much to research the topic much, but assume I know little and fill me in." Maggie slowed down and switched lanes as the mountain highway began to wind upward. Brigit commented on the beautiful scenery—rocky inclines and gorgeous evergreen trees, fast flowing rivers, and stunning waterfalls. She drank in the beauty and peace around them as she listened to her friend.

"I think the term 'crazy quilt' is a dumb name for these quilts. I think they should be called 'heirloom quilts' or something more honorable," Brigit began. "But they're called that because they have no specific design. Most patchwork quilts use a pattern, but crazy quilts have no pattern on purpose. That's why they look kind of haphazard. They also use all kinds of fabrics, unlike other patterned quilts."

"My family's crazy quilt had all kinds of fabrics in it— especially lots of wool, since my ancestors were sheep farmers back in Ireland," Maggie said. "But it also had some cottons that were plain or with prints or plaids, and even brocade and lots of linen material. Wow! It's amazing what I remember when I think about it."

"Definitely," Brigit agreed. "The best crazy quilts were made by hand and not on a machine, and some had all kinds of interesting additions to them—buttons, bows, crochet work, and other embellishments such as embroidery. I guess they did look kind of crazy!"

"Come to think of it, my family's had buttons and embroidery," she said. "I even got to sew some buttons on it when I was a little kid. The only thing I remember that was not random was the Kelly green yarn ties at the corners of the quilt blocks."

"Oh, they used to do that, too," Brigit agreed. "It's really quite creative, kind of like a Picasso or something. The quilters could express themselves any way they wanted to, and that's why I think crazy quilts became popular. It was a way to show off their stuff!"

Maggie laughed. "Did the quilters only use old clothing and cast offs?"

"Not always, though that was a great way to remember the family story before the days of cameras," Brigit said. "But quilters often used it as an art form, sometimes buying expensive or interesting fabrics just for fun."

"My family sure didn't have the money to do that," Maggie admitted. "They were quite poor, except for the Caulfield side."

"Hmm...you'll have to tell me about them later," Brigit said. "Anyway, from what I remember, crazy quilts were first made as costumes, not as bed quilts. Back in the 1100s, Venice had an annual carnival, and everyone dressed up. The people used crazy quilting to make colorful costumes. Cool, huh?"

"Way back then? I thought crazy quilts were an 1800s thing," Maggie said as she noticed a tiny coffee shop that was painted bright pink and purple. "Hey, let's stop for a coffee and a break, okay?"

"Sounds good to me. Let's do it, but the inside better not be pink" Brigit said, turning up her nose. "This is a little too Pepto-Bismol colored for me."

Maggie laughed. Her friend always made her laugh. It felt good. Freeing. Life-giving.

After a coffee break, the two women continued driving, and Brigit continued sharing details about history, which was one of her favorite things to do. Intermittently, one or the other would comment on the views of the mountain streams or rolling hills, the tiny hamlets, or the pretty countryside. The scenic drive both calmed her spirit and invigorated her at the same time.

Brigit returned to their earlier conversation. "The 1800s were the pinnacle of the crazy quilt fad, for sure. They were even featured in the Philadelphia Centennial Expo. After that, magazine articles came out on both sides of the crazy quilt fad—praising it *and* condemning it. Figures. Even back then, people had their opinions."

Maggie laughed, enjoying Brigit's humor. "But I thought Queen Victoria had something to do with crazy quilts."

"Oh yeah," Brigit chuckled. "I forgot about that. Queen Victoria was a hoarder...had a ridiculous amount of stuff and they couldn't even get into her rooms. They even had to hold court in the corridors of Windsor Castle. Crazy!"

"But what does that have to do with crazy quilts, other than she was kind of crazy," Maggie asked, giggling.

"Well, there are whole books out there, if you want all the crazy facts," Brigit joked. "But from what I remember, Victoria's influence was global, and she collected mementos of all kinds of things. Crazy quilts also collect family mementos, I guess. People in those days never threw anything away, so when a piece of clothing or whatever was no longer usable, they'd cut out the fabric that wasn't worn out and used it in quilts and other things."

"I guess the quilts were kind of like collages, huh?" Maggie added.

"Exactly," Brigit agreed. "A collage that sort of parodied Victoria's clutter!"

Both laughed and enjoyed a few minutes of the scenery in silence, but Brigit could never let too much silence come between them. It was just her way. Brigit continued. "The richer ladies of the day showed off their quilts, either laying them on the parlor sofa or decorating the wall. Poorer families decorated their beds with them."

Maggie slowed down and pointed to a roadside diner. "How about a bite?"

"Good idea. I'm famished," Brigit stretched. "That place looks a little more normal than that pink coffee shop."

Maggie nodded as she turned into the roadside café with picture window and a sign that said, "Brandy's Bistro." Maggie held the door for Brigit who bowed dramatically and winked as she passed. Once they looked at the menus, they talked about the fun antiques scattered around the bistro shelves until the waitress came up.

After ordering soup and sandwiches, the two chatted about their kids and their hectic schedules and their ever-present financial challenges. Maggie shared about Anna and the shop and her mom, and Brigit shared about her work and her sister's health issues.

Then they returned to their quilt conversation. Brigit loved sharing her knowledge and she had lots to share about this one.

"I think crazy quilts are really cool because you can look at them and almost see how people lived back then," Brigit said after swallowing a bite of her sandwich, "and if you know the family story, it's all the more of a treasure."

Maggie's eyes teared up, and she could barely swallow the bite of her sandwich. Brigit saw that she'd hit a nerve. She reached across the table and squeezed her arm. "Sorry, Maggie."

"It's just that, well, I'm such a failure." She looked down at the table.

"Stop right there, girl!" Brigit said, loud enough to turn the heads of a couple nearby. She took Maggie's hand in hers and lowered her voice. "You are not a failure! How could you know that Bill would even dare to take it? Cut yourself some slack, girlfriend, or I'll cut it for you!"

That made her smile. She was grateful for friends who could shake sense into her when she needed it, and Brigit had always been that kind of friend. Brigit would defend her, support her, and love her.

The ride home was filled with lighthearted chitchat and lots of laughs. Brigit even had a few ideas about where to look for the quilt, and she gave Brigit tips on slowing down and de-stressing after work. As she pulled into Brigit's driveway, Maggie hugged her. "Thanks for being a walking encyclopedia, Brigit, but most of all, thanks for being my friend."

"The pleasure's all mine, girlfriend!" Brigit winked and waved goodbye.

Maggie's head was swimming as she drove home. *Just like the crazy quilt, I guess I'm treasured too, at least by my friend! Today was just what I needed.*

CHAPTER 11
MARGARET

IT WAS TRUE. Michael had run away.

Margaret, James, and the children stayed in Newry that night, hoping to find Michael lost or simply sulking, but still in town. When Michael was not to be found, the family sorrowfully returned to the farm, not knowing what else to do. They prayed and cried. They fretted and worried.

Margaret's mind raced and sleep evaded her as she imagined all sorts of perils befalling her son. Though she understood his apprehension about emigrating, she could not fathom why he would run away. Exhaustion eventually took over and she fell into a restless sleep, waking up often.

In the middle of the night, she suddenly sat straight up. An idea dawned on her. She shook James awake. "He's gone to see Robert! He's gone to Kilkeel!"

"Of course," James agreed, rubbing the sleep from his eyes. He slammed his fist into the mattress. "Our lad has been moping around all winter, holding in all his frets and fears. I am through with this nonsense! I should have known he would go there. I will go at the break of dawn and fetch him home."

"Please do not be too vexed with him, husband," Margaret pleaded.

Before sunrise, James had already prepared the wagon to leave. She could see he was angry but she sent him off in the fog of the spring morn, with a heel of bread and a hunk of cheese. The journey would take nearly half the day, but with each passing mile, she knew James would be closer to ensuring that their firstborn was safe.

* * *

Once in Kilkeel, James checked at the boarding house where he knew Robert stayed, searched through the small town, and then went to the docks. It was there James heard the news.

"Robert left with a young lad this very morn," the elderly bearded man said. "Up and left his job, he did. Said he was going to the New World."

"Which way was he traveling?" James asked, frantic to know where to look.

"West, to the Mournes," the man said, tipping his hat and bidding James good day.

"Much obliged, good sir." James shook the man's rough, wrinkled hand.

James anxiety grew by the moment until his hands began to shake. Oh, how he wished for a sip of Irish whiskey or even Poteen just then, but he quickly shook off those thoughts with a shake of his head and a prayer sent to heaven.

James had no answers but he was done. Done with pampering the unrealistic imaginations of his eldest lad. Michael knew they would emigrate to the New World. Why wouldn't he settle his heart and turn toward the Sailing? Why be he so stubborn?

James unclenched his aching jaw and headed west along the main road, and it didn't take long for him to find Robert and Michael walking along the dusty road. Relieved to see them both but still shaking from anger, James pulled his wagon to a stop and hopped out, wishing his face weren't hot and red with anger. As he looked at his son, Michael's face held a mixture of fear, surprise, embarrassment, and shame planted firmly on it.

"'Tis much heartache you have brought to all of us, lad," James scolded, a little too loud and harsh. "We thought you dead or taken, and your mum has shed many a tear. We all have. You must stop this foolishness at once, or we will have a meeting in the woodshed, that we will. We might have one anyway for the pain you have rendered us!"

"Forgive me, Father," Michael choked out. "I have wronged you. I was wrong." Michael bent his head in contrition and stood silent. James thought he looked to be awaiting a slap right there.

James's anger eased; his son was safe. He let out a noisy sigh, shook out the tension in his hands that had been balled up in fists, embraced Michael, and instead of a slap, he mussed Michael's hair. His lad embraced him and broke into sobs saying, "I'm sorry. I'm sorry," over and over again.

James shushed him but continued to hold him as he turned to Robert. "Forgive the intrusion, brother. Your nephew loves you."

"Michael is repentant. He is contrite, brother. He had quite a fright and has learned much along his journey of transgression. We just now be on our way to return to your farm." Robert smiled. "If you are keen with it, I will stay with you until the Sailing."

Michael wiped his eyes and smiled in expectation, and James smiled too. "We will all rejoice in your presence, brother," James said.

On the ride home, Michael told his father about how he had left them at the Cathedral, walked along the River Newry, and caught a ride with a farmer going to Warrenport and then another to Kilkeel. He apologized over and over and admitted that he had been scared, lonely, and had time to think about the implications of being separated from his family forever. "I ne'er want to leave me family, Father. I love you all more than I love this land. I learned that and much more on me way."

James laughed in relief. "Me lad, you must learn to accept the changes that come in your life, else you will always be disgruntled, for life is full of changes."

"Yes, Father, I have much to learn," Michael admitted.

For the remainder of the ride home, James and Robert helped to answer the questions Michael had. James tried to handle his son's fears and worries with patience, care, and skill. Indeed, by the time they got to the farm, James could see a marked improvement in Michael's countenance, and he raised a mighty thanks to the Lord above.

James, Robert, and Michael returned to a dark cottage late in the evening. Everyone was asleep, but when the three men opened the door, the family awoke with a joyful start. A late-night celebration ensued, with cups of warm milk and much love.

* * *

A frenzy of activity filled the following weeks, especially for James. With the farm sold to the baron and emigration imminent, the comfort of his brother Robert's light-hearted presence and his strong arms were a great help around the Hawkins farm as they prepared for the local fair.

The Hilltown Fair was a semi-annual event that the entire family enjoyed, but this year would be different. Each day, he and the family prepared for the big day.

"The Fair will be not so festive this year, family," James warned them. "We must work hard to sell all we can—the animals, the tools, and anything we not be taking with us—all that might fetch a price."

The fair was held on April 21st, Easter Monday. It was a day of celebration, not just as an extension of Resurrection Sunday, but also as a way to reconnect with friends and neighbors after the long Irish winter. People from near and far would descend on the small village of Hilltown to buy and sell, to enjoy Irish culture, and to jabber the day away. Because they would not have time to enjoy the festivities or chat with the neighbors, the thought of it was a melancholy one for all of them.

James, Robert and the lads prepared for the journey to the fair while Margaret and Susan prepared for the Easter Sunday dinner. Taking their animals to Hilltown would likely be an arduous journey, and they discussed how to manage it.

"We will fill the wagon with the goods and the wee lambs and the chickens that we need to sell," James said during dinner. "Robert, you and the children will prod the animals along, for it will take time for them to walk the nearly four miles to Hilltown."

"We will all do our part, Father," Michael said. That night they went to bed early, ready for a busy day.

Margaret awoke the next morning with a terrible headache, likely due to the incessant strain of her needlework and the stresses of change. "I will stay here with the wee ones, James. You take Michael, Susan, and Ned, and God be with you," Margaret said as they filled their bellies with oatmeal and hot tea.

James kissed his wife and wee ones farewell, and they were off.

On the way to the fair, the thick hedgerows and moss-covered stone walls along the road kept the animals from wandering far. But when they came to the big, brown bog, James worried that the animals might stray.

"Hold them fast, lads and lass," James called from the wagon. "Bring them close and do not let them stray into the bog."

Thankfully the animals didn't wander, and all of them dutifully plodded on. When they finally came to Hilltown and saw the fair in the distance, James's heart rejoiced with excitement as well as a bit of trepidation.

"Well done, all of you," James commended. "'Twas a difficult job you did this fine morn. I am proud of you all.

And now, on to even bigger things."

James had already discussed their duties. Robert and Michael would be in charge of selling the animals. First, they all went to the far end of the fair grounds and found a large pen for their cows and calf, pigs, sheep, and chickens.

"Oh blathers!" Michael said, laughing as he shut the pen gate. "They be quite the menagerie, don't you think, Uncle?"

"'Tis true, lad," Robert said. "Let us pray the good Lord favors this day with blessings."

After settling the animals, James took Susan and Ned and set them up to sell their wares. The shovel, spade, and hoe. Several of Granna's things and Mum's needlework. A few dishes and pots, goose feather pillows, and clothes. Whatever might fetch a price for the Sailing.

"'Tis such an exciting day, even if we have to work." Susan shook her head, her braids flying in the breeze.

"We be real merchants, just like the grown-ups," Ned replied, grinning.

James laughed as he gave them final instructions and then bid them farewell to find out the news of any possible sailing vessels. As he walked toward a group of menfolk, he took in the view. The atmosphere at the fair was open and friendly, as he, or anyone, would expect of the Irish. Even in difficult times, these hard-working, sensible folk were there to socialize, celebrate, and enjoy all things Irish. It was a grand affair, and quite a noisy one at that.

The small, makeshift stalls of meats and sweets, eggs and butter, hats and shawls, quilts and crochet work filled row after row, leading to the animal pens at one end. At the closer end of the fair were the entertainers—the jugglers, musicians, and storytellers—all throwing caution to the wind at the same time and creating a cacophony of Irish joy. The sound of the tin whistle, harp, fiddle, bodhran drum, and uileann pipes gave heed to all who wanted to dance the reel or the jig or the lilt, and James secretly wished he had time to partake of the revelry. Fine Gaelic music and song filled the air, while the jugglers drew the wee ones to their wonders, and the storytellers spun Irish yarns about the folk heroes of old.

James chatted with the men but heard no helpful news. But when he returned to check on Susan and Ned, Susan was excited beyond measure. "Look, Father, that woman just down from us be selling brogues and boots just the right size for Michael and me! And she has portmanteaus, too. We already sold a few things and have these ha'pennies. Can we get them, please, Father?"

"I will speak with her, but we must wait until we have sovereigns in hand from the sale of these things and of the animals." He pointed to their wares. "Patience, lassie. God will provide. There are many strange faces here from Ulster and even Leinstar. Perhaps they have come with sovereigns and a mind to buy our things."

As the day wore on, James kept searching for information and checking on his family. Susan and Ned had sold many of their wares. Robert and Michael did well, too.

"The baron's cook bought most of the pigs and chickens," Michael told his father. "'Fattest of the lot, they are,' he said. I be glad we fattened them through the winter and was happy to collect these sovereigns from the man." James patted Michael on the back and gave him hearty thanks.

Robert added to the good news. "A nearby neighbor bought the cow and calf, and he kindly offered to let us keep them for milk and cream until we sail. Only the sheep are left, but no one seems interested yet."

"Why are there no buyers for the sheep, Father?" Michael asked.

"'Tis still early, barely after lunch, lad," Father said. "Be mindful that patience be a virtue."

James left and hurried to talk with the other menfolk he knew. He inquired of the ships and the sailings and the dangers of an Atlantic passage, and he learned all he could for the days ahead. Though he enjoyed a pint of ale with the men, he remembered the hurt in Margaret's eyes when she confronted him. He slowly, carefully, and wisely nursed just one pint as he chatted with his neighbors.

"There be a fine new ship sailing on the twenty-second of May, me friend," said an acquaintance, Sean Boyd. "She be called the *Tom Bowline*, and here be the newspaper print, *The Belfast Mercury*, that tells the tale. I am traveling to Belfast this week to put me name and that of me family on the list of passengers."

James took the newspaper from Sean and read the announcement:

> *"Ship Tom Bowline, Belfast to Quebec, to sail direct from Belfast on twenty-second of May.*
>
> *The favourite and fast-sailing ship, Tom Bowline, 1,200 tons burthen, William Gray, Commander. This superior new British-built ship is now in Port, is only on her first voyage, and will be punctually dispatched from Belfast for Quebec, on the above date.*
>
> *The Tom Bowline will be fitted up in the most superior style for the accommodation at Cabin, Second Cabin, and Steerage Passengers, and will be provided with the following scale of provisions, free of charge, which is included in the rate of passage money: 25 pounds Biscuit, 10 pounds Flour, 50 pounds Oatmeal, 5 pounds Sugar, 5 pounds molasses."*

Feeling the hand of Providence place a firm grasp on his shoulder as he finished the article, James said to Mr. Boyd, "I would be much obliged if I could travel with you and put our names on the list as well, friend."

"With pleasure, James," said Sean with a slap on the back. "It would be a great joy for us to voyage together."

After discussing the details, James returned to find that Susan and Ned had sold nearly all their goods. "Father, look, the ground be almost bare, so much we sold!" Ned said. "And look at the sovereigns!"

"Lord be praised!" he said. "I will return presently, after I see how Robert and Michael have fared, and then you two can go and enjoy the festivities."

On the way to the pens, James stopped by the booth with the boots and chose a pair for Susan and Michael. He also bought brogues for little Mary and John. "'Twill need them to keep the splinters of the ship deck off their tender feet," he said to the saleswoman. He then bought two large cardboard suitcases, portmanteaus, for the voyage, but he quietly hid his purchases in the wagon to surprise the children.

When he got to the pens, James was glad to hear that the sheep had been sold to the baron. "You have done a great deed, lads!" he said to Robert and Michael. "The baron has indeed become our benefactor. May we ever thank God for the man."

James released Michael to join Susan and Ned and to watch over his siblings. Meanwhile, he told Robert about the *Tom Bowline* and the providence of meeting Sean Boyd.

"We have been blessed beyond measure this day, brother," Robert said. "The Sailing 'tis but a month away! Margaret will rest easy at the good news."

Later that fine day, he tied the cow to the wagon, knowing the calf would stay close to her mum, and they all began the joyful journey home. On the way, Robert drove the wagon while James showed the children his purchases and the shiny sovereigns. He commended each of them for their fine work, and then he shared the news of the *Tom Bowline* with the children. Even Michael seemed to realize that God had a hand in this, and they all rejoiced in the good fortune that came their way at the Hilltown Fair.

None of them could wait to tell Mum the news. None more than James.

CHAPTER 12
MAGGIE

MAGGIE HAD NEVER FELT as excited about starting any job. She woke up extra early to give herself plenty of time to get ready, then she quickly ate a bowl of cereal and gulped down a cup of coffee, eager to get started with her day. With this job she felt safe and loved by her new employer, Anna, and that made all the difference to her.

As she clicked her seatbelt in place, she noticed a button had fallen off her favorite jacket that she wore especially for her first day of work at Anna's Antiques.

Great! First day and I can't be late. If only I had Grandma's button tin. She pulled out of the driveway as she remembered the button tin.

Maggie would never forget the day her grandmother let her choose buttons from that button tin to sew on the crazy quilt. She was only eight then, but it made her feel like such a big girl. There were a variety of sizes, shapes, and colors, and she wasn't sure what to choose. There were buttons made of wood, pearl, glass, bone, plastic, and others. Her memory of that day was quite vivid. She could almost see them now.

She had painstakingly picked out eight buttons—one for each year of her life—four wooden ones and four pink pearl ones, her favorite color. Then Grandma had patiently helped her sew each one onto the family crazy quilt in places that accented their resting spots. She was proud and thrilled to be able to contribute to her family's crazy quilt, and Grandma had made her feel special by letting her do it. She—like her mother, grandmother, great-grandmother, and great-great-grandmother—had made her mark on the family heirloom. She smiled as she drove into the parking place reserved for Anna's Antiques.

Grandma always made me feel special. Anna does, too.

Her first day as Anna's assistant was a busy one. Anna took much of the morning showing Maggie how she priced things, how to work the antique cash register, how to strategically place certain antiques around the store, and other important details of working in the shop. While Anna waited on customers, Maggie watched her engage people in a way that seemed to make everyone feel welcome. Anna was gentle and patient, and Maggie felt valued. Important. Appreciated.

Anna's like a cup of cool water. A lot like Grandma.

As was her daily custom, Anna closed the store for an hour and a half for lunch, again inviting Maggie to join her. She began to get the impression that Anna enjoyed her company as much as she enjoyed hers.

"I'll bring lunch for us next week," Maggie offered.

"That would be lovely, dear," Anna replied.

As they enjoyed chicken salad and, of course, tea, Maggie listened as Anna shared about her own Irish family heritage.

"My ancestors were Irish *and* Catholic, not a good combination in the 1700s," Anna said. "Back then, there were terrible laws restricting the rights of Irish Catholics, and my family felt the brunt of those laws. They lost most of their land, and they couldn't even vote or go to school! Can you believe it?"

Maggie shook her head. "My ancestors were farmers and were pretty poor, but I didn't know there were laws that kept the people from prospering or getting educated. Who made those laws?"

"Mainly the British, I think, to keep the Catholics in their place." Anna sipped her tea. "Catholics were the majority of the population in Ireland, but the Protestants held most of the power and often used it against the Catholic majority. They simply kept most of the Catholics from succeeding and prospering, and they even confiscated their land if they protested!"

"No wonder so many Irish people emigrated to America!"

"Indeed." Anna agreed. "By the early 1800s, reforms began to come that would change some of these laws, but the damage was already done to many of these families. They had subdivided their land among their boys many times, until there wasn't enough land to farm. Moreover, they'd been downtrodden for a long time and they felt trapped by their society and its unfair laws. The people were dirt poor, uneducated, and hopeless."

"Was your family like that?" Maggie asked.

"They were poor tenant farmers, yes," Anna continued, "They lived on the west coast of Ireland, and that was the area that took the worst brunt of the famine. They had a cruel land agent who was supposed to collect rent for their English landlord. But the agent used his position to exploit the entire village terribly. For many years he required them to pay much more money than the landlord had actually set, and the agent got wealthy on the pain of those poor people. Many families were 'turned out' of their tiny cottages and became homeless because of him.

"Then, one day, the landlord came from England for the first time ever, and the agent was caught red-handed." Anna smiled. "The landlord found out what the agent was doing and turned him out of the great manor house he was living in!"

"Sounds like he got his payback, and I'm glad."

"He did, but many other agents never did." Anna shook her head. "And as long as many of those landlords got their rent, they didn't really care what happened on their land."

Anna checked the teapot and went into the back room to refill it, leaving Maggie to stew over the unfairness of it all. When she returned, Anna found her with a pinched brow and crossed arms.

"That's wrong!" Maggie fumed. "Why didn't the government do something?"

"They finally did." Anna sat down. "By the early 1800s, a commission reported that the Irish had suffered more than any other people in Europe. The report stated that Ireland had become a hostile place in which to live. By 1829, laws were finally passed that allowed Irish Catholics to vote, be educated, join the army, own property, and inherit land. Finally, they were even allowed to become lawyers, teachers, and judges—jobs that were kept from them for a century or more!"

"It sounds like the English treated the Irish much like the American Southerners treated people of color during that same time."

"Pretty close, dearie," Anna said. "With the many generations that endured such terrible discrimination, the system forced those poor Irish people deeper and deeper into poverty. They had to work deathly hard to pay the rent and the agent's fees, but they only had a tiny patch of land to grow food for themselves. The easiest crop to grow was potatoes, and that's how they got into trouble when the Potato Blight came and destroyed their entire food supply. Can you imagine eating only potatoes year after year? I think maybe that was the proverbial straw that finally broke their backs, and that's why those many Irish emigrated from their homeland to other countries."

Just then, Anna's phone rang. She excused herself from the conversation, answered the call, and then returned to the table where she fell deep in thought.

"I can't blame those poor people for wanting to leave Ireland," Maggie agreed. "What a helpless way to live. Their only chance must have been to move across the ocean and give up what little bit they had to find more opportunity."

"All of us have seasons of feeling pretty helpless and hopeless," Anna said, her soft blue eyes piercing Maggie's. "I sure felt that way when my husband died, but I've found that the trials of this life are often blessings in disguise. Often, the worst times make way for a brand new life—one that you never could have imagined. Just think, I never would have had this shop—or met you—for heaven's sake! But I couldn't see any of those things as blessings until I began to embrace the changes that were forced on me, and believe me, I did some kicking and screaming in the process. I just couldn't see that God really was orchestrating my situations to actually bring beauty out of the ashes of my broken world. I guess the Irish had that same life lesson forced on them."

"I guess so," Maggie replied. *Does God have His hand on me as well?*

"I know it is difficult for you right now, dearie." Anna placed her gentle hand on hers. "But God truly does have a plan to give you hope, Maggie. Try to embrace the changes that God allows in your life, and hold on to His promises that He will never, ever, ever leave you."

"I will, Anna. Thank you."

As the two cleared the table, Maggie thought her words. *There are always others who've had it tougher than me.*

* * *

For the rest of the afternoon, Maggie shadowed Anna as she waited on customers. Anna graciously welcomed her customers to browse around, sharing tidbits about whatever they were interested in and somehow sneaking a comment in about "the good Lord" or "if the Lord wills" or "He's faithful" with such ease that it amazed Maggie.

Near closing time, an old, homeless man stepped through the door, reeking of alcohol and sweat. Maggie froze, unsure how to respond to him, but Anna just kindly spoke with him and then guided him to the door. As she said goodbye to him, Anna pulled out a few bite-sized candy bars from her pocket and slipped then into the man's hand. "God bless you, brother," were her last words to him as she closed the door and quickly locked it.

"Well then, another good day of serving God and mankind." Anna wiped her hands on a nearby tea towel and smiled at Maggie. "And a good first day for you, too, dearie!"

"Thank you for this opportunity, Anna. Really." Her eyes glistened with gratitude. "You don't know how much I appreciate it."

"I appreciate the help, Maggie," Anna said. "These old bones are getting more and more tired with each passing month. Before you go, I'd like to invite you to join me for a lecture on the Irish Diaspora at The Irish Shop on Sunday afternoon. I hear it will be a good one, that is, if you're not busy."

"I happen to be free, and I'd love to join you! Thank you for the invitation," Maggie said.

"Let's meet here at one o'clock, and if you don't mind, you can drive us both to The Irish Shop."

"Great! I'll look forward to it, Anna." Maggie impulsively gave her a quick hug before heading for the door.

A perfectly perfect first day! Maggie jumped into her car, feeling tired but fulfilled. *What will tomorrow bring?*

CHAPTER 13
MARGARET

JAMES WAS RELIEVED. Margaret was pleased about the news of the *Tom Bowline* and of knowing that the Boyds would be on the journey with them. Though Margaret didn't know Sara Boyd well, she told James that she thought her to be a God-fearing woman who was kind and temperate. She admitted that was also glad their little girl, Meera, was close to Mary's age. The two families would journey together, and that seemed to bring his dear wife a measure of comfort.

Two days after the fair, James joined Sean Boyd on the journey to Belfast to sign them all up to sail on the *Tom Bowline*. The men drove to Hillsborough, stayed the night with Sean's cousin, and arrived at the Belfast docks before noon the next day. As the luck of the Irish would have it, the *Tom Bowline* office was easy to find, and the two men signed the paperwork without a problem. James secured the last two second-class staterooms, while Sean chose to sail in steerage.

"The good Lord be with us both, friend," James said as they jostled their way back to Hillsborough. "I fear that steerage may be a forlorn place for you three."

"We must suffer through," Sean said sadly. "Our funds be

low, and we must save for our future in the New World."

Along the dusty road, the two men talked about the New World, about plans of how to get their families to the ship, and about the long and dangerous Sailing. After staying again for the night in Hillsborough, Sean and he were both excited to tell their families that they left Sean's cousins long before dawn and arrived home before dinner.

"We have two cabins and they are topside, me love." James squeezed her tight and lifted her off her feet. "They be in the aft of the ship, but they are not in steerage and we will fend well."

The children squealed and danced with joy around the tiny cottage until he called them together to pray. "Settle down, and let's ask God's favor to continue with us, all the way to Wolfe Island."

James took great care to assure his wife and children that the trip to Belfast, the ship, and the accommodations with Sean's cousin would be fine and that they would fare well. "We will overnight in the byre of Sean's cousin, but it be clean, warm, and dry," he told them.

The days passed all too slowly as their anticipation grew. They prepared as best they could, but much of the time they were simply waiting for the Sailing. Then, on the first of May, a letter came from Uncle John.

"'Tis Providence this letter came before we sailed, or we would not have received it." Margaret squeezed her husband's rough hands. Immediately, the entire family gathered around the table as James read Uncle's letter.

April, 1851

Dear Family,

My excitement grows daily as I await your arrival. Yet I know between then and now there will be difficult times ahead. Saying goodbye to all you know. Journeying to the port. Sailing for the first time. It'll not be easy. All will be well in due time.

Be strong and courageous! Do not be afraid or terrified, for the Lord goes with you. He will never leave you or forsake you. Just as Joshua and the children of Israel crossed the Jordan to possess their new land, trust God and follow in His ways as you cross the Great Ocean to possess your new land. When you arrive, you will find a land flowing with milk and honey here in the New World.

Many an Irishman from the Old Sod have settled here on Wolfe Island. It is an island not unlike our own Emerald Isle, but it is much, much smaller. There be faults in this place, to be sure. But it is far better than our beloved homeland, and she will give you a new start. Treasure the memories of old, but embrace the promise of the new. Bring your faith, your family, your future hopes, for truly He will give you a bright future as you make the journey.

Until I see you face-to-face, you will all be in my prayers.

Uncle John Hawkins
Wolfe Island, Canada

As James finished the letter, he sighed, smiled, and patted little John's head. "Truly, 'tis the greatest gift to our children—to give them a start of their own," he said, holding the letter to his chest. "Though the way be difficult, it be far better for our children there than in this poor land that has already betrayed a great many."

"I will go with joy, but it will be a sad day to know I'll never again be setting me eyes on me beloved Ireland with such a great sea betwixt us," Margaret said.

"I can't imagine not seeing the larks on the Mournes and the smell of the peat in the hearth," Michael said sadly. "Me heart faints at the thought of it. 'Tis grievous indeed."

"Or the hills, blue with the blossoming flax that I'll ne'er see anymore," Susan added, her voice soft.

"I still want to find a four-leaf clover to take with me," Mary reminded them.

"Let's all go into the fields and help Mary find her

treasure," Ned said as he scrambled to his feet.

"Aye! Let's do," they all seemed to say in unison.

That afternoon, the children found not one but six four-leaf clovers! Margaret ceremoniously pressed all six of them into her father's favorite book of Irish poetry.

James nodded in affirmation. "We'll take them with us, children. One for each of you to remember our beloved homeland."

A few weeks later, on May 10th, the family celebrated Ned's seventh birthday with their last picnic in the Mourne Mountains. The springtime buttercups, golden whins, and pretty primroses were blooming abundantly on the heather hills, and the air was fresh and clear. It was simply the loveliest of days. The older children ran to the highest hill, straining their eyes toward the east, hoping to view the sea on which they'd sail, but to no avail.

"I cannot see the sea, Father," said wee Mary.

"'Tisn't too far, sweet lass," James said, stroking her hair. "We will sail on her soon enough."

The anticipation of the days ahead captured them all. That afternoon, while the wee ones slept on a blanket under a tree and the four older children played tag, James and Margaret talked and laughed and thoroughly enjoyed a precious day of leisure, the first in a long time.

"Oh, for more days like this." Margaret reached over and held his hand.

"May there be many ahead on the wee isle that will become our home," James agreed, lifting her hand to his lips for a kiss.

* * *

On the following Sunday after church, the small community of Hilltown, as well as many other friends and neighbors, hosted "An American Wake" for Margaret and the family, as the Irish came to call the farewell gatherings they often had for those sailing to the New World. The Boyds also joined the feast of departure, and it was a fine time indeed.

Neighbors had brought what little they had—a little pot of champ, a small kettle of Irish stew, a bit of roast mutton, a few bowls of nuts and berries, and Irish soda bread. And Ian, of course, brought his Poteen. Handing James a large glass, Ian toasted the Hawkins family. "Cheers to the travelers!" Ian said loudly.

Margaret looked at James and purposely shot him a look of concern. But she was not to worry, for James winked and barely took a sip of the toast.

"Thank you," she later whispered to her husband.

"'Tis a feast like we've not seen since the harvest, Mum!" Susan said.

"And Irish stew?" Ned said, enjoying every bite. "'Tis me favorite."

Margaret enjoyed the chatter, childhood games, and a fair bit of laughter, but then the painful goodbyes and prayers for the two families brought sadness as well. For those who stayed in Ireland, this was the death of the "Irishness" for those who left. To those who were leaving, it was a mixture of sadness and of promise, for the New World was known to be a land of opportunity and hope. The mixture of emotions threatened to overwhelm her.

But then, as the Hawkins said their final goodbyes and climbed into the wagon, their neighbor, Thomas Stewart, walked up and offered his hand to James. "Thee will be missed, James, but be assured, I will take good care of the cow and calf."

"Thank you, Thomas," James replied. "You have been a good neighbor. May the good Lord bless thee."

"Do tell, have you a place for your sheepdog?" Thomas asked, casting a glance at Margaret.

"Such a vexing decision has not been made, to be sure," James said, eyeing the children with concern. Truth was, she and James had put off deciding what to do with their precious Buddy for fear that the children would be overwhelmed by the loss of the dog who had been such a special part of all their lives.

"Might I have the privilege of caring for him?" Thomas asked. "I will ne'er let him forget you, that I promise."

Michael jumped up from his seat with a beaming grin. "Oh, will you, Mr. Stewart? We'd be indebted to you." The other children nodded in agreement, obviously relieved that their canine friend would have a good home.

"You see the answer before you," Margaret said, laughing in relief.

"We will bring them all by on Sunday morning," James added as he bid the horse toward their home.

* * *

The week in between Sundays was busy with packing and planning for the journey ahead. Margaret wrapped the largest piece of cheese she had to take along, and James smoked the last lamb and dried the meat to take on the journey. They would bring jugs of water and the two lanterns, besides the crates, the portmanteaus, and the large trunk, into which they packed their most precious possessions—their pictures, books, and, of course, the quilt.

"The rest can perish in the sea, but not these, Lord," Margaret whispered as she wrapped the quilt and pictures carefully. "Please keep them, and us, safe." James heard her prayer and whispered a hearty, "amen" as he planted a quick kiss on her cheek.

Soon the final Sunday on their beloved Emerald Isle came, and after a teary farewell, Margaret waved as James and Michael stoically left to deliver the cow and calf—and Buddy—to the Stewart farm. Margaret prayed for her son, for she knew how much her eldest loved his dog.

Once home Margaret and the family spent the rest of the day carefully loading the wagon with all the worldly goods they would take with them, as well as the few things that the Boyds would be taking to the New World.

"We must be ready, for at daybreak, the Boyds will be here

and we will set out on our journey," James said stoically. But he held his thought, *and to forever leave the land that we love.*

Even before the sun rose, Margaret was up and busy setting things right, making their final breakfast in the home that had been theirs for such a long time. It was a somber time in the tiny cottage. Everyone silently ate and then readied themselves for the journey, save baby Meg, who seemed unaware of the changes to come and unconcerned for the days ahead.

When all was in order and they had nothing to do but sit and wait for the Boyds to arrive, Margaret slowly looked around, longing to remember it all, to preserve it, and to carry it with her to the New World.

She walked around the farm alone, determined to sear each detail in her memory—the tiny, stone cottage with its thatched roof that James had faithfully patched year after year. The moss-covered well with the water bucket swaying in the breeze. The broken, old pitchfork left leaning against the byre. Even the chicken coop and outhouse. A great many memories to capture. In her mind's eye, she faithfully recorded the gently rolling fields and the pastureland. She would remember. She would never forget the Irish life she was forever leaving behind.

When the Boyds arrived at the farm, the Hawkins piled in the wagon and left their farm for the last time, carefully easing their way onto the road they had traveled all their lives.

"Farewell, home," Mary said, waving as they went. "We will miss you." The children all joined in one last wave, and tears were had by all, even by the wee ones.

"Oh how we will miss you!" repeated Margaret, holding baby Meg to her breast and joining her tears with the others.

They silently passed the farms and fields and hills they had known all their lives. And in the distance, Margaret saw Mourne Mountains, majestic against a bright blue sky, seemingly beckoning them to stay. But the beautiful sight of the fertile meadows and groves, and the gentle slopes with their emerald beauty were soon spoiled by the squalor and the run down shacks, the poverty, and the dismal villages they passed on the way to the Boyds' cousins in Hillsborough.

"This is why Father bid us to leave, James," Margaret said as she saw a sickly woman and her wee ones sitting by the roadside in rags. "'Tis sad to see it."

Throughout the long day of travel, Margaret sorted through her many feelings of sadness in leaving their homeland, their friends, and their life. That grief seemed to permeate the air they breathed, but she didn't know how to stop it. Though she was finally excited about the future, she was also sad and fearful of the journey ahead. But the stark reminders around them of suffering and hardship gave her a sense of resoluteness. Amid the pain of letting go, she held on to hope for a good future for her family.

After spending the night in Hillsborough, at the byre of the Boyds' cousin, the Hawkins and the Boyds traveled on to the city of Belfast, as the many emigrants had done before them.

Yet when Margaret caught her first sight of the bustling city, her heart skipped a beat and she thought of Newry. Her birthplace seemed but a wee town compared to Belfast, and it took her breath away.

CHAPTER 14
MAGGIE

As THE RAIN PELTED her car on the way to church that Sunday morning, Maggie began to think about turning back, going home, and being done with the church thing. Her Sundays used to be special days filled with church, family, and rest, at least when Bree was there. But she no longer looked forward to going to church, especially when she had to go alone. She felt out of place among all the happy families and couples.

How I miss Bree.

Alone was not her favorite place.

During church her phone vibrated, and she peeked at the number. *Unknown.* A minute later, a voicemail appeared. *Probably some marketing call,* she reasoned as she listened to the announcements.

The pastor talked about prayer, and Maggie was inspired to use her drive time to pray on the way to pick up Anna that afternoon. She especially felt the need to pray for Briana, and the more she prayed for her, the more her heart ached. Though Maggie prayed for her many times throughout each day, today seemed different. She was burdened for her daughter, praying for her safety and for her health. As the rain beat down on her windshield, her prayers poured out over the steering wheel, passionately imploring heaven to keep her girl safe.

By the time she got to Anna's Antiques, she sensed a peace that passed her own understanding. Anna was waiting just inside the door, and she came out before Maggie could turn off the engine, umbrella in hand.

"Good afternoon, dearie," Anna said, slowly getting into the car. "Are you all right?"

"I'm fine, thanks." Maggie shrugged her shoulders. "I'm just a little worried about my daughter. Zimbabwe is a world away—dangerous and foreign. It's probably a silly mom thing, but still, I can't stop thinking about her."

"My parents must have felt the same way when I was in Kenya with two small children at my side," Anna said. "Let's pray together for her, right now."

Anna took her hand and prayed aloud for Briana's health, safety, and more. Then Anna prayed for her. Anna's words gave her faith, peace, and strength.

Then Maggie remembered the voicemail.

Before she put her car in gear, she said, "Will you excuse me, please? I forgot all about a voicemail that came in earlier."

"Of course," Anna said with a smile. Anna dug into her handbag and put lotion on her hands while she dialed her voicemail.

Maggie waited for the voicemail to connect, and then she heard her daughter's voice! *I missed a call from Briana? Argh!*

Briana sounded weary but happy. She said the team was going back to the remote village where they were before, but she'd try to call the following weekend. Bree made sure to tell Maggie that she loved her—and not to worry.

Not to worry? Maggie pushed the save button and told Anna about the voicemail.

"I promise to join you in praying for your daughter every day," Anna said confidently, "and I can't wait to meet her!"

"Thanks, Anna. You two will love each other."

On their way to the lecture, Anna talked to her about a call she had gotten the day before—an invitation from her daughter to visit her and the grandkids back East. "On the first of the month, I'll be closing the store for a week," Anna said.

Maggie nodded. She was happy for Anna but sad for herself. *A whole week without Anna's wisdom, and no paycheck.*

"Maggie," Anna said, breaking into her thoughts. "Why don't you think about visiting your mother that week? I think it might be good for you to get away before Briana gets home."

"Good idea. Maybe I will." Maggie agreed. "If Mom can help me with the ticket, I have some vacation time at my other job."

The two chatted freely on their way to The Irish Shop, just a short distance from Anna's Antiques.

At the store, Anna briefly introduced her to Quinn McConnally, owner of The Irish Shop. He was tall, thin, and dressed impeccably. Maggie thought he might a bit older than herself, but his gentle blue eyes and welcoming smile put her at ease immediately. He welcomed them both and encouraged them to look around.

His beautifully decorated store had a huge picture window that let in the summer sunshine, which made the glass display cases sparkle with all things Irish. Even the shelves were tidy and pleasant to the eye. Maggie felt right at home and was glad the shop was closed that day.

She and Anna meandered together through the shop, looking at everything from T-shirts with silly Irish sayings to lovely jewelry with the Irish Claddagh on it.

"Mom has a ring like this one." Maggie leaned in to take a closer look. "It symbolizes love, loyalty, and friendship."

"I guess your Irish upbringing runs pretty deep, eh?" Anna replied.

Both women laughed and continued to look around. Then Maggie saw the quilt.

A large, beautiful quilt hung above the wall displays in the center of the store. It hung on a thick wooden dowel and

SUSAN G MATHIS

looked similar to the Irish Chain quilt her grandmother had shown her when she was little, but this one appeared to have a double chain.

She pointed to it and addressed Anna. "Isn't that just beautiful?" Before Anna could answer, Quinn got their attention.

"Let's get started, shall we?" Quinn announced. "Please take a seat, and we'll start in a few minutes."

Maggie and Anna went to the corner of the store where chairs were arranged in a perfect semi-circle and found two seats in the second row. About ten others joined them ranging in age from a teen to senior citizens.

"Today I'd like to talk about the Great Irish Famine of 1845 to 1852 and how it led to the Irish Diaspora," Quinn began as he perched on a stool. "But to get there, I need to back up a little and talk about what led up to those terrible days."

Quinn welcomed the audience to participate. Maggie liked that, and his voice sounded kind and soothing.

Quinn talked about how the poor Irish people believed that the potato was an answer to their prayers—one single source of food that could be grown in great quantity with little work and last a long time. He reiterated much of what Anna had already told her. Moreover, most of the poor were tenant farmers who didn't even own their land—they just rented it—and had to pay high rent.

A man in the back of the room stated, "I thought they were also sheep and cattle farmers. What about them?"

"You're right. Thank you," Quinn said, nodding. "The Irish hills were excellent for grazing cattle and sheep, and many of the poor farmers raised these animals. But most of the meat and leather and other products from the sheep and cattle were exported for the British use. The best Irish land went to raising animals and produce that was exported and sold to pay the high taxes, while the marginal land was left for the poor Irish use. It was a sad sort of affairs for those poor people."

"And we can't forget that there were those uncaring landlords and corrupt land agents," Anna added, with obvious anger in her voice.

"Exactly." Quinn paused to take a sip of water. "Most of the food that the struggling Irish produced was shipped to the British and others overseas, even while their poor neighbors starved. Corruption was rampant, and then, in 1845, the Potato Blight came and destroyed the only thing that was left for the poor Irish to eat—potatoes!

"Can you imagine?" Quinn continued. "These already poorest-of-the-poor Irish families wake up to their near-harvest, smelling a terrible sulphur smell in their gardens, and they find brown spots all over their potato plants. Then their crop simply rotted to nothing, seemingly before their eyes. Their entire year's food supply—gone!"

"What did they do?" Maggie asked.

"Even though the farmers grew other crops, they had to sell most of them to pay their rent or they would be evicted, homeless, destitute," Quinn responded. "And that winter was bad. Many became homeless and many, if not most, died.

"In 1846, over 75 percent of the harvest was destroyed by the Potato Blight, and in 1847, the lack of seed potatoes led to even more starvation. By 1848, the harvest was only about 60 percent of what was needed, and the famine continued to ravage the country.

"But what's tragic is that the famine should never have happened in the first place," Quinn said, struggling to speak. He paused to take a breath, emotion flooding his face. Unbidden tears welled in Maggie's eyes in response to seeing Quinn's anguish over the tragic truth of what happened to all those people.

"Ireland had extremely fertile land and the country could have produced enough food to feed every Irish mouth. The landlords and their wicked agents didn't care! They caused death and suffering for millions!"

Quinn paused, obviously trying hard to regain his composure. He ran his fingers through his blonde and graying hair and sighed.

"Such a tragedy, an unnecessary tragedy!" Maggie whispered to Anna.

"None of the other crops were affected by this blight. Just the potatoes," Quinn continued. "There were plenty of oats and barley. Plenty of meat and cheese. But all of that was exported! And the meager relief efforts took a long time and were a pittance of help. Instead of keeping some of the good crops in Ireland to feed their destitute countrymen, the powers that be exported them and let the people starve! Can you believe the callousness of these people?

"Well, after they realized that others around the world were questioning the ethics of this, then they allowed American Indian corn to be imported, but this food was hard for the Irish to digest and many became ill from eating it. Then the government began national work projects, but they were not much help either. The work was hard labor with little pay, and many died of weakness, lack of food, and disease.

"Just imagine thousands of gaunt figures—their ashen skin and those sunken cheeks and eyes staring blankly, as they starved. Children no longer played or laughed. Entire villages became silent with the sound of impending death. For a while, there were so many people dying that many villages didn't even bother to have wakes; they just buried their loved ones in shallow graves without any service or ceremony. About a million died during those years. A million people on that tiny island nation! The hopelessness must have been overwhelming."

"And even if they lived through the famine, what kind of future could they foresee, especially for their children?" Maggie asked.

"True, and a sobering reality. Thank you," Quinn said. He looked down for a moment, appearing to gather his thoughts, and then continued. "The soup kitchens helped, but that caused another problem altogether. Most of the Protestant churches ran the soup kitchens, and many of the

Protestant 'Soupers' simply wouldn't feed Catholics unless they converted to the Protestant faith.

"Then the relief ships came. They brought food from America, but more importantly, they allowed passage back to America."

Quinn stopped, took another sip of water, sighed, and paced the floor. Several people cleared their throats and shuffled in their seats, obviously uncomfortable with all they were hearing. Maggie looked at Anna, who was dabbing her eyes with a hankie.

"Over a million Irish were forced to emigrate during that time. They had to leave their homeland, the land of their birth, or die!" Quinn continued. "By the way, they emigrated *from* their country, not immigrated *to* another country. They didn't *want* to leave; they *had* to leave or they would perish."

Quinn stopped and shook his head. Maggie watched as the audience seemed to hold their collective breath, waiting for him to continue. When he looked up, his face shone with compassion and sadness.

"Hundreds of thousands emigrated, mostly to America and Canada," Quinn continued. "But they also emigrated to Australia and New Zealand, South Africa, the United Kingdom, Mexico, Brazil, and Argentina, among other places. Thank God these nations took these poor people in or else whole families wouldn't be here today!

"It's sad, really, for the Irish cherished their Emerald Isle, and most had never traveled more than a few miles from their villages. The thought of traveling over the great Atlantic Ocean to a strange land was simply terrifying for them. But they were dying. They had no choice.

"Unfortunately, many of the travelers were so emaciated and sickly, that a lot of these people did die during the voyage," Quinn said sadly. "Worse yet, a lot of the ships were poorly provisioned, and some of the ships' captains treated the passengers no better than they had treated their former cargo—the slaves. The papers began calling these sailing vessels 'coffin ships,' and that scared the Irish all the more."

"Why didn't the Irish just fight back and take their land from those greedy British?" asked a teenage boy a few seats over from Anna.

"They were starving and weak, and they had no weapons and few legal rights, remember?" Quinn said. "Good thought, but undoable at the time. The Irish had been pushed down for many generations and had no fight left—and no means to fight."

Quinn paused and looked each member of the audience in the eye. His misty eyes were intent, pleading for them to understand. When he got to Maggie, she could barely look at him.

"To conclude, what can we learn from all this that will really matter to us in the twenty-first century?" Quinn asked.

Anna was the first to speak. "Jeremiah 29:11 is one of my favorite Scriptures, and I think it applies to the Irish Diaspora. It says, ' "For I know the plans I have for you," declares the Lord, "plans to prosper you and not to harm you, plans to give you hope and a future." ' I think God used this terrible tragedy—as He uses difficult times in all our lives—to give many of the Irish people a brand new start, to prosper them in ways they never could have prospered in Ireland, and to give them hope for their children and their children's children. If we look at history since then, we can see that the Irish have prospered and made great contributions all over the world because they were forced to leave their little island home."

"But that famine was pretty radical stuff," the teenage boy said. "They *were* harmed—as I see it."

"Yes, but they were 'harmed' by man's sinful greed and callousness and the unfair laws made by man—not by God," Anna responded.

"Well, I think that what we can learn from all of this is to never let government control our lives like they did to the Irish!" said a gray-haired man in a pinstripe suit.

"God and government," Quinn said, smiling. "I guess that sums things up pretty well. I want to respect your time and close when I said we would so we'll end it here. Thank you for coming today, and I hope to see you next month as we continue to discuss emigration and more about the ships."

After a standing ovation, Quinn thanked everyone personally and gave each person a flyer about the next lecture. Maggie shook his hand, and then Anna did, too, as she said, "You're quite a speaker, Mr. McConnally. Thank you for sharing your insights."

"And thank you for sharing God's truth with the audience," Quinn said with a wink of gratitude.

Quinn turned to Maggie, and she pointed to the wall. "That quilt's just beautiful, Mr. McConnally. My grandmother had a similar one, only it didn't have a double chain."

"Thank you, but you can call me Quinn," he said, smile lines accenting his kind face. "My grandmother made it. It's called a Double Irish Chain quilt, and it's a variation of the Irish Chain, which I assume your grandmother had." Quinn tilted his head closer to Maggie's as he continued. "See how the blocks are laid out on a diagonal in a checkerboard pattern with two blocks each at all four corners? It's quite a treasure, don't you think?"

"It's amazing. Are you selling it?" she asked.

"Goodness, no," Quinn replied. "I had it on my bed for years, but I spend most of my time at the store so I thought I'd enjoy it more here. And I also thought others who came to the shop could admire it as well." Quinn looked at her intently, even graciously, until she felt a blush rise in her face.

"It's a family heirloom, a priceless treasure," Quinn said. "It was part of my inheritance when my mother died."

"I'm sorry for your loss," Maggie said, "but yes, you do have quite a treasure there."

"Thank you, Maggie," Quinn said. "It was nice to meet you, and I hope you'll come again."

"Nice to meet you, too, Quinn," she said as she and Anna said goodbye and left The Irish Shop.

CHAPTER 15
MARGARET

THE BELFAST HARBOR was a noisy, dirty, smelly mass of confusion.

"What have you brought us to, James?" Margaret said, looking to and fro and recoiling at the sight of it all. Stacks of barrels and crates and cargo. Passengers eager yet frightened. Ships and boats and dinghies. Sailors smelling of rum and sweat. Dead fish and seaweed clogging the murky water. Yelling. Cursing. Pushing.

"Me lamb, we will only be here for the day and night, and then we will board the ship," James reminded her. "I will take you and the children to the boarding house directly, while Robert, Sean, and I sell the horse and wagon and sort the details."

Margaret swallowed her annoyance as James promptly took them to a boarding house near the harbor while the men and lads waited in the wagon. The place was loud and busy, but it was clean. The one rented room would be crowded, but it would do. Thankfully, Sara invited Susan and Mary to stay with them in their room. Margaret made a lunch of cheese, bread, and water. Then she put the wee ones down for a nap.

The men returned before dark, pleased that they had a

buyer for the horse and wagon, even though the price was a scandalously low offer. It was obvious that both men had spent some time at the pub, but Margaret didn't say anything to James.

He be carrying the weight of the world on his shoulders, I suspect. Heaven help him.

That evening, the two families shared a simple meal of dried mutton, cheese, bread, and water. After making makeshift beds for the lads, Margaret and James settled into the one bed with the wee babe. Margaret lay in bed amid the foreign sounds of the boarding house and the city, so she slept little that night while the others slept soundly. But she rested as best she could, wondering and worrying about the days ahead.

In the morning, the two families rode in the Hawkins' wagon for the last time.

"There be our buyer," James said, sounding relieved.

"I feared he would not come." Margaret admitted.

James nodded and quickly unloaded all their worldly belongings. When they rounded a high wall of crates to head for the ship, Margaret's jaw dropped as she saw the vast ship that would become their home for the next month or more.

"'Tis much bigger than I had imagined, James." Her voice trembled. "We have never entered anything so grand, save the Newry Cathedral." Her heart brimmed over with trepidation of the unknown, but she tried to hide it for the children's sake.

The dreary, dirty, smelly docks felt all too chaotic for her, a quiet farmer's wife. Its hundreds of barrels and crates, passengers and sailors, and porters and carters simply overwhelmed her. With wide eyes and open-mouthed astonishment, the children and the Boyds clearly felt the same way, save Ned. *Always the adventurer, my Ned.*

But for Margaret, the saddest part was seeing the many destitute families sitting by the wayside, hopeless and rejected. The sailors had cast them away and they were not allowed ship passage, either because of poor health, lack of funds, or lack of space, she supposed. She was thankful that her uncle and James had already secured passage and had planned well.

"When can be board, James? This be such a frightful place!" Margaret's voice cracked and she bit back tears as her husband shrugged his shoulders, bidding her patience.

As she looked at the others, Margaret could see that the lot of them could not wait to get away from it, too. Thankfully, they were able to board the ship that same day, a day before the actual departure.

But before boarding, the doctors on shore inspected them for disease, poking and prodding and invading their privacy terribly. After a long while, they finally got a stamp on their tickets and turned their luggage over to the porter. When it was all completed, Margaret and the family, and the Boyds, walked to the proper dock. The heaviness of the moment, of the depth of her loss, weighed on her with each step.

The Hawkins and Boyds climbed into the dinghy that would take them out to the *Tom Bowline* anchored in the harbor, and the next day, the ship would take them onward to a strange and foreign land. As they drew closer and closer to the ship, Margaret's apprehension grew stronger, but she remained silent and kept back the flood of tears that wanted to be free. Everyone stayed silent, except Ned.

"What a marvel, Father!" Ned stood up and then immediately plopped down after losing his balance.

"Stay put, son," James warned. "You haven't your sea legs yet!"

Once they were on board the great vessel, the Boyds were shown to steerage at the bottom of the ship, while the Hawkins family was taken to their cabins to await their belongings. They followed a swarthy sailor to the aft of the ship who pointed out their second-class rooms.

Margaret stood outside the door and looked at their living quarters, side-by-side but not adjoining. The "staterooms" were tiny and plain to say the least. The simple straw mattresses and the two rough wood berths nearly filled the room, and although she didn't really know what she had expected, this certainly was not it! The cabins were narrow and there was just room enough to put a small chest between the edge of the two-feet-wide berths and the wall, and a few things underneath the bottom berth. The two berths were one above the other in each room. That was all.

Margaret stood with her family in the doorway, overwhelmed and reticent to enter. It looked more like a closet than a stateroom. But it was private and it was theirs for the journey, she reasoned. She looked at James knowingly, she squared her shoulders, and she took a deep breath.

"Robert, Michael, Ned, and I will stay in this cabin," James said, pointing to the nearer stateroom and sounding as cheery as Margaret had ever heard him. "Me wife, lassies, John, and baby Meg, you will be in the other cabin. See, each cabin has a tiny porthole, and you may be able to keep the door open in fairer weather."

"How shall we get on, Father?" Mary asked, looking into the dark room.

James took control of the jarring situation quickly but gently. "It be grand compared to steerage, as you will see. It be topside, and it be ours. Be grateful for Uncle's generosity, child." Unfortunately, as soon as James walked into the tiny cabin, he hit his head on the hurricane lantern that hung from a hook on the ceiling. In two fatherly steps, he retreated to the doorway rubbing the crown of his head and looking rather sheepish.

"Children, listen to your father," Margaret interjected, "and mind this: You must wear your brogues or your boots at all times, for look at the slivers on these decks! Be mindful of all the rough-hewn wood about. You will be given bits of oranges and lemons to keep the body from gut rot, so be sure you eat it all. And take care that none of you leave our side without permission."

"And we all must pray for a safe passage. God will guide our family," James said. Right then, James took her hand, and they all formed a small circle. They prayed for safety, for strength, for health, and for all who would travel with them, including the Boyds and the captain and the crew. They ended the prayer, and Margaret sensed a newfound peace, just as the crew brought their belongings.

Margaret and the family had a bite of food they had brought with them and settled the wee ones down for a nap before beginning to unpack the few things they could.

"How wise it was to bring these lamps and quilts, Mum," Susan whispered, careful not to awaken the napping wee ones. "The darkness be black, even at midday, and the ocean's dampness chills the bones."

"Though the quarters are narrow, there be room enough to put the trunk there by the wall to keep our sewing goods and our quilt present to work on," Margaret said, keeping her tone light. "And we can put these two crates under the berth to hold a few conveniences."

"And if we take care, we can dress without knocking our knuckles and elbows against the wall or on the edges of our berth," Susan responded, cheering up.

Margaret placed a tender hand on her daughter's cheek and said, "You are me joy and me crown, child! Now let us unpack our portmanteaus and put them under the berths."

Margaret assessed what might fit in the two cabins and what needed to go in the cargo hold. The Hawkins' cabins were in the extreme aft of the vessel, and although passengers had the run of the entire ship, there was little place to go.

When all was done and the wee ones awakened, the Hawkins and Boyds reconnected on the main deck after naptime.

"Children, take great care not to get in the way of the crew," James warned, "for they be hard at work and we mustn't disrupt them." The children nodded in agreement, even the Boyd's pale and petite four-year-old Meera, her scant brown hair blowing in the wind.

"And watch out for one another," Margaret added. "Michael, Susan, and Ned, take heed to the wee ones and do not let them wander near the rail or go down into steerage."

Sara told her about their accommodations. "Meera and me

be sent to the women's area, and Sean was directed to the men's area." Sara frowned. "I know Sean warned me we'd have to live apart, but it still be scary with all those strangers a staring at us."

Margaret placed a hand on Sara's shoulder and said, "Sean be just past the curtains, and we be just up here, me friend."

"Others have already claimed the far corners of the ship," Sara continued. "They have the most privacy and be far from the wooden latrines that I know will reek in the stuffy, dank hold. But I found the best berth I could for Meera and me. Let me show you."

After showing one another their accommodations, the two women returned to the main deck and stood by the deck rail, not knowing what to do. They watched the children play and the sailors load barrels and boxes and bags and trunks, and Margaret couldn't help but think of all they had left behind.

The afternoon went quickly and night fell before long. The sailors worked late into the evening, but the expectation of their morning launch kept Margaret awake more than the noise. She felt the ship move slightly in the water and fretted about the voyage while listening to her children sleep soundly. How would they get along for a month or more?

* * *

Margaret awakened early but it was midmorning before all the passengers and crew were on board and ready to sail. Then the gangplank was put out, the ropes and the cables unfastened, and the ship began to move along slowly. She surveyed the growing crowd and wondered if every passenger and crewmember had joined them on the deck.

Margaret turned away and steeled her heart to say goodbye to her Emerald Isle and all she had ever known. She would never again see the green heather hills or the purple Mournes or the thatch-roofed cottages. She looked beyond the bustling port and dirty bay, straining to see the hills one more time. But the city filled her view. She shook herself free of the sadness and remembered her mission.

They were setting sail for the New World!

While the steam tugs gradually towed the ship out to sea, the crew searched for stowaways and the officials took their names for an immigration list. Then the ship's doctor inspected passengers again. She wondered if they'd ever be done poking, prodding, and inspecting them.

The Hawkins and the Boyds stood at the rail as the ship slowly left the harbor and then the bay. When Margaret caught a glimpse of the faraway cliffs and the green hills of their homeland, she wept. But to her surprise, Michael stiffened and tried to be brave. She watched him and wondered what was going on in his young mind. *Me Michael be betwixt and between a lad and a man!*

As their homeland got smaller and smaller and finally disappeared from their sight, Michael could contain his sadness no longer. Margaret took her eldest in her arms and they cried together. The others joined in. While she knew that they must all turn their hearts toward the western horizon, to their new homeland, to the other side of the world, in that moment there were no words, just tears.

Before long a few men began to sing melancholy ballads of their homeland and of the emerald hills and of the rocky cliffs. They crooned of the wretched Potato Blight that ruined their fields and caused them to have to take this voyage. A few women joined in with moans and groans that sounded all too similar to the keening for the dead, and Margaret wished she could shut them all out.

But then, singing and dancing and celebration commenced, as if the entire lot of them were purposely willing themselves to turn to the new chapter that was beginning in their lives. As if each one of them who was grieving his or her Irish past seemed to be choosing, one by one and then as one people, they embraced the changes that had befallen them—even while their hearts were heavy and their minds were clouded with fear of the unknown.

Margaret watched as a group of musicians began to play a

bit of festive Irish music. Even Uncle Robert joined in and added his tin whistle to the moment. Dozens began to dance and move in pairs down the deck. Couples and children alike danced around the ropes and jigs and past the busy sailors who shook their heads but probably wished to join them. More than a few cried. Others kissed. All were lost in the emotion of the moment.

"Can we join them, Father?" Mary asked.

"Do, and with our blessing," James replied.

Dozens of children ran and played around the groups of people, kicking up dust and jabbering happily, seemingly unaware of the dangers and challenges ahead. But then the winds and the moving deck halted the celebration.

The warmth of the day gave way to the cool of the evening, and Margaret knew it was the last time they'd see their beloved homeland. The ship rounded the northernmost tip of their country, she and the others watched the sun set for the last time on their Emerald Isle. Stars begin to pop out, and she lifted a prayer of protection to the One who made those beacons of light. As night fell, the teeming sea of Irish humanity slowly grew silent, save a few whispers and whimpers and many tear-filled cries.

Just then, the tapestry of stars gave no comfort to her, and nearly every Irish lad and lass and man and woman wept for the sadness of leaving their beloved Ireland. After they had expended their sorrow and said farewell to their homeland, Margaret and the family regretfully turned to their berths to awaken to life at sea.

CHAPTER 16
MAGGIE

MAGGIE COULD BARELY contain her excitement the following Friday when she got to work. "Your suggestion to visit my mom was brilliant, Anna!" She'd barely walked through the door but was prattling on like an excited schoolgirl. "Mom bought me a ticket to go see her, and I had no trouble getting the time off from my other job. Thanks for suggesting it."

"I'm glad you'll get to visit your mother, dearie," Anna said. "Lord knows we need our moms now and then, especially during troubling times."

"That's for sure, but I am nervous about what she'll say when I confess that I've lost the quilt."

"Honesty is the best policy, Maggie," Anna said. "From what you've said about your mother, I'm sure she'll understand."

Maggie loved working at the antique store and was getting more and more comfortable with her work there. She enjoyed working with the customers, and she thoroughly cherished her time with Anna. She even delighted in dusting and tidying up the store during the slower times.

She had brought a crockpot of chili for their lunch that afternoon, and they savored it while they chatted together.

"How did you learn about all these valuable antiques?"

"Come with me," Anna said, leading her to the far corner of the back room. At the end of her small desk was a shelf full of books. "Feel free to read any of these books. I find them quite informative and have learned a lot from them through the years. I also watch Antiques Roadshow quite often." Anna laughed, and her laugh sounded like the tinkling of fine china.

"Thanks, Anna. I will," Maggie said, looking through the titles.

Customer after customer came to peruse the hidden treasures at Anna's Antiques and the day flew by. One customer bought an antique quilt, the one with the diamond pattern. But while she was paying for it, her little girl knocked over a china figurine, sending it crashing to the floor in a shattered mess.

"Devyn!" her mother scolded. "What have you done?"

The little girl burst into tears. "I didn't mean to. It slipped," she cried, big tears running down her tiny cheeks.

Maggie wasn't sure what to do, but Anna was at the little girl's side in a jiffy with a tissue in hand, ready to console the poor child.

"Don't cry, little one," Anna said, smiling and handing her the tissue. "Accidents happen. You mustn't let a little mishap cast a gloomy cloud over this delicious day." Anna patted the girl's head and led her to her mother's side.

Then Anna turned to her mother. "That figurine's not of any great value. Don't worry your pretty head over it." Then, noticing her purchase, Anna said, "I trust you'll enjoy your quilt for generations to come. I bought that at an estate sale right here in Colorado Springs, from a woman whose family settled here in the 1800s!"

"I believe I will, ma'am," the woman said, "and thank you for being so kind."

"My pleasure," Anna said. "God bless you both!"

As mother and daughter walked out the door, Maggie got busy cleaning up the mess and wondered at the gentleness she had just witnessed.

"What's a day if we don't offer a bit of kindness to another?" Anna said to Maggie.

Saturday was much the same as the day before, busy with customers and little time to rest or chat. After Anna locked up the store and prepared to leave it closed for a week, the two women wished the other a safe journey, good vacation, and a wonderful time with family.

On the way home, Maggie began to grow more and more excited—and apprehensive—about visiting her mom.

What will she say when I tell her about the quilt? Will I disappoint her or will she get really angry? She worried all evening and throughout the night.

By Sunday, she had worked herself into a frenzy, nearly obsessing about how she would break the news to her mother.

* * *

On Monday, Maggie traveled to her mom's, and after renting a car and driving an hour, she arrived just before dinner as she had planned. Her mother, Elizabeth Graham, had moved into a small condo that Maggie had visited only once before, and it still felt strange to her. But when she walked in, she cheered up. Her mom had a lovely homemade meal prepared for her arrival. Maggie dropped her bags, hugged her mom, and sniffed. The smell of the delicious meal wafted through the air.

"I thought I'd make shepherd's pie," Elizabeth said, her dark eyes twinkling with delight. "I know it's one of your favorites."

"It is. Thanks, Mom." Her mother had set a candlelit table in the dining room with her good china and silverware from her grandmother. Maggie appreciated the gesture, but she ate her meal quietly, saying little and eating less. Her pent up anxiety was more than she could bear.

"What's wrong, sweetie?" her mom asked, putting down

her fork and looking into Maggie's troubled eyes. "You're never this quiet, and you seem to be hurting. What is it?"

Maggie burst into tears. "Oh Mom, I'm so ashamed."

Her mom went over to her and held her tightly. "Now, now. There's nothing that can be as bad as all this fuss. I'll make a pot of tea and we'll talk."

Maggie inhaled and tried to calm down as her mother went into the kitchen to put on the kettle. Then the two left their half-eaten dinner and moved into the cozy living room. When the kettle whistled, her mom excused herself to prepare the tea, but before long she returned with teacups and a teapot, ready for a long overdue face-to-face conversation.

"I...I don't have our family's crazy quilt anymore, Mom," Maggie confessed. "It's gone, and I'm sorry. I failed you and our family." She cried as if someone had died. She couldn't help it.

"Is that all?" her mom said calmly, trying to soothe her daughter. "Now, it's really not as tragic as it seems."

Maggie looked at her mother blankly, not believing that she wasn't getting scolded. She had built her quilt predicament into a huge mountain, but her mother made it seem like it was more of a molehill!

She's not angry with me? She doesn't even seem disappointed. Maggie was incredulous. She told her mother what she thought had happened and how she had been searching for it ever since she found it missing.

Though she had told her mother earlier about her job at Anna's, she hadn't told her how she had found her new position, until now. "And in the midst of looking for the quilt, that's how I got my new job at Anna's Antiques!"

"I wondered how you found a job at an antique shop," Elizabeth said, smiling. "I think God has bigger plans with you and the quilt than you know. And it sounds like His blessing, Megs."

"Well, the job is anyway," she conceded. "Anna's such a caring and wise person, a lot like you!"

Her mom smiled, obviously grateful for the compliment and even more grateful that her daughter no longer seemed to be carrying such a heavy burden alone.

"I have something to show you," Elizabeth said.

Maggie watched as her mother slowly walked into her bedroom. Her mother's slow movements, her plump round figure, and her salt-and-pepper hair reminded her that her mom was aging fast, too fast. She was thankful to have this time with her and glad to have her shame eased, even a little.

A few moments later, her mom emerged from her room with a handful of photos. "I've been going through those bins in my closet, and I found these," her mom said, handing her one of the pictures.

"This picture's the only one I have of the quilt, and though it's not a great one, maybe it'll help you find it—if the Lord sees fit," she said. "I'm glad I pulled it out of the bin. I almost didn't."

"Wow! Thanks, Mom!" Maggie was thrilled to have a photo to show people as she searched. She took out her iPhone and captured a few pictures of the photo.

She studied the picture, an old black-and-white of her great Aunt Mabel holding the quilt on her lap. The quilt lay folded into a large square and wasn't even the real focus of the photo. The photo was faded and a little blurry, but it showed a good piece of the crazy quilt—the various patches and embellishments, the quilt's edging and a small part of the backing as well. In the picture, one could faintly see the yarn ties, buttons scattered about, and a bit of embroidery that looked like writing, though it wasn't apparent what it said.

"The edging was dark green wool, and the backing was maroon, remember, Megs?" her mom asked. "And remember those ugly, bright green ties?"

"Oh yeah," Maggie said, drawing on her memories.

"And see that embroidery?" Elizabeth asked, pointing to some cursive writing along the visible edge of the quilt. "It gives the dates of the Hawkins's sailing from Ireland to Wolfe Island. I remember your grandma telling me about it when I was a little girl."

Her mother went to get a magnifying glass out of her desk, and then the two women tried to see what it said. They could make out the words *May* and *June*, but the dates were too blurry.

"What do you remember, Mom, about the family I mean?" she asked, wrapping herself up in an afghan and picking up her teacup.

"Let's see." Her mother paused, seeming to pull up thoughts that had been long ago filed in her memory. She flipped through the pictures in her hand and showed her another photo, even older than the first.

"This is a tintype of your great-great-grandmother, Margaret Hawkins," her mom said. "She was in Canada by then, and she's older, but it was she who started making the crazy quilt and then came here from Ireland with her husband, James, and six young children."

"It must have been a hard trip with all those kids," Maggie said. "I mean, it's not like those ships were Royal Caribbean cruise ships."

Her mom laughed, a happy, girlish laugh. Maggie always loved hearing the music of her mother's laughter. It eased her tension and she sank more comfortably on the sofa, enjoying the warmth of the afghan around her shoulders and her mom's company.

"I'm sure it was a terribly difficult journey," Elizabeth said. "From what I've seen in movies and read in books, the ships back then were just awful, more like slave ships than cruisers! They were really small and dangerous, and it took a month or more of treacherous travel."

Her mom looked through her photos again and pulled out a picture of an old Irish cottage. "I took this picture back in the '80s when I went to Ireland with your dad, remember? It's a picture of the Graham cottage in County Sligo, not the Hawkins' cottage. But I imagine they are rather similar. Irish cottages were all made pretty much the same back then."

"The cottage looks really small, but I love the stone work

and the thatched roof!" Maggie said, studying the photograph.

After snapping a picture of it on her iPhone, she handed the photo back to her mother. Candles flickered on the mantel as she flipped through the stack of photos her mom handed her. But then a dark thought crossed her mind. Her mother must have noticed the change and asked her what she was thinking.

"I've messed up my life, Mom," she admitted, setting down her teacup and pulling a tissue out of its box. She dabbed her eyes and blew her nose. "My marriage is gone and my family's destroyed. And now I've failed this family, too."

"You haven't failed the family, Maggie," her mom said. She promptly shut the photo album she'd been flipping through. "How could you have known he'd take it? You couldn't! Stop torturing yourself over this." Her mother's tone implored her to listen to reason.

"This is but a chapter in your life, a change, and, I admit, a big change," Elizabeth continued, pausing for a moment. "But you didn't choose this divorce. I watched you fight for your marriage for a decade and a half. You couldn't make him stay faithful." Her mom let out a huge sigh and continued.

"Megs, I know how much you hate change. You always have. I remember when I moved your room around while you were at summer camp that one year, you came home and were in a panic for a good week or more!"

Both women laughed as they recalled the time when that happened. She was glad to let go of the stress that seemed to cling to her, and she blew her nose again.

"You just have to begin to embrace change, Megs. *Choose* change and move on in life," her mother said. "Otherwise, you won't be able to turn the page to the next chapter in your life. Think about it, Maggie. Your life's like a long book that's yet to be finished. You have many more chapters to write, and I trust you'll write them all with God's help."

"I want to, Mom," she said, "but this chapter's one I'd rather delete from the manuscript!"

"I know, and I wish all this weren't in your story either," her mom said. "But it is, and you can't change that. All you can do is accept that God has allowed it to be a part of your story—the divorce, the quilt situation, all of it. I believe God can use bad things like this to change you and then help others down the road."

"How can God use me, a broken person with a broken marriage and a broken family?" she asked skeptically. "I don't get it."

"When the time comes, you will, my sweet girl. You will," Elizabeth said. She kissed her daughter on the forehead and smiled at her, cupping her chin in her wrinkled hand. "Trust him with your tomorrows, Megs."

The two quietly got up, cleared the dishes, put on their pajamas, and readied for bed. Maggie was making up the sofa when her mother appeared in the doorway.

"I have a great idea!" She said, her eyes bright with excitement. "You brought your passport with you as I suggested, right?"

Maggie nodded.

"Let's take a trip to Wolfe Island tomorrow!"

CHAPTER 17
MARGARET

MARGARET'S BIRTHDAY was May 24th, just two days after they sailed. The family celebrated her with plenty of hugs and a joyful sing-along on the main deck. Uncle Robert played the tin flute while the family sang old Irish ballads together. Fellow passengers—those who weren't seasick—joined in the festivities, but only a few adults had their sea legs enough to dance to the tunes. The children fared best of all, and many young lads and lassies kicked up their heels at the sound of Uncle Robert's whistle.

As the ship plowed its way closer and closer to their new home, the constant sway of the ship and the water sloshing against it was far different from anything Margaret or the rest of these Irish farmers had ever experienced. Indeed, seasickness was common. Many of the Irish passengers began to adjust after several days, but many never did, especially those in steerage.

"You must learn to rock with the ship, not fight against it," Uncle Robert warned the children as they stood by the rail, "or your bellies will complain and empty their contents. You be lookin' a bit green around the gills, Michael."

Michael nodded but said nothing. Margaret put her arm

around him as they watched the foaming billows of ocean waves and felt the rhythm of the ship. She took in a whiff of her surroundings and turned up her nose. The salty brine smell permeated the air, their clothes, their bunks.

"I be going down to steerage to see to Sara," she told James. As she descended the narrow stairway, her eyes had to adjust to the darkness, her nose to the stench, and her nerves to the fearful surroundings.

"I cannot lift me head," Sara complained. "'Tis been days and I cannot stand the ship's sway. I can barely lift me head off me berth."

Margaret wiped her brow as Sean came to take over. "Let me take wee Meera and tend her so you can rest."

Susan happily took charge of wee Meera, even letting Meera sleep with her one night to let Sara rest. Whenever Sean wasn't caring for Sara, Margaret continued to go below decks and tried to nurse Sara back to health, but Margaret found the women's steerage area a terribly depressing and smelly and scary place.

Margaret was grateful that these were not her quarters; she could barely stand to be down there, even for the purpose of aiding her friend. The jute curtains that separated one area of steerage from another swung to and fro, lurching with the ship's movement. But the curtains did little to stop the smells or the sounds of sickness.

Because of all the sickness, as well as the rumors of the immigrant ships being "coffin ships," health and safety became the two main objectives for each person who found passage on the ship. The ship's captain and the crew had rules for cleanliness and for airing out the berths, and they had to be strictly followed. Margaret added rules of her own.

"You must not touch anything unclean," she warned her children, and she insisted little Meera listen as well since she was below decks with the wretched mess more often than not. "You will likely see vomit and blood or other vulgar things while you are on the ship, and you must not go near any of it. And you must not share your food—or anything—

with anyone, even your brothers and sisters."

Margaret fretted at the foreign noises of ship life as well. The constant ocean breeze was enough to knock the wind out of a person's bagpipes. And the endless creaking and groaning of the timbers and planks haunted her day and night. She despised the sailors' salty speech, and she was often tempted to side with a few of the passengers' negative talk. The cadence of ship life was sorely monotonous, the musty moldy straw mattresses irritated her nightly, and it unnerved her to hear the wooden plates of the deck shifting and clashing together day after day.

One day, Susan and Mary came running to the cabin, breathless. "Mum, just now, the ship swallowed up a woman's hem!" Mary cried. Margaret smiled and answered Mary, explaining what had happened.

"Child, the plates between the floor beams often open just enough to keep the ship strong," James added. "They might catch the hem of a dress and then shut again, trapping the poor woman in its grasp. But it will release her presently, don't you fret my wee lassie." James hugged her as did Margaret. Then little Mary relaxed, and all was well.

* * *

For Margaret, the 3000-mile, six-week journey was indeed full of strange and scary experiences, and she marveled at how optimistic many were. In spite of the miserable conditions and hardships, most of the emigrants had faith. She heard them talk about their dreams of a better world for their children. She saw that they looked for a better tomorrow, a land of plenty where food and land and work were abundant and landlords were few. And if they weren't sick, they played cards, sang, danced, and talked. Margaret, however, fought her dark thoughts day after day.

Indeed, she became introspective and nostalgic and barely left the cabin, preferring to stay in the tiny space with baby Meg. Little John usually stayed with them, for the poor lad was often seasick. No matter how much James tried to pry her and the wee ones out, Margaret refused to leave. She knew she was becoming a recluse, she knew they were beginning to worry about her, but she couldn't help it.

"I cannot bear the wind in me face, nor the salt on me tongue," Margaret admitted. Or she would excuse herself with, "I must protect the wee ones from the dangers that be outside these walls."

Margaret knew that James tried to distract the children from her sadness by creating a sense of adventure for them, and he often talked about God's plan for their lives. She was glad he did but felt helpless to change her mood.

"Remember Noah, children?" James said one day. "God led him to take his family and two of every animal to a new land, just like us. Noah did as God asked but their boat ride was even longer than ours, and he saved the animals from the flood."

"There are cows and goats and chickens on our ship, too, Father," Mary said.

"But who was the captain of Noah's ship, Father?" Ned asked.

"Noah was," James replied, "and his lads were the crew!"

James kept the children laughing and helped them all stay positive. The children adapted more easily than Margaret. For Michael and Ned, the *Tom Bowline* was an engineering marvel, and before long they had explored much of the ship, made friends with a few of the crew, and enjoyed a bit of sea life together.

* * *

One day Ned met the captain's son, Murtagh. Though the lad was nearly eight and much taller than Ned, Margaret was grateful her wee explorer had a friend on the ship. Murtagh's respectfulness endeared him to her, even if he did seem a bit rough around the edges.

When Ned asked about Murtagh's name, Murtagh proudly

announced to the whole family, "I be named such because it means 'skilled in the ways of the sea' like me father."

"'Tis a fine name, me friend," Ned had replied.

Murtagh had told Ned—and the rest of the family—that the *Tom Bowline* was a brand new ship. While on deck together one afternoon, he pointed way over the railing toward the propeller. "Lookie here. Them old ships had side-wheelers for propellers, but this here ship has a new screw propeller. It makes more noise, but we can go a heap faster. And them old ships didn't have a covered deck like this. People could be swept out to sea on them old ships. I saw it happen with me own two eyes!"

In the weeks that followed, Ned spent more and more time with Murtagh. Ned learned all about the crew—the captain, first mate, second mate, the steward for cabin passengers, the carpenter and cook, and the seamen and the apprentices. Most of the crew learned to tolerate the two boys, and Ned and Murtagh enjoyed many young-laddie adventures together. And in the evenings, Ned often shared his newfound knowledge and experiences with his mum and the rest of the family.

"Come, Michael," Margaret overheard Ned say one day. "Murtagh said he'd take us to the ship's secret places."

"I be nearly a man, Ned," Michael scoffed, refusing the offer. "That be child's play."

Ned went alone and Murtagh showed him all around the secret places of the ship, down into the cargo hold and around the animal pens, even up in the crew's galley and sleeping area—even into the captain's chamber where his valet caught the boys red-handed. Ned told his mum that the valet had scolded Murtagh, saying, "You be catchin' a whippin', boy, if your father finds you taking a passenger 'round these here parts." That ended any more visits to the secret places and Margaret was glad of it, though she couldn't help but feel gratitude that little Ned had found a friend to play with.

* * *

During the voyage, when Susan wasn't helping to care for the wee ones, she spent a lot of her time with Uncle Robert, learning how to play the Irish tin whistle. The instrument, also called a penny whistle because it cost just a penny in Ireland, always brought her and most of the Irish folks she knew both comfort and melancholy thoughts of home. Susan caught on quickly and started sneaking down to steerage to play for the people, just to bring them a bit of relief from their constant misery. And although it was dark, damp, and smelly down there, she wanted to help them, and she did.

A few times, while the wee ones napped, Susan helped her mum sew a patch or two on the quilt. She enjoyed working on the quilt, but she didn't like being cooped up in the tiny cabin. Very often, Susan opted to be out on the deck or down in steerage whenever she could. To her, the tiny cabin felt like a cage, and she felt uneasy inside its walls, for she saw her mum grow more and more sullen as each day passed.

"Remember the heather on the hills and the bleating of the sheep, Susan?" her mum would say. Or "Oh for a sup of fresh, warm milk from our cow."

Despite her mum's melancholy, day after day Susan and the other children ran and played on the deck. The activity passed the long, miserable days on the ship and helped the Hawkins children stay reasonably healthy.

Wee Meera was not as lucky. After her mother recuperated, little Meera had become ill and the two stayed below deck for many, many days. Margaret and James forbade Susan to visit her, as did the crew, for the ship fever had struck steerage with a vengeance.

Then Susan overheard a conversation between the ship's doctor and another of the crew. She could smell the smoke of their pipes and the salty air of the ocean waves as she leaned in to listen to the men speak.

"The woman was dead in her berth this morning," the doctor said, "and I fear there may be many more like her. We threw the body overboard before the sun came up."

"We shall throw the lot of them overboard if they endanger this passage," said the other man, coldly.

Susan tiptoed a little closer and cocked her head to hear more, but the wind carried bits of the conversation away from her hearing. She heard words like danger and disease and death, but that was all.

In two shakes of a lamb's tail, Susan ran to her father for comfort.

"They threw someone overboard without a proper burial." Susan trembled all over. "For the sharks and fish to eat her," She burst into tears and held onto her father tightly.

"There, there, child," James consoled. "'Tis the way of sea life I suppose. You must stay far, far from steerage passengers from now on, even from Sara and Sean and wee Meera. The ship fever be a fearful thing!"

* * *

James took full control of the children since his wife stayed in her cabin most of the time. For many days after the first death and burial, James encouraged the children to be extra cautious. Susan and Mary stayed close to the cabin, afraid of the ship fever and of running into any of the steerage passengers. Michael and Ned ventured a bit further, but a deadly pall had fallen over the ship, and rumors of more and more deaths became a near daily occurrence.

James drew his family closer to their cabins with each passing day for a great many of the steerage passengers were sick, frail, and wailing in pain. Meera was one of them. James found Sean above deck and spoke with him from a distance, fearing he may carry the pestilence. After hearing how bad things were, he gathered the family to pray for little Meera and for all those who were sick.

After their evening meal, James quoted a Scripture verse. "Malachi 4:2 says, 'But for you who revere my name, the sun of righteousness will rise with healing in its rays. And you will go out and frolic like well-fed calves.'" Then he lifted his head to the heavens and said, "Oh for such a day!"

For days afterward, James spent time with Margaret, trying to coax her from her private pit of despair. He prayed for her, and even the children asked God for their mum to smile again. But he saw little change, and Margaret often begged him to leave her alone.

James and Robert continued to spend much of their time watching the children on the decks or in their tiny cabin while talking about how they would settle the family on Wolfe Island, what they would plant, and how they would manage in the New World.

James watched his wife helplessly and, he had to admit, sometimes with a measure of frustration as she continued to hide away in the small cabin, her emotions ebbing and flowing, much like the ship. How could he help her?

* * *

One day, the dawning morning peeked through Margaret's thick glass porthole, pushed through the crusted salt on its pane, and cast rays of pink and orange on the rough-hewn wall. She awakened to the day, and she felt like a new woman, a woman with a heart full of faith, lightened from a load of fear and foreboding. She didn't really understand what had happened, and she couldn't explain it to James or the others, but something within her had changed.

"Thank You, God, for pulling me out of the pit. I knew I couldn't have done it myself." Margaret said, looking up to the sky.

Margaret could smile again, and she could see how the family rejoiced. The day was one of the warmest, sunniest, calmest days they'd had since they had left Ireland. She spent much of the day outside with her family, enjoying the view of the sea as it gathered like a cloud and flattened out before the ship rocked back and forth, moving forward and onward toward their new home. She inhaled the fresh air and enjoyed the sunshine and laughed with her children, her husband, and Robert. It was as though her season of grief had passed and she could breathe again.

That evening, the lantern in their cabin swayed with the ship in the darkness, and it cast eerie shadows on the rough walls. But instead of being afraid, the children made a game of it, grabbing and grasping at the shadows as if they were playmates.

"'Tis good to see you play, children." Margaret said, laughing gently. The children were happy, and for the first time in a long while, so was she.

When the children were asleep, Margaret met out on the deck with James. The bright full moon climbed higher and higher in the dark, navy sky and the moonshine glittered on the water like jewels. She laid her head on her husband's chest and breathed the cool ocean air.

"I feel free, James, safe, and I thank you—and God." Even as real concerns for the future still weighed on her, Margaret was content. James smoothed her hair and kissed her forehead. She listened to the sound of his heartbeat. She knew whatever the future held for their family, they would face the unknown together.

CHAPTER 18
MAGGIE

MAGGIE HADN'T VISITED Wolfe Island since she was a little girl. The thought of seeing where her family had settled captured her imagination and she could barely sleep that night. She woke early, showered, and dressed way before she heard her mother stir.

"Morning, Mom!" she said cheerily. "I'm ready to go whenever you are."

Still wiping the sleep from her eyes, her mother laughed. "Well, give me a chance to have some coffee and get out of my bathrobe, okay?"

"Sorry. I'm just excited, that's all," she said. "Take your time."

"Glad to hear it, sweetie," her mom said as she poured her coffee and headed back to her room.

Elizabeth did take her time, at least that's how it felt to Maggie. But they were off within the hour for a short, twenty-minute drive to Cape Vincent, NY, to take a ferry over to the Canadian island. They drove their car onto the ferryboat, and before long they were on their way to Wolfe Island.

"For some reason, I just hadn't put it all together," Maggie confessed. "I thought our family settled in Cape Vincent, not Wolfe Island."

"When the Hawkins came from Ireland, they settled on Wolfe Island and became Canadians," her mom explained. "But when Margaret's daughter Susan got married, she and her husband, Patrick, moved to the U.S. and settled in Cape Vincent. That's how we ended up being Americans."

"Ah, I get it," Maggie said, smiling. "I could have been a Canadian if great-Grandma Susan hadn't moved here!" After a short pause she added, "I guess I also didn't realize that the island was quite as close to Cape Vincent as it is." Maggie and her mom hugged and got back in their car to drive off the ferry.

"Amazing, huh? In just fifteen minutes, you're in another country!" Elizabeth said as they drove off the ferry and waited to go through customs.

After clearing customs, they were on their way to the largest community on the island, Marysville. Maggie opened a brochure about the island as Elizabeth drove.

"Wolfe Island forms a natural boundary between Canada and the U.S. at the entrance to the mighty St. Lawrence River. Though Wolfe Island is the largest island in the Thousands Islands, yet it is only eighteen miles long by one to five-and-a-half miles wide. It currently has a population of just fourteen hundred people," Maggie read.

"What do these people do in the winter?" her mom asked as they drove along the main road where she could see only a few dozen small farms.

"In the winter, the ferries don't run because of the ice on the river. I guess they're stuck on the island. Can't image it, can you?"

Elizabeth shook her head. "I doubt we still have any relatives left here. At least, I've never heard of any."

"I think I'd get island fever if I couldn't reach the mainland for six months out of the year!" Maggie crinkled her nose in displeasure. "Let me read a little about the history of

Marysville," She cleared her throat and began. "Marysville was named after Mary Hinckley, a ferry operator, tavern keeper, postmistress, and midwife. She was a widow with seven children who married Archibald Hitchcock, Jr. They had four more children." She looked up. "Eleven kids!" she exclaimed. "Incredible. And she managed to do all those other jobs, too."

"Your great-great-grandmother, Margaret, had twelve children," her mom glanced at her. "And her daughter Susan had eleven."

"I just can't imagine!" Maggie replied as they drove into the center of Marysville and stopped at the general store. "Let's stop here and see what we can find out."

Her mother decided to wait in the car and read more of the brochure while Maggie poked her head into the store. The general store seemed to be the only one in town, and it was a busy place indeed.

"Welcome! Can I help you?" asked a middle-aged woman wearing jeans and a flannel shirt.

"Hi! I'm Maggie Dolan. I'm just visiting the island for the day and doing a little sight-seeing. My ancestors were the Hawkins, and I wondered if you know of any Hawkins who live here on Wolfe Island?"

"You bet! Mark or Brian or Erik?" asked the store lady.

"I...I don't know," Maggie said. "I really didn't know if there were any of them left on the island."

"There sure are. Here's the phone book." The store lady reached behind the counter and then handing her a thin directory. "Feel free to call them all. You can use our phone if you need to."

Maggie was perplexed and a bit giddy. She decided to give it a try. It was as if she were on a treasure hunt. First she called Mark and Rosilyn Hawkins. There was no answer, and she left a message. Next she called Erik Hawkins, who didn't answer. Finally, she called Brian and Sybil Hawkins, and Sybil answered the phone.

"We'd love to meet you! Come on up to Hawkins Hill and

let's visit!" Sybil said cheerily. She gave Maggie the directions, and they were off to meet their long-lost relatives!

"I can't believe we have relatives I never knew about!" exclaimed Elizabeth.

"This is really weird but really cool," Maggie said, excitement pulsing through her.

They drove along the pretty island shore and past several village streets. It appeared that they were leaving the village and going into farm country again, but then they turned onto the street Sybil had directed them to. Once they got up to Hawkins Hill, Brian and Sybil were waiting outside their home. They all greeted each other warmly, happy to meet one another. Brian and Sybil told them that Rosilyn and Mark lived across the street, and said that Erik was off the island for the day.

"I'm sorry. I don't know much about our family background," Brian confessed. "But you should go and talk to our cousin Nora. She's eighty and knows everything about everything." Sybil gave her a call, while Brian provided directions to Nora's house.

"Thanks a bunch!" Maggie said, attempting to shake her newfound cousin's hand. The big bear of a farmer gave her a solid and sweaty hug instead.

"Come and visit again," Sybil insisted, waving as they drove out of the driveway.

Maggie and Elizabeth looked at each other in astonishment, and then they both started to giggle. Maggie couldn't believe the day they were having! After a quick lunch of fish and chips at a café, they drove along the shore to Cousin Nora's house on the far opposite end of Marysville.

As they turned into the driveway, they noticed the large newly cut front lawn that led up to the small blue-and-white house. Various lawn decorations and birdhouses cluttered the front, but a large "welcome sign" stood like a soldier near the front stoop.

"Well, come on in," Nora said, welcoming the two women. Although it was the afternoon, Nora still wore her housecoat and slippers. The frail woman was bent over and slowly walked with a cane as she led them into a living room that held an abundance of decorations and memorabilia. They all sat and introduced themselves, and then Nora wasted no time spilling out her wealth of information about the family.

"Patrick Hawkins was the first Hawkins to come to the island in 1831," Nora said. "He leased a place on Mill Point in 1832. Patrick's first son was my great-great-grandfather, and his second boy, John Hawkins, was your great-great-Uncle John. That makes us rather distant cousins."

"Did John Hawkins marry and have a family?" Maggie asked.

"He married a woman named Ann," Nora said, "but that's all I know about them."

"Please tell us more about the island, Nora," Elizabeth asked.

Maggie pulled out her iPhone and jotted notes as fast as she could on her notes app. She loved history, and this wasn't just any history—it was her family's history!

"Wolfe Island has several important places," Nora began. "The grand Ardath Castle was here on the island. It had twenty-five rooms and was built in 1823 by a Mr. Grant, I believe." Though Nora had had a stroke a few years earlier and struggled to walk, there was nothing wrong with her memory or her tongue. "But it burned down in 1935. Patrick—he would be your great-great-great-uncle—owned a portion of the Ardath land at one time."

Nora was silent for a moment and then said, "Oh, and here's another fine tidbit. During the Civil War, Wolfe Island was along the Underground Railroad route. But I don't think that our family was a part of hiding runaway slaves."

"Do you know anything about our relatives, James and Margaret Hawkins, who came from Ireland?" Maggie asked. "And do you know about the family quilt that they brought with them?"

"Don't know nothing 'bout that, but by the time your kin came from Ireland, there were many, many poor people here on the island," Nora said. "Because of that awful potato famine, there were hundreds of poor Irish farmers who settled here. Most often they came with little more than the clothes on their backs."

"How many people lived here back then?" Elizabeth asked.

"Don't rightly know," Nora said, furrowing her brow, appearing to think hard. "I suspect around the 1850s and 60s there were more here than there are today. Besides Irish, there were Scots, English, French, and others. And during the war, there were the 'skedaddlers.'"

Maggie looked at her mom and both shrugged their shoulders in sync. Then Elizabeth asked, "Who were they?"

Nora cackled at the ladies' response. "Oh, they were the war dodgers who didn't want to fight in the American Civil War, but we islanders took 'em in just the same. Oh, and there were a few Fenians, a secret revolutionary group that wanted to go and fight the British to free Ireland from its rule. Fat chance that was going to happen. Them British were ruling the world back then."

"Wow! That's fascinating, Nora." Maggie shifted in her seat.

Again Nora laughed, her cackle made the two women laugh with her. "I could tell you stories from now until the harvest! Lived here all my life, and I know just about everyone who's come and gone from here, and a few who wished they had."

Nora's mouth went dry, so she got up to get each of them a glass of water, and Maggie jumped up to help. Though Nora's home was small, it sat just across the street from the narrow channel between Wolfe Island and the tiny island of Simcoe.

"What a beautiful view you have," Maggie said, glancing out the picture window as she took two of the glasses from Nora and walked back to Nora's cluttered living room.

"That cottage across the way's mine, too," Nora said pointing out the window. "You should rent it next summer."

"We'd love to!" Elizabeth smiled and winked at her. Their cousin was quite a find.

"More you say?" Nora said, not really asking. "Well, that general store you went to? The Baker family owned the store for 140 years, and it's the only place to get most of our goods. It has food that's sold by the pound, brandy, sewing supplies, hair products, and lots of household goods. But back in them days, you could even order furniture, or you could barter and get what you needed with eggs, butter, honey, or things like that. 'Course, you can't do that now. And in the winter, the store's stock gets pretty low until spring, when the ferry starts up again."

"How do you live on an island that you can't get off of for several months during the year?" Maggie dared to ask.

Again Nora cackled, yet she was endearing nonetheless. "Ever heard of plannin', girl? You stockpile what you need and plan to hunker down for the winter, that's all. Ain't nothing to it."

Maggie laughed, though she still couldn't imagine it.

Nora continued rattling off even more information. "Schooling didn't come to the island until 1845, but since your kin came after that, they probably got a good education. Back then there were lots of tradesmen and workers— wheelwrights, blacksmiths, carpenters, builders, boat builders, mechanics. There were even three taverns and a summer hotel, and a couple of doctors and three churches. It was quite a bustling town, Marysville was."

Maggie looked at her iPhone and realized the time was flying by. Her mom had warned her that they had to get to the ferry before the last run or they'd be stuck on the island all night. She looked at her mom and mouthed, "It's late" so her mom could attempt to wind up the conversation kindly.

"This has been wonderful, Nora," Elizabeth said, rising from her chair. "I didn't know we still had cousins here on the island, and it's been fun to learn all this about Marysville."

Nora got up and went to her bookshelf. "Here's a book about Wolfe Island and here's a video on the St. Lawrence's

Lachine Canal, where your kin probably came through to get here," Nora said, handing them to Elizabeth. "My gift to you. I think you'll enjoy learning more about our island and watching how hard it was to travel up the St. Lawrence River. Our relatives endured a lot to make this fine island what it is today. It's quite interesting."

"Thanks, Nora," Elizabeth said, gathering her things.

"And you should visit Mill Pond on your way out of town," Nora suggested. "That's where John Hawkins lived, and I suspect that's where your relatives settled when they came."

After Nora gave Maggie directions to the pond, the three women hugged, exchanged contact information, and thanked one another. Maggie took a few pictures on her iPhone, and she grinned at the thought of finding their newfound relatives.

"We've got enough time to see Mill Pond, right, Mom?" Maggie asked as they drove down the road.

"A little, but we need to get to the ferry in time for the last passage," her mom said. "I'll direct you to the pond. Thanks for driving. I'm a bit tired."

Maggie and her mom chatted excitedly about all they had learned, thrilled to have "new" cousins in their lives. Finding Mill Pond was easy, thanks to Nora's directions, and when they turned down the road Nora instructed them to turn on to, they passed a large swamp of cattails, a vast grove of trees, and a few wild turkeys. Then they came to an open area with a pond on one side and summer cottages on the other.

"Look there, Mom! Aren't those birds Great Egrets?"

"You're right," Elizabeth said. "Aren't they're beautiful! I wonder if the Hawkins saw such beauties back then?"

Maggie looked around. "But there's no farmhouse here." She was disappointed not to see the homestead of the 1850s.

"Probably long gone. Ah, well, we'd better head back to the ferry while we can. We've seen and learned more than we ever imagined, haven't we, sweetie?" her mom asked.

"It's been an amazing day." Maggie said. "Just amazing!"

CHAPTER 19
MARGARET

NED COULDN'T BREATHE. The undercurrent grabbed at his legs, pulling him under the waves, tossing him to and fro like a bit of driftwood. The bone-chilling cold made his teeth chatter and gooseflesh pop out all over his body. His lungs screamed for air.

Terror coursed through his small body. How could he have fallen overboard? What happened?

I'm going to die!

The current fought him, and his limbs felt like heavy weights. He tried to turn his body around to see the ship, but was helpless amidst the foaming waves. Suddenly two strong and seasoned sailors appeared and grabbed ahold of him. Slowly they pulled him to the buoy waiting for them. He clung frantically to one of the men, feeling like a wild animal. Then everything became fuzzy and slow, as if fading into a dream.

Ned could barely sense that he was being hauled up onto the ship. All he wanted to do was sleep. Sleep and dream warm, pleasant dreams. But then he felt his body on the cold, wet deck when a sailor slapped his face and yelled, "Foolish boy! Are ye with us yet?"

Ned could barely hear him, and he couldn't seem to respond. Somehow he felt separated from his body, and he wanted to rest.

Then the sailor bent his head back and blew into his mouth! He pushed on his chest as the man tried to force the water from within him. He wanted to scream, "Stop! It hurts!" but he couldn't. He tried to push away, but he seemed disconnected from his limbs. He couldn't open his eyes. He couldn't breathe. He couldn't speak. He could barely hear. He couldn't even move his hands. The sailor pushed and blew over and over again until he finally choked, spit water, and then slowly opened his eyes. He looked around and saw a sea of faces hovering near and looking at him.

"Foolish boy!" the sailor said loudly. Then he shook his head, got up, and walked away.

* * *

Margaret stood by the railing, chatting with another passenger when she heard a splash. Her heart nearly stopped. She knew, just *knew*, it was Ned. She turned and watched in horror as two sailors dove into the ocean after him, and she feared the worst. She stood there, paralyzed in fear, hands pressed hard against her open mouth. She know the water was terrifyingly frigid, even on this calm day at sea. How could her lad survive such a plunge?

Once they dragged his tiny body up onto the deck, several sailors tried to revive him. Margaret watched as one of the crew held her back. Her family joined her as they waited for what seemed like hours to see Ned revive. Finally, finally he did.

Margaret knelt and gently lay Ned on her lap, cradling him in her arms. "I am here, lad," she assured him. She stroked his cheek and brushed the hair from his face. "What in heaven's name happened?"

"Murtagh was trying to show me the propeller, Mum," Ned said weakly. "I...I guess I leaned over too far."

"God be praised that you live!" Margaret said. She picked up her boy as a passerby stared and shook his head in disapproval. She didn't care. He lived.

Each one of the family members touched him gently and told him of their love, but Ned buried his head in his mum's arm and cried. She held him tightly until James urged them both to go to their cabin.

After Margaret brought him to his cabin, took off his wet clothes, put on his warmest garb, and tucked him into bed, the family gathered in the tiny cabin. The lot of them rejoiced to see Ned alive and present with them. Ned appeared to be both pleased that they all cared, and more embarrassed than ever that the thing happened in the first place.

"It was Providence those two sailors were there to fetch you out of the deep, Ned," Margaret said.

"And it was Providence that you were there, Mum," Michael added. "If you had been in here in the cabin and not out catching a breath of air, poor Ned would have been alone."

"And he might have drowned had you not taught him to swim last summer, Michael," Mary added sounding proud of her brother.

Margaret knew that Ned heard the conversation, but he didn't respond. He was shivering, chilled to the bone, and near tears. She shooed the family out, and got busy trying to warm him.

"I love you, son. No foolish mistake will ever change that." Margaret kissed his brow, rubbed his skin and hugged him tightly. When he finally stopped shivering, she tried to get the sea salt off him by rubbing his skin and working her fingers through his hair. Ned relaxed at her gentle touch and individual attention, and he began to cry quietly in her arms until he fell asleep.

Margaret hovered over him, watching him breathe. She stayed in the cabin the entire afternoon. Only wee Meg's hunger could distract her from caring for her son.

Finally Ned awoke as the sun was setting and immediately began to shiver again. Even in early June, the damp cold of the ocean and its constant wind seemed to chill him to the bone, especially that night.

Indeed, the cold of "the plunge," as Margaret and the family came to call it, seemed to set deep into the very core of Ned that evening. There was no fire, no relief from the cold. Instead of going to bed as they usually did, the entire family huddled together on or near Ned's bunk with him. They tried to warm his body with their body heat. Even little John cuddled close and rubbed Ned's arm with his tiny hand. Finally, Margaret sent them off to bed while she kept him with her and cuddled him in her bed.

Her closeness and the straw mattress seemed to help a little. So did the blankets and quilts they had brought with them, but Ned shivered all night. Of cold or of fear, Margaret could not tell.

"Dear God, have mercy on me laddie, please!" Margaret whispered over and over. She spent a fitful night half awake, half asleep, holding and stroking her son to keep him warm. The next day, she beckoned the ship's doctor to check him out, and the doctor gruffly said he was a foolish lad but fine.

For days after, Margaret kept Ned close to her in the cabin, and she noticed he was unusually quiet and docile. Then he developed a cold and fought a fever. She spoon fed him broth and oatmeal and watched over him diligently, worrying that she might lose her lad. Thankfully, within days, Ned was up again and well. Still, Ned became sad and fearful, and, she guessed, regretful and embarrassed.

Margaret worried that Ned was too quiet, too still. That was not her son's way. Yet she knew all too well what fear could do. She had been there just days ago. She tried to get him out of the cabin, but he wouldn't leave. When she tried to coax him out of his shell, he only turned toward the wall and stayed silent.

James tried too. "Master Murtagh has been asking for you,

Ned. Why don't you find him and set his heart to rest."

"Nae, Father," Ned answered. "I best stay here."

Waves of guilt and regret and sadness washed over Margaret during this time as well. As she tended her son as best she could, offering him comfort and care, it occurred to her that for most of the trip she had been terribly sad and introspective. She was caught up in her own pain and neglected her divine duties as Mum. She had been faithless and fearful and felt as though she had failed her son—all her family.

Margaret sincerely wanted to change. She wanted to fully accept the new life they were sailing toward. But she needed God's help. She pondered and prayed, but she seemed to be talking to the wind.

Then she thought about what St. James had said, "You must believe and not doubt, because the one who doubts is like a wave of the sea, blown and tossed by the wind." The idea hit her hard—she was that doubter, tossed by her thoughts and emotions and memories. At that moment, Margaret bowed her head and asked God to help her trust, move forward, and leave her losses behind. She would no longer be tossed here and there. With God's help, she *would* change!

That evening, Margaret took the family quilt out of the chest and called the family to her side. "I've been a foolish woman," she said, tears choking her. She held up the quilt and continued. "This be our past, I know, and it be important. But you, me dear family, are me present and me future. I know that now. I nearly lost me boy, but God has shown me my waywardness. Forgive me."

James took her in his arms and held her close. The family joined him, and they all hugged her and showered her with their love and appreciation. Then, after a blessed round of "I love you's," the children went off to sleep, while she lingered for a long time just outside the cabins with James, holding each other and speaking softly.

Margaret kissed his cheek. "Thank you, James, for being

strong and sure whilst I be wayward."

"You have been in pain. I know that. But I be glad to have you back, me lamb. I have missed you," James confessed.

The next morning, Ned seemed more chipper than he had been since the plunge.

"I think I shall find Murtagh today," Ned told his mum. "Will you come with me, Michael?"

"I shall, brother," Michael said, smiling at the invitation.

* * *

Ned was happy to let Michael guide him, for now, he knew he needed that guidance. Ned now wanted his brother close as he ventured out around the ship.

It wasn't hard for Ned to find his friend, Murtagh, but it took some time for the two to reconnect. Ned felt pangs of guilt and remorse, and he knew Murtagh did, too. From the moment the plunge began, Ned had worried that Murtagh would get a whipping if his father, the stern and commanding Captain Gray, had found out he was a part of the foolishness. Ned silently vowed not to tell but was afraid to ask if it had happened.

Ned and Murtagh stood together on deck, not knowing what to say. Ned kicked an invisible ball and Murtagh looked at him but said nothing. Observing the awkwardness, Michael involved the two in a game of tag, and soon they forgot their troubles and happily played together as friends.

"I be worried sick, Ned," Murtagh admitted later as they sat on the rough deck, catching their breath. "I thought you might die, but your father said that wasn't true. Then I thought you hated me, but now I see that isn't true either. You can tell me father it was me fault if you want to."

"Nae, 'twas me fault," Ned corrected. "Let us let it be in the past and we will heed it no more."

Michael left the two boys alone to talk about what they had been doing while they were apart, and Ned told Murtagh about the book he had just read.

"I cannot read. I've had no book learnin'," Murtagh sadly admitted.

"I can show you how! Oh let me show you how!" Ned said, excited to give Murtagh something to set his heart to rest. "Me sister Susan taught me, and she can help you learn, too!"

From that day until the day they landed in the New World, Ned and Murtagh met every day to have what they called, "cipherin' time." Susan joined them often, especially when Murtagh was struggling to understand such things as blends and other nuances of the language.

And the lads never again talked about Ned's plunge into the sea. It was in the past.

* * *

Days turned into weeks, and Margaret noticed that the monotony of ship life began to take its toll on all of them. She tried to veer them in a productive direction, but it wasn't easy.

James and Robert occupied their time dreaming of their new life and talking with a few of the other men. But James also took time to talk and dream with her.

Michael spent much of his time with Uncle Robert. He later told his mum about hearing tales of fishing adventures and sharing dreams of one day working for the railroad in the New World.

Margaret shook her head. "Ever since you heard about the railroad being built in County Down, you and your uncle be consumed with railroading. I know you want to one day work on the railroad, but I wish you would stay near, Michael."

"I shall be close while I grow, Mum," Michael assured her with a hug. "Do not worry."

Susan needed no prodding to be productive. It was in her bones. She busied herself with the tin whistle and she continued to teach Mary her letters and sounds. The tiny teacher told Margaret that she was determined to have her sister reading long before they got to Wolfe Island, but Mary had a short attention span and distracted easily. When Susan wasn't helping Murtagh learn to read, more often than not, she took up her tin whistle and practiced the tunes her uncle had taught her. Then, whenever she accomplished the newest tune and practiced the others, she would beg her uncle to teach her more.

"Can we please sew on the quilt, Mum?" Susan asked one day. "I don't want to forget."

"We have no more patches to add," Margaret replied. "We have sewn all Grandfather's and Granna's pieces on it and have none left."

"But what about Ned's breeches?" Susan suggested. "They are too torn from the plunge to be used for John, and they would be a good reminder of God's care for us."

"What a fine idea!"

That afternoon, while the wee ones slept, she and Susan cut two pieces of fabric from Ned's breeches to be sewn onto the quilt. She let Susan do all the sewing, and Susan was proud to sew one of the patches onto the quilt all by herself. The other piece of fabric was set aside to go into the quilt at a later time.

As for wee John and baby Meg, they kept her busy most of the days and she was glad of it. Margaret sighed as she looked down at her two youngest sleeping peacefully as she darned a sock. "Soon, me sleeping ones. We will be there presently."

* * *

One day, Margaret feared that Meera might be next to pass on and she prayed fervently that she would not. The small child had fallen ill once again. Though her father, Sean, came topside often to visit with James and her and let them know how she was, Sara almost always stayed below deck, trying to nurse her child back to health. The fever was taking its toll, and between the set sail and now, six women and lassies and three men and lads had gone to their watery grave.

Then a knock at the cabin door came before daybreak, and Margaret rose quietly to answer its call.

"She's gone to God," Sara said, whimpering and barely getting the words out. "Will you join us to say goodbye? The sailors want to bury her before dawn."

"Of course, Sara," Margaret said, holding her grieving friend in her arms. "May we all join you?"

"It must be now," Sara said. "Dawn be not far off."

Margaret awakened James and the lads and hurried the lassies to join the Boyds on the main deck, while Robert stayed with the sleeping wee ones. The sadness of the two families was displayed with keening and crying, prayers and silence.

As the sailors tossed Meera's tiny body into the deep, Margaret held Mary and Ned's faces to her skirts. She could not bear the thought of them remembering such a sight.

"Who will hug Mrs. Boyd now, Mum?" Mary asked, sniffling. "And who will give her kisses when she be sad?"

"God will be with her and Mr. Boyd, child, and we will be their friends," Margaret replied, though her voice shook with heartbreak for Sara and Sean.

"Will I die, too? Will they toss me in the deep too?" Mary asked. "I be near Meera's age."

Margaret knelt down on the rough deck and held her lassie close. "Nae, me love, nae. You are healthy and strong. Little Meera was sickly and weak."

"But John be sickly, too," Mary asked. "Will he die?"

"Nae, me child, nae. God will hold us all close," Margaret said with as much assurance as she could muster, holding her wee Mary close and praying for God's care.

CHAPTER 20
MAGGIE

MAGGIE AND HER MOM arrived home just before dark. Maggie was tired but thrilled to have had such a special day on Wolfe Island. Her mom was too.

"Let's put on our pajamas and check out that book Nora gave us," her mom said.

"Sounds good, and if we're not too tired, we can watch the DVD, too," Maggie replied.

After changing and grabbing their nightly cup of chamomile tea, the two women sat on the sofa together.

"What a fun day!" Maggie smiled. "I had no idea we'd meet relatives and learn as much as we did. I only wish we'd learned something about our ancestors...and the quilt."

"History and culture are a part of all peoples' stories," her mom countered. "We didn't learn details about Margaret and James's life, but we learned a lot about Wolfe Island, about living on a little island like that, and about our extended family. That's all a part of who Margaret and James—and their children—became. And who they became is a part of who we are today."

"How's that? We don't live on an island, and we aren't anything like them."

"We're Irish! Our green blood runs deep," her mom said, laughing. "Remember growing up? The St. Patrick's Day celebrations, the Irish music, the stews and the potato dishes? Where do you think they came from? Grandma learned them from her mom and she from hers—Margaret Hawkins!"

"Oh, I get it! But now that I don't have our family quilt, I have nothing to pass on to my daughter and granddaughter and great-granddaughter. I've broken the chain."

Her mom paused and looked deeply into her eyes, the way she always did when she was trying to make a point. "You can pass on your heritage in lots of ways. With the food you make, the stories you tell, and the things you celebrate. Don't let this one mishap taint the power of leaving a legacy for those to come."

"I guess you're right," Maggie admitted.

"Let it be, girl. Let it go!" Her mom said as she opened the book Nora gave them. Maggie sensed that the conversation was closed and turned to the book in Elizabeth's hand.

"That was nice of Nora to give us these gifts, huh, Mom?"

"Absolutely. We'll have to send her a thank-you card."

The two women spent a long time together perusing the book, *Wolfe Island: A Legacy in Stone* by Barbara Wall La Rocque. The book detailed historical account of the island, from its formation to present. The author's father had done much of the research, and there were pictures, stories, and documents included in the book.

"This is a treasure trove of information!" Elizabeth said, yawning. "But I don't think we'll get too far with it tonight."

Maggie ignored her mom's yawn, took the book, and read from it. "Listen to this: 'The treacherous three- to six-week ocean crossing, often without sufficient provisions or fresh water, left many in a weakened state of health.' Wow! It sounds as though it was a tough voyage. And then it says that after stopping in Quebec City and Montreal, the passengers got on a *bateau*."

"What's that?"

She continued to read. "'The *bateau* was the only river conveyance available in the 1700s and 1800s to transport groups of people, provisions, and cargo too large for a canoe. These flat-bottomed vessels…were built by the French craftsmen at Lachine.'"

"The DVD Nora gave us is about the Lachine Canal and the St. Lawrence," her mom said.

"It says here that 'the bateau were open boats, forty feet long and six to eight feet wide and it was navigated 'by powerful French-Canadian boatmen who entertained the passengers and themselves with traditional river songs synchronized to the pull of the oars.'"

"That must have been quite an adventure," her mom said. "But not one that I'd want to go on."

Maggie nodded. "I can't imagine my great-great-grandmother, Margaret, her husband, and six children—and the quilt—on a boat like that for a week or more!"

Her mom seemed caught up in her thoughts, so Maggie waited for a few moments to give her mom time to think. Then her mom asked, "What did they do at night? Where would they sleep?"

"Hmm…" Maggie scanned the page. "They had 'four men to row and one to steer'…Ah, here it is, 'At nightfall the voyageurs would cook and sleep on the beach while their passengers sought sheltered lodging.'" She paused. "There weren't hotels back then, were there?" she asked.

"I doubt it. Probably stayed in a farmer's barn or something." Her mom yawned and shifted in her seat. She laid her head on her daughter's shoulder and rubbed her arm. Maggie smiled and squeezed her mother's hand. Then she continued to read. "'The incredible feat of ascending five sets of rapids 230 feet above sea level between Lachine and Kingston took about ten days.' Yikes!"

Maggie noticed her mother was falling asleep, so she

placed a sticky note on that page and closed the book. She sipped her lukewarm tea while listening to her mother's rhythmic breathing, silently lost in imagining what such a journey must have been like.

Suddenly her mother stirred and awakened. Elizabeth smiled sheepishly. "I guess that trip took more out of me than I thought."

Maggie nodded. "That was just a day trip. Here I am fussing about my present lot in life, my pain and the changes that have come in my life. Yet all of that's nothing compared to what our own relatives went through!"

"We all have our burdens to bear," her mom stretched and said. "Yes, the Hawkins had a lot of hardships—much more than we can probably comprehend. But that doesn't diminish the pain and the challenges you're going through. I had to endure the deaths of two husbands, and it was awful. But I don't really know the pain of divorce and betrayal like you've experienced."

"I guess people's changes and tragedies and hardships shouldn't be compared with other peoples' troubles, should they?" Maggie said. "Still, the Hawkins must have been pretty desperate to actually *choose* such huge changes. I'm not sure I'd be brave enough."

Elizabeth took her daughter's hands in hers. "Oh, I think you're braver than you believe, Megs. Yes, you hate change, and a lot has been forced upon you. But you are seizing opportunities—like taking that job at the antique store. And though you have many more changes ahead of you—like becoming an empty nester in just a few years—I know you'll be just fine."

"What about getting used to being a single mother now?" She stood and paced the room. "Seriously, I never thought I'd have such an embarrassing title."

"It's only embarrassing if you look at it that way, and if you choose to resist the changes that have come your way," her mom said gently. "I had to accept being a widow—and a single mother—twice."

"I...I never thought of you as a single mother," she said, embarrassed by her obtuseness. "Sorry, Mom."

"That's fine," Elizabeth said. "The point is, 'It is what it is.' And you can fight it or embrace it. From experience, I know that embracing your situation is a far easier way to go."

"I'm still learning a ton from you, Mom. Thanks." She sat down and rested her head on her mom's shoulder. "I sure love you."

"You, too, Megs," her mom said, kissing her daughter on the forehead. "You too."

* * *

The next day flew by quickly, filled with errands and appointments that her mother had made. By that evening, Maggie set the table and poured glasses of water, glad to enjoy a quiet dinner with her mom, the last night before she had to fly home.

"Let's watch that video Nora gave us, okay, Mom?" Maggie asked, finishing her last bite of chicken casserole. "That was delicious. Thanks."

"You're welcome, and yes, let's watch it," her mom said.

As they settled next to each other on the sofa and watched the video, the two women learned that the Lachine Canal opened in 1825 and was enlarged in 1848 to let boats travel up the grand St. Lawrence River and bypass the treacherous Lachine rapids. The canals opened the great river to navigation all the way from the Atlantic Ocean to Lake Ontario.

After finishing the video, Maggie said, "I can't imagine how scary that must have been for those people to travel upstream on flat boats, through canals and all that! And with kids no less."

Just then, her cell phone rang. The number registered "unknown," but she took the call anyway.

"Hi, Mom," Briana sounded tired. "It's really early here, but it's the only chance I have to reach you before we go back into the villages. I didn't wake you, did I?"

"Oh, Bree! Honey! It's great to hear your voice," she said, snapping her fingers and grabbing her mother's attention. "I'm at Nana's, and we're both thrilled to get your call."

"Say 'hi' to Nana, okay? And tell her I love her," Briana said.

"I'm going to put you on speaker. You don't sound well. Are you okay?"

"I've felt better, but I'm okay, Mom. Don't worry." Bree sounded exhausted. "I think I might have a touch of the flu, that's all."

Maggie put Bree on speakerphone and let her mom hear the news with her. Bree told them about their treks into the jungles and villages that had the worst poverty she had ever seen. "The children were often dirty and have flies all over them, and many have swollen bellies, which is a sign of severe malnutrition," Bree said, her voice cracking. "And there's no electricity or running water. No sanitation or anything modern. Please pray for them, Mom and Nana. It's tough to see those little ones like that."

"We'll pray for both you and those you are serving, Bree," Elizabeth said to her granddaughter. "We've got lots of time to pray, and we'll get others to join us."

"Thanks, Nana. Please pray this awful headache goes away, too. I can stand feeling nauseous, but it's hard to work with a bad headache. Hey, sorry, but I need to go."

"We'll be praying, Bree," Maggie said, choking back tears. "Take care of yourself, babe. I love you!"

"I love you both, too!" Bree sounded like she was going to cry, too. "I'll try to call whenever I can. Bye."

As the line went dead, Maggie looked at her mother. She looked concerned too. Maggie wrapped her arms around herself, worried about her daughter, sick and far away.

"She has several more weeks there, Mom," Maggie said, overwhelmed at the thought. "What if she gets really, really sick?"

"Now's the time to trust and not to fear," her mom

insisted, though Maggie could see unease in her eyes as well. She gave her daughter a comforting hug. "I know it's easy to get consumed with the 'what ifs', but worrying won't help Bree. We need to pray and trust God. He loves her and He's with her."

Her mom took her hands and she prayed for Briana, for her, and for the people of Zimbabwe. Her mother's prayers were filled with faith and strength. When they finally finished, Maggie thanked and hugged her mother, and then they both went to bed.

But Maggie obsessed about Bree for many hours, tossing and turning, until she finally got up and made herself another cup of tea.

She took a sip of her tea. *I wonder if Bree's getting the proper food and rest? Who will be there to help her if she's really sick?*

She went back to the sofa sleeper and after a restless night, she got up weary and anxious. At breakfast, Elizabeth encouraged her again to trust God with Bree's life. As she packed her bags to head back to Colorado, her mom shared about her own journey of trust.

"I knew you were having marital troubles for a long time, Megs," her mom admitted. "But what could I say? I was on the other side of the country, and you stayed silent about it all. And when one of you was sick, or when you had that car accident a few years ago? Oh, I felt helpless! I had to choose to trust God with your life and with Briana's life! I wasn't with you, but I prayed for you and Bree all the time. You know that, right?"

"I do, Mom, and I appreciate it." Maggie zipped up her suitcase. "I'm sure I've given you lots of reasons to worry and and pray."

"That's true, and I've not always left off the worry and fretting part," Elizabeth said, smiling. "But the point is, learn from me, sweetie. God has Bree right in the palm of His loving hands, and He will keep her and take care of her better than you ever could."

The two hugged and said their goodbyes, and Maggie

drove her rental car to the airport. As her plane burst through the clouds into the bright blue sky, she looked out the window and smiled. I trust you, Lord. Please keep Briana safe.

CHAPTER 21
MARGARET

MICHAEL'S BIRTHDAY, June 16th, faithfully dawned
sunny and warm. He shifted in his bunk, waiting for Ned to
wake up. He was glad he was a year closer to manhood, but
he felt impatient, even moody, that morning.

Ned finally awakened and whispered, "Michael, let's go for
a hosin' and start your birthday right."

Michael agreed and the two went to the main deck in their
under drawers, hoping the boatswain would give them a good
dousing while the sailor cleaned the deck. He did, even
playfully chasing the boys, as well as a few others who joined
them, with his spray.

The incessant ocean wind had settled to a gentle breeze. It
was a fine day. And while Michael enjoyed the hosin', it did
little to dispel the gloom that hovered over his head that
morning.

Susan had secretly learned how to play "Happy Birthday"
on her tin whistle, a new and modern song their Uncle
Robert had heard on the Kilkeel docks back in Ireland. When
he and Ned came back from their hosin', she struck up the
tune and the family celebrated him with a song.

Yet Michael still felt anxious, frustrated, and bored. He

missed being in the fields with the sheep, and on the ship he felt like a caged animal. He was tired and cranky and he didn't like the journey they were on one little bit.

"Barely halfway there, but it feels like a lifetime," he mumbled to Ned as they watched the steerage passengers cook their food on the far deck. "Can't wait to get off this ship and be free. Look at these people, still struggling like back home."

"'Tisn't so, Michael," Ned countered. "At least they eat when they aren't seasick, and they're heading to a new start. We are, too."

Michael shook his head and slumped down onto the hard deck. Uncle Robert joined them, sitting down beside him. "'Tis a fine day for celebrating me eldest nephew." Robert patted him on the shoulder.

"I'd rather be celebrating anywhere but here," Michael grumbled. Ned rolled his eyes, got up, and walked away.

"Why be glum, me laddie?" Robert asked. "It be a crackin' day with the sun out shinin' warm against our skin and only a wee breeze. 'Tis a fine day, I tell ye."

"Can't help it, Uncle. This be a horrid lot we live, especially on a birthday such as this. People dying around us. Sickness all around. The ship creakin' and groanin' like a dying old woman. Nowhere to be alone. This be no life for me."

"This be only for a short time, Nephew," Robert reminded him, "and this passage will take us to a new life where you will have a fine future. Ireland buried hope long ago."

"It wasn't buried when I be in the fields with me sheep," Michael said. "There be much for me in Ireland, sitting in the soft green grass and walking the heather hills and hearing the birds chirp and watching the clouds blow to and fro. That was me hope. Not this."

Just then a few children walked past them, thin and frail, stains on their ragged clothes, looking weak and tired even though it was still morning.

"Even these lads and lassies be weary of it all," Michael complained.

Before Robert could speak a word, those same children began a game of tag, running and laughing.

"'Tisn't true, lad. You just be havin' a dark cloud hangin' over your head," Robert said. "See, these wee ones be full of life even though the voyage be hard. We all long for the rolling hills of Ireland and for the smell of the earth. We all miss the bleating of the sheep and the solid land beneath our feet. We all miss our red-hot peat fires and oatcakes and lamb stew. But it only be a season we must suffer in order to get to the New World."

"I miss the apples and fat white potatoes, too," Michael whined. "But most of all, I long for home and me safe stone cottage and me bed."

"Ye must turn your heart away from all that, lad, or it will kill any ember of hope that may grow within your breast!" Robert stated. "Turn your heart to your new home, for it will bring your future, a future full of good things."

"God has been cruel to the Irish," Michael said flatly.

"Nae, lad," Robert corrected. "It be man's sin and selfishness that has caused the Irish famines and blighted future for these many. 'Tisn't God. Remember Joseph? God may have allowed hardship to come to the lad, but it was for his good and the good of many others, as he came to see much later. Yea, this journey we be on is one of hardship, but God will bring good, as you will come to see later on. Now, I beg you to still all those negative thoughts within you. Throw them overboard and bury them in the sea! That be me birthday wish for you, Michael."

Robert placed his hand on his shoulder and gave it a gentle squeeze. Then he got up and said, "Heed, what I have said, lad!" And then walked away.

Michael sat there a long time, thinking, even praying. He watched the bony bodies and emaciated faces of those who came topside from steerage to get a bit of relief from the stifling, rancid air below. Some had hollow eyes and a pallid complexion that warned him of sickness and hunger and pain. And then he looked at his healthy body and said, "Forgive me, Lord! I be whole and well. I mustn't complain."

Ned shook him from his introspection, jolting him away from his quiet altar. "Will you please come and talk with Murtagh and me?"

"Aye," Michael said.

When the two lads found Murtagh, the captain's son was full of information that he had overheard his father tell his mates that morning about the voyage down the St. Lawrence. Murtagh had only been on this journey twice, he said, and it was still new and interesting that he was bursting to share his wisdom with his friends.

"The St. Lawrence be a mighty river, lads, grander than most any river in Europe," Murtagh said. "The Captain says we'll be rounding into the Gulf in but a week!"

"We will see land?" Michael asked, thrilled at the thought of finally seeing firm ground again. "Will we stop and set our feet on firm ground?"

"Yae and nae," Murtagh said. "We will see land presently, but it will be far away, and we will not go to port. We will continue, past America, past Nova Scotia that be in Canada, and then on and into a narrow strait. There you will see the land of Newfoundland on one side and Cape North on the other."

"In a week, you say?" Michael asked, rubbing his hands together in excitement.

"If there be no storms or tempests to slow us, yae," Murtagh said. "But then starts the exciting part."

"Tell us, Murtagh, please," Ned begged.

Murtagh smiled and began. "The mighty St. Lawrence has a big, big mouth but a small, small throat." Michael could see that Murtagh loved telling stories, and he loved being the keeper of valuable information. After all, he was the captain's son, he reasoned.

"Once we pass the islands, we start going down the mouth, and there it gets narrower and narrower as if it's going to suck you up," Murtagh said, waving his arms and being as dramatic as possible. "You can see land on both sides, on a clear day, and then we stop for inspection when we see the Grand City show off her pretty self."

"What Grand City?" Michael asked.

"She be called Quebec, and she's a beauty," Murtagh said. "But she be a strange lady, for everyone there speaks French!"

"How will we get on in such a place?" Ned asked.

"Oh, we'll not stay there," Murtagh corrected. "We journey on to Port Montreal where you will get off the ship and we return to Belfast. And that's where the dangers begin for you."

"Danger? What danger?" Ned asked.

"The rapids and the bateau," Murtagh said. "I haven't ever been past Port Montreal meself, but I've heard tales, fearsome tales, of the treacherous journey beyond."

"Do tell," Ned said.

"Another time." Murtagh looked at the sun, high in the noon sky. "I must sup with the captain, or he'll give me a whippin'. Happy Birthday, Michael. May the Lord shine His face upon ye."

Murtagh ran off, leaving Michael and Ned to absorb the news of the journey ahead. What dangers could he mean?

As Michael pondered the meaning of it all, Susan and Mary came to fetch the lads, for their family had planned a special afternoon for him.

* * *

Margaret rocked wee Meg as she listened to her husband and brother-in-law. She enjoyed it when James and Robert settled into their old, comfortable ways of bantering back and forth, telling stories together as a team. The entire family sat on the deck, enjoying the warm sun and cool breeze while the wee ones slept on their father's and mum's laps amid all the noise of the passersby. It seemed that they could sleep anywhere.

The two men told stories of the New World, old stories as well as the few new stories they had read of or heard about from those on the ship, whose friends and relatives had already settled in Upper Canada. They shared all the details they could possibly recall of the letters from Uncle John and others who had cast a bright light on the New World. And, to be honest, they may have told a few tall tales beyond the facts in the excitement of it all. Margaret smiled as she watched the camaraderie between the two brothers.

"The New World be a Promised Land where a man can work for a fair wage and buy his own land," James said proudly. "And it be a land where the soil be quite rich and so the toiling be much easier."

"It be a place where working as a carpenter or a fisherman—or a railroad man—can gain a man one dollar and fifty cents a day!" Robert bantered as he winked at Michael when he emphasized "railroad man."

"And there in this Promised Land, education be better and food be cheaper and much more abundant," James said, smiling at his scholar, Susan.

"A man can buy land and build a home and own it, and he never has it taken from him. For there, in the New World, there be no landlords," Robert said. "And the taxes be only a quarter of Ireland's taxes."

James continued to paint a picture of plenty, of a bright future. But then he turned to the Bible. James talked about the patriarchs of old, Abraham and Moses, who had traveled to distant lands seeking a better life for their families. He talked about how God led them through troubled places—deserts and foreign lands—and how they found a future for their people. And he talked about what they had to leave behind and what troubles they had endured. But James always, carefully came back to God's promises and provisions.

As Margaret listened to James and Robert, she purposefully scooted close to Michael, rubbing his back and praying for him. She longed for her son to find that same sense of peace that she had found and knew he lacked. She prayed for God to open his heart to embrace the changes to come, as He had done for her.

Margaret noticed that Susan and Ned sat entranced, thrilled to listen to their father and uncle tell such tales. Obviously, they didn't need convincing, for they were excited about the adventure they were on.

Little John, Mary, and baby Meg awakened as the family seemed to be more at peace than ever. Margaret could see the joy on their faces and hear it in their voices. As the wee ones gathered on laps of love to hear more about their future life together, she turned her face to the richest hues of orange and red, colors only an ocean sunset could bring. She felt grateful for such a day as this.

CHAPTER 22
MAGGIE

THE FOLLOWING SATURDAY, Maggie was making plans to visit several antique stores to look for the quilt when the phone rang. It was an "unknown" caller, and she answered before the third ring.

"Bree?" Maggie said, expectantly.

"Mrs. Dolan?" a man's voice asked. "This is Sam Mason in Zimbabwe."

Her adrenaline began to rush through her body. "Yes?"

"I'm the director of the mission project here, and I need to talk to you about your daughter, Briana," Sam said.

"Yes?" It was all she could get out right then as she dug her nails into the palm of her hand and bit her lip.

"I'm sorry, but your daughter's ill, quite ill," Sam began. "She's in a tiny village clinic quite far from the capital, but she's being taken care of. We have one of our leaders with her twenty-four seven."

"What?" Her heart raced. Her palms began to sweat. "I...I just talked with her yesterday!"

"I know, but malaria got a grip on her," Sam said.

Malaria? That's deadly! Maggie's mind began to race, but before she could think any more, Sam continued.

"Malaria is a mosquito-borne infectious disease, and yes, Briana was taking her MefloQuinne. But she must have been bitten by the wrong mosquito," Sam said, trying to lighten the conversation. It didn't work.

"Unfortunately, Briana has a bad case of it," Sam continued. "She has a high fever and chills, muscle pain, and a severe headache. Right now, she's on an IV and meds, but she needs lots of prayer."

"Bree said she had the flu and a headache." Maggie's voice cracked with emotion.

"That's how it begins, but it was advancing as you spoke, yes," Sam said.

"Is she in danger?" Maggie asked, tears filling her eyes.

"Yes," Sam replied honestly. "Please pray and get others to pray. God's with her. I will call you tomorrow with an update. God bless you, Mrs. Dolan."

"Tell her I love her, please," she pleaded.

"I will," Sam promised. "Goodbye."

As Maggie hung up, she put her head on the table and wept. *Dear God! Please help my Bree. Please heal her!* She sat there, paralyzed with fear and worry, unable to call her mom, or anyone, for a long time. She tried to pray, but worry kept bombarding her thoughts.

Finally, she decided she just had to have some emotional support. She called her mom and then a few friends and told them about Bree. Each one tried to console her, and each promised to pray and gather more prayer support. She even left messages for Anna on both the store and her home phone, for she had forgotten to get the number for Anna's cell phone. Finally, she hardened herself, called Bree's dad, and left a voice mail. When the calls were done, Maggie was alone.

Alone to deal with it all—just God and her.

She looked at her "To Do" list on the table. She grabbed it, crumpled it up, and tossed it aside. *Forget the errands and the quilt. Nothing matters now but my daughter!*

She picked up her Bible, searching for answers, for strength, for faith. Though she usually read from her iPhone Bible app, there was something comforting about holding the

Bible in her hands just then.

She made a cup of tea, had another good cry, and braced herself for spending a day alone with God and the fear that gripped her. She flipped through her Bible, trying to find solace. But the house was deadly quiet and the quiet seemed to shout at her, "Your Bree is far, far, away, sick and alone!"

Maggie got up and paced the floor, but it was still too quiet. When that didn't help, she put on some Christian music and turned it up…loud! That did help.

She spent a long time soaking in the truth of those songs, truth about God's love and mercy and care. Then she scrolled through her "favorites" playlist and found what she was looking for.

"This is for me!" she said out loud. She listened it over and over again. She listened to the song's encouraging words about having faith through trials and holding on to hope. She cried over it. She sang to it. She prayed it. When the next song came on, the words of that song touched her in a new way. The words and music began to fill her with faith.

Maggie decided to call Brigit for support. She turned down the music, called her friend, and got her right away. After tearfully filling her in on Bree's situation, Brigit talked about how her divorce and the nasty custody battle had been a defining season for her. Brigit moaned. "I actually screamed at God, Maggie. I was so mad at Him. I was terrified that I might lose my kids. But I reached a point where I felt like I had to give them to God, or I really *would* lose them. I learned to be utterly honest with God and surrender all of it to Him through that awful time. You can, too. Do you want me to come over?"

Maggie shook her head. "Thanks, but I think I need to be alone with God today."

"You're probably right," Brigit agreed. "Well, I'll be praying for you, Megs, and if you need a hug, I'm here for you."

"Thanks, friend. I appreciate it." She hung up and somehow knew that this day, this weekend, this situation would become a defining time in her life. She switched off the music, and got down on her knees.

"Lord," she prayed aloud, "I hear You. I need You. I want to do this right for once. Bree needs You, Lord." She broke down and cried, but then she continued to ask God for help, especially for Bree. When all her prayers were spent, she dried her tears and turned to her Bible. It lay open to Psalm 23, and she pondered its words.

Maggie's thoughts and her conversation with God were honest and painful. She shared her anger that God called Bree to the mission field but didn't keep her safe. She admitted she was frustrated about dealing with finances and finding the quilt and worrying alone, without Bill. She told God how she struggled with knowing who she was, and how to trust Him, and what to do with her life. She even complained that these were certainly not the green pastures or quiet waters that the psalmist David spoke of. They were more like the valley of the shadow of death.

The shadow of death?

She could barely bring herself to think about that, but she willed herself to read on.

"'I will fear no evil,'" she read aloud, "'for You are with me.' And I know You are with Bree, Lord!"

Maggie got up and made a bowl of soup, but as she ate, her throat tightened and her brow furrowed and she was again bombarded by worry and fear. *What if Bree...dies?*

With that thought, the tears came as a torrent, tossing her into despair like she'd never experienced before. Sure, it had been painful when Bill left, but in the secret places of her heart, there was a bit of relief as well. He would no longer be there to torment her with negative, hurtful comments, accusations, and attitudes. He would no longer bring his critical spirit around to poison the atmosphere.

This was different. This was Bree!

She tried to shake the fear that began to choke her, the fear that chained her to a prison of *what ifs*. She got up and paced again. She screamed. She cried. She even tried worship music. But nothing seemed to help.

What if?

What if Abraham had refused to give up Isaac?

The thought shocked her like an ice-cold bucket of water being thrown in her face. Startled, Maggie got up and went to her Bible. She flipped through Genesis until she came to chapter 22. She read about Abraham's test, how the Lord asked him to slay his son.

Unimaginable! But…is God asking me to give up my Bree? Unthinkable!

She continued to read about how Abraham actually prepared to obey God, chose to obey Him. He saddled his donkey, brought the wood for the fire, and took his precious son Isaac with him. For three whole days he journeyed through his own valley of the shadow of death, knowing what God had told him to do, and Abraham actually determined to obey—no matter what.

Even while Abraham was there, walking with his dream child, and knowing that he would kill him? Impossible! She shook her head, tried to dry the tears that wouldn't stop coming, and continued.

"'We will worship and then we will come back to you,' Abraham said to his servants." She stared at the words.

"Oh, what I would do to have the kind of faith Abraham had!" she said aloud. "I can't fathom losing my child, much less be willing to bind her, slit her throat, and burn her on a fire of my own making! Oh Lord, what do You want of me, of Bree?"

To her, it seemed as though God was silent, but she continued to read Abraham's story, desperate to find an answer to the agony in her heart. She read out loud, as if she wanted the walls of her home to hear.

"'Do not lay a hand on the boy,' he said. 'Do not do anything to him. Now I know that you fear God, because you have not withheld from me your son, your only son.'"

Maggie knew, then, what God wanted of her.

"No!" she yelled. "I cannot bear to lose my daughter! I've

lost my marriage, my family, and many of my things—even my family's quilt. But none of that...none of that compares to losing Bree—and You know it, God!"

Maggie couldn't believe she was even considering such a thought. She cried and fought it until she could fight no more. For hours she wrestled with the knowledge that God wanted her to put everything—including Bree—in His hands. Finally, late into the evening, she fell into a deep and troubled sleep.

* * *

It was the early morning hours when Maggie awoke, eyes swollen and heart heavy. When she became conscious enough to remember the day before, she began to weep yet again.

"I can't, Lord," she said, lying in her bed and looking at the ceiling. "You know I don't have the faith of Abraham. Please help me."

She got up and showered, exhausted from the emotional war within her. Her head ached. Her heart ached. She even felt nauseous at the thought of wrestling with this yet again.

But Sam said he'd call today!

She grasped ahold of a thread of hope. And grasp she did. She turned her thoughts to that call, and she busied herself until it came.

Yet the hours passed all too slowly. She looked at her iPhone hundreds of times. She charged it. She checked to see if the ringer was on and if there happened to be any missed calls or voice mails—even though she kept it within her reach the entire day. In the meantime, she prayed and read and tried to be strong.

Finally her phone rang. "Hello?" she said frantically.

"Mrs. Dolan?" Sam answered with crackling sounds muffling his voice.

"Is she better?"

"Unfortunately, Briana's much worse. I am very sorry to tell you this. I promised I would call, but that's all I know right now," Sam said hesitantly. "We must pray and wait. I will call you tomorrow."

The crackle of the phone stopped, and she sat stunned, too afraid to even cry anymore. *That's all he could tell me? Nothing but THAT?*

Maggie was furious now, mad at the shortness of the call. Mad at the news. Frustrated that there was only bad news. And she was angry that God hadn't healed her daughter.

"Where are You, God?" she raged aloud. "Alive but worse? What kind of a loving God would do this to a beautiful girl who's serving You on the mission field?"

Though she felt embarrassed to verbalize her fears and doubts, her anger and frustration, it felt good to get it all out. She continued to vent her emotions and her thoughts for a long while, shouting and arguing with God, who seemed to be silent. When she was finally through, she washed her face, made a cup of tea, and decided to return to the story of Abraham.

"Abraham looked up...and saw a ram," Maggie read, "...and sacrificed it as an offering instead of his son."

Okay, God, she bargained. *You don't have to help me find my family's crazy quilt. It's Yours. It's my ram. But please, please spare my daughter.*

She knew that it was an unfair bargain. *Sheesh, a quilt for Bree? Who am I kidding?* She rolled her eyes in disgust.

"You can't take her, God," she said through her tears. "You provided a ram for Abraham. Provide for Bree and me. Please."

* * *

In the wee hours of the night, Maggie awakened with a start. She lay in the dark, thinking about Abraham's story, about her story, about her God. She knew, just as she knew that first day, what God was asking.

He wanted it all. All.

She prayed in the darkness of the night with tears of

surrender. *She's Yours, God. I'm Yours. If You choose to bring her home in a pine box, I will choose to praise You. I don't know how, but I will.*

It was said. Finally. From the bottom of her heart. With all her will. With all her mind, knowing what it might mean for Bree, for her.

They were His. His alone.

Maggie fell into a peaceful sleep, but she was awakened to the shrill ring of her phone before the sun rose. She scrambled to answer it.

"Hello?" she said, unable to hold off the yawn from her mouth.

"Mrs. Dolan?" Sam said with a lilt in his voice.

"How's she? How's Bree?" Her voice trembled but surprisingly, her heart felt calm.

"I'm happy to report that, just hours ago, Briana's fever broke and she gained consciousness," Sam said. "The doctor thinks she's through the worst of it. It will be a long recovery, but she's going to make it, praise God!"

She couldn't speak for several moments, but when she regained her composure, she said, "The Lord provides! Please tell Bree I love her and will keep on praying for her."

"I will," Sam said. "It will take time for her to be able to travel. But when she's strong enough, we will bring her back to Harare, and then she'll be escorted home by one of our staff. We will be in touch as soon as we know more. God bless you, Mrs. Dolan."

"Thank you," she said, feeling emotionally spent but grateful. "And God bless my Bree."

CHAPTER 23
MARGARET

JUST THREE DAYS after Michael's birthday, James stood by the railing and watched as billowing banks of ominous clouds began to gather.

"I can smell it in the air, Father," Michael said. "A storm is at hand."

"Aye, laddie," James said, his forehead creased with concern as he looked up at the sky. "We have a fearsome trial ahead of us."

Rumors of an impending storm struck fear in the hearts of every passenger and crewmember alike. The ship was close to land, and the dangers were many. Reefs. Rocks. The jagged shoreline that could smash a ship to bits. The crew put ropes out, all around the deck to have something to hold on to, and they instructed the passengers to secure their belongings and to brace for days of rough seas. But the worst was the knowledge that the steerage passengers were sealed below. Just knowing they were locked in that dark, dank belly of the ship made James shiver and pray for Sean, Sara, and the others.

Thank God we have topside rooms; please keep our brethren safe.

"There will be no food, no water, no relief, just you mind that," said the cabin steward gravely. "Prepare well for the days ahead."

An eerie, dark sky signaled the coming storm. And the rhythmic whoosh of the ship cutting its way through the sea became irregular, teasing them with a changing force that pulled the vessel from side to side instead of straight ahead. The air grew damper and colder, and the green froth of the angry waves melted the passengers resolve to be brave.

The ship crested, rising with groans and creaks and moans of the wood.

Then fell, hitting the waves hard and crashing.

Then climbed again.

The cabin steward returned from battening the hatches and hurriedly said, "Captain says the ship will stay firm in the tempest's fury, but I am to warn you of the dangers ahead. This be a bad storm, and you must not leave this stateroom, under any condition, until the storm has passed."

James hugged his wife and then hugged the children. After a quick prayer together, he went to his cabin and shut the door. James hurried to secure their belongings, hoping to beat the storm's impact.

Then seawater began to flood the decks, creeping into their tiny cabin.

Moment by impending moment, the atmosphere thickened. The turbulent motion increased, and their stomachs soon responded. Dizziness. Sweat. Vomit. James and the lads all succumbed to its fury; all but Robert felt its wrath.

The storm tossed the ship violently, and they could barely stay in their berths. Though James knew the dangers, he crawled on his hands and knees from cabin to cabin, trying to help his family. But he, too, was tossed by the tempest with each wave, sometimes going airborne and other times being slammed hard against the rough cabin walls. He tried to find the rhythm of the lurching sea, but there was none. The ship pitched and tossed uncontrollably until all of them, even the crew, began to fear for their lives.

Anything not tied down was tossed wildly around the tiny

cabins. Boots became projectiles. Tin cups flew like birds. The angry sea and its heaving waves actually tossed them out of their berths more than once.

James opened Margaret's cabin door. "I must tie the wee ones to you else they may be tossed hither and yon!" James shouted over the storm's howl. Without asking, he took Margaret's apron and tore it into strips of cloth. Then he tied baby Meg and little John to their mum. He did the same with Mary, tying her to Susan. And as he left, he shouted that he would pray that this would keep them safe.

Then James became terribly ill. Ned clung to Michael instead of to his father. All of them grew sicker and sicker with each mountainous lurch of the ship. The heaving waves became as sea monsters, pitching and rolling them to and fro.

Everything was wet. All of it reeked of vomit. James and the others worried and wondered if they would actually make it to the Promised Land. He wondered if the nightmare would ever end.

* * *

Margaret thought her wee John would not make it through the storm. He grew weaker and weaker as he heaved and retched until he had nothing left. And then the wee lad grew feverish and silent and listless. Hours later, John's eyes rolled back in his head and he started convulsing wildly. She prayed and tried to help him, but the storm within him and the storm around him left her not knowing what to do.

"I will go, Mum, and fetch Father!" Susan shouted over the storm.

"Nae, child," Margaret cried. "'Tis much too dangerous. Even your father dare not go out in such a tempest. Stay here and care for Mary. And pray. All of us must pray."

Margaret was alone. Alone with four sick children, as she herself was sick. What could she do? Who could help her?

The sound of the storm's fury was so loud that she could only hear its wail. Not the children's cries. Not their prayers.

Not their moans.

All she could do was pray. She cried out to the only One who could help. She asked for her son's life. She asked for deliverance. She asked for peace.

At that moment, wee John settled into a corpse-like stillness, not even responding to her anguished grasp or piercing wails. John had fallen into a deep sleep, and only the slow, rhythmic rise and fall of John's chest alerted her that he was alive.

She thanked God that he lived still, but she wondered if her other children would survive this terrible ordeal. If she and James would even live to see the New World. As she continued to pray, her eye caught sight of the steamer chest, and she wondered if the quilt would make it to the New World to be passed down to the next generation and to tell of their story.

Baby Meg, little John, sweet Mary, and even Susan had finally fallen asleep, and Margaret was left alone with her thoughts. She touched Susan's matted hair and gently pulled it off her face. She ran her hand along the strip of cloth that still tied Mary to her sister like an umbilical cord. She kissed Mary's tiny face, careful to not touch the goose egg on her forehead caused by a projectile that had found its mark there.

Then she ran her hand along the cloth that held John safely to her and touched his chest, just to make sure he was still breathing fine. Thankful that he was, Margaret turned to her baby Meg, still tied and faring better than the rest.

The storm still rocked the ship. It still swayed and creaked and moaned. The stench from the vomit was nauseating. She looked around her tiny cabin and saw that water had saturated many of the things that had flown around the cabin and landed on the floor.

The storm was yet to be over. Yet to give up its anger. Yet to free them of its fury and fear.

But she knew what God was asking her to do.

Margaret knew she had to give it all up, give it all to God. She knew she had kept back a part of her heart that still longed for her homeland, for safety, for security. She knew she had to once and for all trust that God would bring her family into the future that they had hoped for, dreamed of, and longed for. But letting go was hard. And embracing the unknown seemed impossible to her, especially with the storm threatening their lives.

She thought of all she had left behind. All she had given up. In the midst of helping her sick children and herself retching between sobs, in the midst of the smells and the lurching and the fury of the storm, she finally, totally let go. She placed her future, and that of her family, in God's hands. Whether they made it through the storm or not, she would trust. Whether she lost everything, she would still love Him.

She laid it all down. All.

* * *

It took nearly two days before the sea finally gave up its anger. But when Margaret awakened on that second day to the quiet of a gentle wind and the rhythmic rocking of the sea, she checked each one of her children and breathed a sigh of relief. John slept peacefully, and she rejoiced that he had come through such a close brush with death. Susan, Mary, and wee Meg slept as well, as if each were in a cradle, rocking them to rest.

Margaret forced herself to find her sea legs, weakened as they were, and go to James's cabin to see how they fared. When she opened the door, not one of them stirred. She checked to be sure they were safe and asleep, and then she returned to the cabin, plopping into her berth in exhaustion.

The storm had passed. They were safe.

She and the family slept for several hours more as the bow rose and fell in contrition for the fury it had cast on the lot of them.

When she and the wee ones finally awakened, one by one they left the reeking cabins to seek some fresh air. Margaret and the children joined James, Robert, and the lads outside, who were already sitting on the deck. James appeared weaker than she had seen him in ages, but the lads looked well.

She took James's hand. "Are you all right, husband?"

"I am well, wife. Tired, but well." James kissed her hand and smiled. "And you?"

"God has dealt mightily with me, and I am well, too," she confessed. "I will tell thee all presently."

As they settled down to visit, John and Mary quickly fell asleep on their father's lap, happy and content to be safe in his arms. Margaret told James, Robert, and the lads about little John's scare and God's work in her heart, while baby Meg nursed ravenously. James and the others listened quietly to the entire tale, sipping water, all of them still weak and worn from the turmoil of the storm.

When Margaret finished her story, Mary and John woke up. They all hugged her warmly in response, and then Ned tugged on her skirt.

"Look, Mum, sea fog," Ned said, pointing to the rolling fog coming over the deck rail. They watched it slowly move toward them, until they could barely see a few feet away. It grew colder and damper, but it felt as though the cool mist had come to wash away all the trauma of the past few days.

"So silent it be," Mary said, popping her thumb out of her mouth.

The fog was indeed peaceful, even refreshing, and it left droplets of moisture on their skin, seeming to bathe them in its embrace. But it blew past quickly, and with its passing came clear blue skies.

"God's bath," said little John as he smiled and rubbed the moisture from his face.

Margaret looked at him and nodded. "God's bath," whispered Margaret.

They sat in silence for a long while, and then she got up and went over to the railing to get away from the reeking, vomit-stained cabins. James shared the news he had heard from the crew. "Two of the sailors and seven of the passengers were lost in the storm. But God be praised, the fever has passed, even with the storm's wake, and for that we must rejoice."

"And the Boyds? How did they fair?" Susan asked.

"They were topside a while ago, and though the sadness of Meera's passing still encompasses them deeply, their bodies fair well," James said. "The crew be preparing victuals presently, and we must try to eat something."

"Might it be oats?" wee John asked.

They all laughed and hugged, and hugged again, happy to be past the fury of the storm.

A few moments later, the family returned to their cabins and found Robert busy cleaning. He had already cleaned Margaret's tiny stateroom and was working on the men's cabin. He had wiped up all the vomit and pulled out the bedding to air and put everything back in its place in her room, and he was doing the same with the other.

"Lord have mercy, brother!" Margaret said, overwhelmed at such a kindness. "You are an angel from heaven above, 'tis true."

Tears flowed down her cheeks as she hugged Robert, and the children joined her as well. James gave him a fine slap on the back and thanked him too, just as the steward brought food and water for them all.

"Oatmeal!" Mary cried.

As they sat on the deck outside their cabins, eating oatmeal and sipping water, Margaret looked down at her dress and then glanced at the children's clothes. She sighed. Soil and stains covered their pantaloons and shirts and dresses. The children's stockings had been darned repeatedly with each successive child's use, and the ragged woolen coats on their backs reminded her of the wretched castaways they had seen on the docks of Belfast.

But they were not there. They were here. Eating oatmeal and safe. All of them. And together. Just days from their destiny. Days until they set foot on the land that would become their home, their heritage.

Margaret suddenly thought of her quilt. She had to know

whether it had weathered the storm in one piece. She got up, went to the steamer chest, and opened it carefully. Then she unwrapped her treasures, wondering how they had fared. She brought out the quilt for all to see.

Laughing in relief, Margaret said, "The quilt is untouched by the tempest's fury but for a tiny corner that got wet. It is safe, as are we. When we settle in our new land, we will add remembrances of this voyage, including me apron you ripped to shreds, James! And I thank you. And that shirt you wear, Robert. You have been a godsend, brother, and we must honor you with our lives."

"'Tis me honor, family," Robert responded. "Thank you for allowing me to journey with you on this grand adventure!"

Margaret smiled. "Let us rejoice in God's deliverance of us all! Our hope and our future are close at hand."

CHAPTER 24
MAGGIE

MAGGIE SAT ALONE at the company picnic table eating her lunch. She watched the clouds roll by and heard the birds chirp, but nothing settled her heart. Finally, grabbed her cell phone and called her mother. "I haven't heard from Sam in three days, and it's making me crazy! I need to know that Bree's okay. Where's God in all this?"

"I'm sure they're just waiting to hear of some progress," her mother said, trying to calm her daughter's nerves. "This is a stressful time, I know. But, do you really doubt God?"

"I guess not," Maggie admitted. "I gave Bree to Him, and I still do. But it's hard not knowing what's going on."

"For sure," Elizabeth agreed. "As her nana, I'm on pins and needles, too. Let's pray and shore up our faith a bit, shall we?"

Maggie felt better but still fragile after the two women prayed over the phone and said their goodbyes. One minute she seemed a bastion of faith and the next a puddle of tears. The waiting felt like torture, but wait she must. She had no choice.

Early Thursday morning, the phone rang. "Hello?" Maggie said, heart pounding with anticipation that it was Sam.

"Mrs. Dolan? This is Sam," he said cheerily. "I have good news! Briana's doing much better. She's eating and walking and gaining her strength. The doctors think she'll be able to travel back to home base here in Harare and then back to you in Colorado next week."

Her relief brimmed over with tears of joy. "Thank God!" she said. "Can I talk with her?"

"Sorry, there's no reception in that little village," Sam said. "Reagan, the girl who's with her, has to send a message to me through a contact in another town. But don't worry, when Briana gets here to our office in Harare, I'll make sure you talk with her."

"Oh, thank you, Mr. Mason," she said. "I can't wait to hear her voice!"

"Keep on praying, Mrs. Dolan. We all are," Sam said. "I'll be in touch soon. Goodbye."

Maggie dried her tears, called her mom to update her, and got ready for the day.

I can't wait to tell Anna about all this and get her input. I sure wish I would have gotten her personal cell number before she left so I could have talked with her during all this mess.

* * *

The next day, Maggie woke up excited to work at the antique store, but she was even more anxious to talk with Anna.

"Anna?" she called out, even before she closed the shop door. "Anna?"

"Dearie! It's a blessing to see you," Anna said, rounding the corner of the back room. "How was your trip?"

"Oh, Anna, I have a lot to tell you!" She set her purse and lunch on a table. Then she immediately blurted out Bree's situation, talking faster and faster until she had to stop and catch her breath.

"My heavens, child! I wish you'd had my cell number!" Anna said. "But God's in control, that I know."

Before they could continue their conversation, customers began to come into the shop. Maggie waited on a few of them and the morning passed quickly. At noon, Anna closed the shop for their daily respite.

"Oh, Anna, I'm sorry. I didn't even ask about your time with the family," Maggie said.

"That's fine. I was interested to hear all your news. But thank you for asking," Anna told her. "I had a wonderful time with my family. It was quiet and peaceful—nothing like your week!"

"Yeah, mine wasn't peaceful, but God met me in the storm." She continued on, telling Anna about wrestling with giving Bree to God. The emotion of the experience overwhelmed her again. Anna placed a caring hand on her arm.

"While all of us should be willing to give everything up, few of us are called to actually make such a hard decision," Anna said. "It sure wasn't easy for me to become willing to put it all in the Lord's hands when I was on the mission field. Losing my husband, my children's father, was the hardest thing I've ever gone through, and I'd hate to see you go through anything like that. Yet I know He'd get you through it if He had destined it."

"I am learning that I have to choose to trust God each moment of every day, and that's really tough," she admitted.

"You're doing what you can, dearie," Anna said. "You've told me that you're reading the Bible and praying day and night and soaking in worship music. It's really all a choice— to plug into God's life-giving power, and it's then a choice to trust. Keep on doing what you're doing, Maggie."

After lunch, a steady stream of customers came in and out of the store all afternoon. Just before closing, a woman came in pushing another young woman in a wheelchair. Maggie greeted them and asked how she could help them.

"My daughter, Lily, wants a teacup," the woman said. "She has MS and struggles to hold things well. If you have something rather sturdy, that would be great."

Lily looked to be about Bree's age, and Maggie's imagination began to run away with her. *What if Bree ends up in a wheelchair? What if she's permanently disabled from this illness? What if?*

What if Abraham…?

She took a deep breath. *I trust You, Father.*

She smiled at the women and led them to a shelf that held teacups. "I think this one might work."

"Dai…sies," Lily said, haltingly, and forcing a big smile. "I want dai…sies." She struggled to take the cup in her stiff and trembling hands, placed her finger in the handle, and said, "This one, M…om."

"Well, I guess you have a sale," the woman said, appearing to be pleased to see her daughter happy. "We've been searching for just the right cup for days now. Lily knows what she wants."

She smiled and looked at Anna, who held up her index finger as if to say, "Hold on."

Maggie took the two to the counter and finished wrapping the teacup just as Anna came with the daisy teapot and an embroidered napkin with daisies on it. "Let's add this to your treasure—as my gift. God bless you, Lily!"

Maggie looked at Anna, astonished at her generosity. *How does this woman make a living? She's always giving things away.*

The mother looked at Lily, who was jostling around in her wheelchair, trying to say something. "What is it, honey?"

Tears began to run down Lily's cheeks, and she became more and more agitated. Maggie began to wonder if Lily was offended or hurt by Anna's gift. She couldn't understand what was wrong and wondered what to do.

"I…people do…n't care for meee," Lily struggled to say. "People do…n't like me. You do!"

Anna bent down to Lily's height and held her shaking hand. "I do like you, Lily, but God loves you more!" As Lily and her mother cried, Anna leaned down and gave Lily her undivided attention.

Anna told Lily about a loving God who cared for her

deeply. She sprinkled her words with Scripture, becoming bolder and stronger with each sentence. Her soliloquy was one of the most beautiful things Maggie had ever heard.

Suddenly the shop door opened and a heavyset man came in, unintentionally interrupting that holy moment. He noticed that something special, something intimate, was going on and said, "Take your time there. I'll be over here when you're done. Take your time."

Maggie handed both women tissues from the box that was sitting on the counter and worked on wrapping up the teapot.

No wonder Anna has boxes of tissues around the store.

"Now you just enjoy these things, Lily, and remember that you are loved," Anna said.

"Daisies are a happy flower, don't you think?" Maggie said, handing Lily the bag with her treasures.

"I am...hap..py...today," Lily said, her dark eyes twinkling with delight. "Thank...you."

"God bless you," she and Anna said, almost in unison. They looked at each other and grinned. Lily and her mother smiled, too.

Maggie turned to wait on the man who was aimlessly looking at linens.

Awkward! Poor man. He sure is gracious.

"Sorry about that. How may I help you?" she asked.

"Hey, no problem! That looked like a special moment, and I didn't want to interrupt it," said the man.

"It sure was!" Maggie agreed. After the man told her he was looking for antique records, she informed him that they didn't have any. But she went to ask Anna if she knew where he might find them. Anna always seemed to know the market.

Anna nodded her head, went over to him, and told the man where he might find the records in a store just a few blocks away. After Anna thanked him for stopping by, the man said, "That was a nice thing you did there with that girl. Made my day!"

Anna smiled and said, "Mine, too. God bless you!" as she

closed the door behind him and flipped around the "Closed" sign. She locked the door and turned to her.

"Well, there are divine moments in every day, if only we will look for them!" Anna said as casually as if she was saying that the sun was shining.

"But how do you know when those kind of moments come along?" Maggie asked, curious about Anna's intuition.

"That?" Anna said. "Oh, that was easy. You could see it all over Lily's face. She seemed sad and forlorn, much like you were that first day you came into the shop." Anna smiled and sat in a cane bottom chair. "We are not here for our own pleasure, Maggie. We are here to be the hands and feet of Jesus. And when one of His little ones is hurting, what can we do but help? That sweet Lily and her mother were hurting. You could feel it the moment they came into the store. You could see it in their eyes and hear it in their voices. It was obvious."

"I felt sorry for them, yes," Maggie admitted, "but I didn't really notice they were hurting or needed something special."

"Oh, you'll learn, dearie. You'll learn," Anna said. "It just takes a little listening to that still, small voice inside. And remember, God loves you no matter what you do."

"Thank you, Anna, for listening to that still, small voice the day I came into this place," she said with a catch in her voice. "My life will never be the same because of it."

"You are quite welcome, Maggie," Anna said. "But I am blessed as well. I have great help and a new friend."

On the way home, Maggie thought about the day. *I can't believe what an adventure this faith walk can be! I watch Anna and see someone who lives her faith as natural as breathing. Will I ever get there?*

It occurred to her that she hadn't worried about Bree for nearly the entire day. She smiled, feeling good about that. Then she said aloud. "I'm glad You love me, and I choose to trust You—no matter what."

CHAPTER 25
MARGARET

MARGARET LEFT HER CABIN and found that the space on deck was already quite crowded. Children chased each other. Women talked. Couples, including Sean and Sara Boyd, stood near the railing, watching, well, nothing in particular.

She and James joined the Boyds. After greeting one another, all four of them seemed to become caught up in their own thoughts of what was and what would be.

As she stood at the rail, Margaret felt the spray of the salt water against her face. With it, she sensed the strength of the new day filling her soul. Indeed, she *could* meet each new obstacle of change with faith, with trust, and with hope. God *had* been there and He *would* be there still. She knew. She determined then and there to meet each new wave, each new storm that came her way by trusting in Him.

"Birds, Mum, birds!" Mary said, running up and pulling on her skirt. She looked at her sweet Mary and saw more joy in her eyes than she'd seen in a long time. She smiled at her as Mary pointed to the sky. As if in unison, Margaret, James, and the Boyds saw a small flock of seagulls. It meant one thing.

Land was near.

Margaret noticed that the group of people close to them

overheard Mary and strained to see what they had been waiting to see for nearly a month—land. The sky was blindingly blue and Margaret squinted as she looked for land, but she looked out past the twinkling waters anyway. Finally, a man, just feet away, spotted it.

"Land, ho!" he said in a booming voice. The entire crowd cheered, and then an older gent pulled a tin whistle out of his pocket and began to play a happy Irish jig. Before long, dancing and singing and celebration overtook the seafarers, weak and worn as they were.

One of the crew came near them, and he patted Ned on the head. "That be Nova Scotia a far out there, wee laddie."

"In America?" Ned asked.

The sailor glanced at Margaret, laughed, and clicked his tongue. "You be needing to study the mappin' of the New World. That be part of Upper Canada, that it be!"

"We're gonna settle in Canada! Do we get off the ship soon?" Ned prodded.

"No, laddie." The sailor grinned and shook his head. "We be rounding the strait past Newfoundland and headin' into the great St. Lawrence afore nightfall. Sorry to say, but 'twill be days afore you set your wee feet on land again."

Margaret laughed at the conversation. They had much to learn about the New World they would make their own.

But then, one of the sailors mentioned that the ship was drawing near a shoal called the Grand Banks where fish were abundant. Immediately, Robert and the other Irish fishermen heard about this, and one by one they tossed in their lines as did several of the sailors. Margaret watched, and after waiting patiently for what seemed like hours, one and then another and then another pulled up big fat fish—cod, dogfish, and others. That night, the cooks prepared a feast like they hadn't seen in many weeks, the first meat they enjoyed in nearly a month.

* * *

Susan didn't care a whit about fishing, and she just couldn't wait to get off the ship and onto land again. She shook her head and scowled as Ned shrugged off the sailor's comments and ran off to play. *How many more days on this terrible ship?*

Thankfully, Susan quickly forgot her disappointment the minute that Michael came to ask her to join him for a jig. Michael smiled and grabbed her hand, leading her into the group of dancers. They laughed and danced and enjoyed the moment, joyfully kicking up their heels and turning round and round. But it didn't take long before they both returned to their parents' side, winded and weary.

"Why can't I jig, Mum?" Susan asked, trying to catch her breath. "What be wrong with me?"

"You are weak from the journey and from the storm. We all are." Margaret hugged her daughter and then pointed to others leaving the fun. "See there? The others are tiring, too. Do not worry, daughter. You will fare better in the days ahead."

As they headed into the great gulf, a lighthouse sparkled in the distance, alighting Susan's heart with eager anticipation. Here and there little islands of rocks jutted out from the bay, alerting the crew to dangerous rocks and reefs ahead. The captain called his crew to attention, bidding them to keep careful watch for such enemies.

Throughout that pivotal day, hope dawned with each new peekaboo view of land that Susan and the others saw as they slowly made their way through the Cabot Strait. On the port side, Susan caught a glimpse of Nova Scotia, and in the far distance she could almost see Prince Edward Island. Almost.

But on the starboard side, the ship actually came close enough to reveal a few tiny seaside villages of Newfoundland, its rocky shores, and the spring green meadows. Susan could even see smoke rising from the village chimneys.

She and her siblings ran from port side to starboard side, but she finally spent most of her time on the starboard side. How she longed for civilization, for land, for life as they had known it! For her, the waiting seemed excruciatingly long, and she was quite weary of the journey.

Susan pointed and jumped with joy. "Oh my! Look at those giant fish!"

"Lassie, that not be a fish," a nearby sailor said. "That be a mammal, a humpback whale! And lookie there. 'Tis a great pod of 'em!"

"Where'd they come from?" Susan asked.

"They migrated up from the warm Caribbean breeding waters to spend their summer days here," the sailor said, laughing at the sight. "Ain't they beauties?"

Susan nodded. She watched the massive creatures. She couldn't take her eyes off the wonderful sight and felt thrilled to be one of only a few on that side of the ship at the moment. What a marvelous secret!

But then word got around the deck, and before long, a mighty mob of passengers, including her family, crowded around her to enjoy the performance of nearly a dozen huge whales. They breached, tail-slapped, and showed off their pectoral fins for nearly an hour. Susan couldn't remember a more exciting spectacle, and her heart surged with joy.

Later that day, Susan, Michael, and Ned stood by the rail to enjoy the lovely views before them. Murtagh joined them to provide his expert eight-year-old commentary.

"The great St. Lawrence gets narrower and narrower, as if she's going to suck you up." Murtagh motioned with his hands, starting out wide and then putting his hands closer and closer together. "Then the grand city of Quebec shows her pretty self and lets ye in." He smiled, pleased with his lecture.

They all laughed, and Susan watched as Michael ruffled Murtagh's thick head of curly hair. "You be a good lad, Murtagh. We be a missing you when the journey ends."

"I fear I will never find a friend like your brother Ned. Not for a long, long time." Murtagh frowned and looked down at his shoes.

Ned hugged Murtagh but Susan quickly turned them back to the river's view. "Look, a ship! Haven't seen another ship since we left Ireland!" She pointed to a vessel passing on their port side in the far distance. The children ran over to the port side railing.

"Indeed!" Murtagh said. "You shall see many vessels in the days to come, for there are hundreds that bring the Irish and many foreign goods to the New World's shores."

"And what be those pretty birds a flying 'round here?" Susan asked.

They watched as the short, stocky birds with big orange feet caught tiny fish in their beaks and then returned to a nearby island.

"They be puffins and you be seein' thousands of 'em, ye will, for that be Puffin Island over yonder." Murtagh lifted his chin, pointing it toward a small island. "Watch how fast and low they fly, lookin' for them tiny herring fish ta eat, that's what they be doin' for it's a breedin' time."

Susan clapped her hands and said, "'Tis good to see feathery fowl again. Afore long, we'll be on land and done with all this horrid life on water."

Several days later, the ship sailed into a wide part of the river. Its sails pushed hard against the mighty river's current and the voyage became rougher than the day before. Susan tried to distract herself by telling Mary and John fairy stories and by playing with wee Meg. But the day seemed to plod on forever.

Yet by day's end, the ship began to head into a narrower part of the mighty river, and Margaret relaxed a little when she could once again see land on both sides.

Susan hugged her mum. "Murtagh was right. It does feel like we are getting sucked into the river's throat! But I like seeing the land near. Oh, Mum, I ne'er want to venture onto the ocean again. Ne'er!"

"Nor I, child, nor I." Margaret smiled and hugged her back. "I suspect we be landlubbers, that we be." Mum and daughter laughed.

Later that afternoon, Susan sat near her mum, little John, and baby Meg with the tin whistle she had borrowed from her Uncle Robert. She played a soft Irish ballad, a song of their homeland. Those who were nearby listened quietly, and they smiled at the wee lass who gave them a kind reminder of what had been. They all seemed to enjoy the melody of Ireland as the ship cut its way toward Quebec and then on to a new life and future.

* * *

The ship's upriver voyage was slow going, but Margaret enjoyed the beautiful views with its rugged, wooded shores dotted with tiny white wooden houses, tiny white churches, and small quaint towns. The waters of the St. Lawrence were clear and blue, and she licked her lips, wondering if the water was good to drink.

By and by the crew hoisted up buckets of freshwater for drinking. Everyone drank as much as they wanted and had more to spare. Margaret hadn't tasted anything sweeter and more refreshing, especially after enduring rations of the stagnant, boiled water they had while crossing the ocean.

After a few days, Margaret saw green plants floating on the water and shorebirds flying overhead all along their journey up the St. Lawrence. Each sign of life made her heart pump with excitement and made her thoughts turn to better days ahead.

Then she began to see stranger things—pieces of clothing and bedding in the water—and she wondered what they could mean. It was a strange sight, but it was more signs of life than she'd seen in nearly a month. She didn't want to miss a bit of it. She stayed outside and at the rail as much as possible, showing wee Meg and John the sights and sounds. Apparently others didn't want to miss anything either, for the deck was often crowded and the collective mood of the emigrants quickly filled with anticipation—as well as a little trepidation.

That afternoon, Margaret overheard a conversation about Grosse Île, the immigration stop near Quebec, and the terrible cholera outbreak that had struck the immigrants in 1832. She had heard fearful tales—that by 1847, the facilities on the island couldn't accommodate all the deathly ill Irish immigrants. To hold them all, the Canadians had built crude, cold infirmaries on their shores.

What if any of her family got sick and was quarantined there? The thought struck fear in her heart, and as she looked at the crowd around her, she was sure that each passenger who journeyed up the river likely felt that same fear.

Margaret tried to brush her cares away, but it was no use. She knew that upon arrival in Quebec, if the ship had anyone with fever, the captain had to fly a blue flag of warning. Any passengers who were sick would be removed and sent to the quarantine facilities. If they didn't follow this procedure, the entire lot of passengers and the crew could be quarantined for weeks on the ship if the inspectors thought it best.

"Thank God the ship fever has passed! Yet many have died on this voyage, God rest their souls, including wee Meera. Thirty days from our homeland until now, and yet we still have a dozen more days before we set our eyes on our uncle and begin a new life." Margaret hugged her babe tightly. Baby Meg cooed at her mum and she smiled back. Margaret sighed and turned her eyes skyward as wee Meg tugged at her apron. "Let us pass through the Isle with ease. Yet, Lord, I will trust you!"

A shipmate interrupted Margaret's thoughts and words. "We be coming round to Quebec presently. Listen up, all of ye," the sailor called out in a loud, commanding voice. "Ye must ready your quarters for inspection. If there be any soil on your straw bedding, ye must throw it overboard. If there be anything unclean, toss it o'er the rail. Secure all your belongings. Wash thyself well, and if you need a hosin' return hither within the hour. Ready thyself to be inspected by the doctor. If any of ye have a fever or sores, you might be quarantined. You must oblige these orders presently!"

Near panic ensued as Margaret, the passengers, and the crew prepared the vessel for inspection. It became a rather frantic affair. The crew scrubbed and swept and thoroughly cleaned everything, and those who helped got an extra ration of sea biscuits.

Bedding and clothes were thrown overboard and quickly swept upstream by the river's strong current. Sailors hosed down the deck—and many of the passengers—and others emptied and scrubbed the latrines.

"That's why we saw bedding and clothing in the river," Margaret murmured as she busied herself. First she tended to the children and cleaned them up as best she could. She washed their bodies, dressed them in the finest clothes that she had kept hidden in her trunk for just this occasion. She combed their hair. Only then did she turn to herself and do what she could to meet her own needs.

Meanwhile, James and Robert cleaned and secured all their belongings. Then they, too, readied themselves for their arrival at the inspection station. And as they waited, apprehension grew.

Margaret warned her brood before they left the cabin to watch carefully. "You mustn't dirty yourselves, children! The inspectors must see clean and healthy children."

The children nodded and left for the rails, and Margaret took time to pause and look around. The cabin looked fit. Their persons looked fine. They were ready. When all was done, she left the cabin to join her family near the rail. Margaret laughed as she looked around and saw that the ship was cleaner than when they had boarded it in Belfast.

If only it had been this fit all month!

The children wiggled and laughed and chatted happily as they watched the ship slow to a crawl. When the ship finally weighed anchor, the crew hoisted the ensign to let the inspectors know the ship was ready. The ship sat silent alongside several other ships, waiting for inspectors to come aboard and judge them fit or not.

"Why is it so quiet, Mum?" Mary asked.

"I 'spect everyone be a wee bit anxious about the inspections." Margaret said, patting Mary on the head. She tried to keep the children and herself distracted, occupied, and clean.

When it was the *Tom Bowline's* turn to be inspected, the medical officials climbed aboard. Margaret's heart pounded. Would the ship be quarantined? The deadly silence on the deck told her that all the other passengers felt the same way she did. Strangely enough, that thought brought her consolation instead of fear. As she waited for her family to go through the inspection process, she prayed for peace.

The inspection process was slow and stressful, but when it was done, only one mother and her small child from steerage were taken to quarantine. Margaret—and everyone else— sighed in relief. In response to their success, a few of the passengers started playing a bit of cheerful Irish music.

Straightaway, the *Tom Bowline* pulled up anchor, began to move, and slowly passed several still-anchored ships. Margaret smiled as their ship sailed cautiously up the St. Lawrence, passing Quebec and then heading on to their final destination—Montreal.

Margaret and the family changed out of their good clothes and packed them away. After the ship passed by what the sailors called the Isle d'Orleans, she finally caught a glimpse of what Murtagh had called "the grand city of Quebec," and she gasped at the sight.

"'Tis a beauty," Margaret whispered as she took wee Meg from James, and he nodded in agreement. As the ship passed the main harbor, she could see Market Hall with its tall columns and red roofs surrounded by a multitude of fine multi-storied stone buildings, none like she'd ever seen. On the hill beyond, a mighty fortress flew its flag, and beyond that, the city proper.

After sailing past Quebec, the ship traveled through a narrow part of the river where Margaret enjoyed the sight of several small villages. They sailed on until they came to a wide opening in the river just beyond the town of Nicolel, and then the river narrowed again. Unfortunately, a cold drizzle sent them in their tiny staterooms for a long while.

Margaret began to feel more and more impatient and anxious cooped up in their cabin. And like her, the children fretted and fussed, wanting to finally set their feet on land again. The growing mood of restless anticipation made it increasingly difficult to keep the children content.

"Are we there yet, Mum?" Mary whined. "I want to get off this boat."

"I'm bored and hungry." John buried his face in her lap.

"I can't wait to be out of this stuffy room." Susan sighed.

"Patience, children, patience," Margaret said, secretly feeling as they did. "In just a few days, we will finally set our feet on firm sod, and we can all rejoice in it."

"But I don't want to leave just yet," Ned admitted. "I will miss Murtagh too much."

Margaret smoothed Ned's hair and bid them all to hush.

That evening they enjoyed a light supper while Margaret and James told them stories to help pass the time. Before long the children fell asleep after such a busy day.

The next morning the sun came out and with it their moods lightened. While the wee ones napped, Margaret and Susan worked on the family quilt, trying to pass the last, long days on the ship. Susan sewed another patch on the quilt—a piece of her mother's torn apron.

"When we settle on Wolfe Island, we must take a swatch of cloth from each of our garments to remember the Sailing," Susan said decisively. "They will hold many a story for us."

Margaret laughed. "If we can find a swatch that doesn't have a stain or a tear, that be a good idea, child!"

Susan laughed, too, but then she looked at her worn clothes and her face grew solemn. "What will they think of us on Wolfe Island, Mum? Will Uncle John be embarrassed and ashamed of us?"

Margaret shook her head and scowled at her daughter. "Shame, child! Be not vain. Many of those on the island have taken this same journey—or worse. All who have traveled through these mighty waters will have mercy on us, and those who have not will surely understand. Just you mind that. And besides, we have our inspection garb in the trunk."

* * *

By the time the ship finally entered the port of Montreal, Margaret and her family had already packed up all their worldly belongings, put on their best clothes, and anxiously awaited the one more cursory inspection before disembarking the *Tom Bowline* once and for all.

The ship had given them a safe passage, and for that Margaret was grateful. It had been their home for more than a month and held many memories, both good and bad. Her eyes scanned the deck as her family stood in line to disembark, and Margaret—and likely many of the Irish emigrants who traveled with her—felt a bit of melancholy in her heart, as well as much apprehension for what might be to come.

Margaret looked at her family and saw a mixture of excitement and anticipation evident on their faces, save Ned. She put an arm around her lad, knowing he would miss his friend Murtagh and the adventures of sailing the sea.

Just then, Murtagh came near and put out his hand.

"Farewell," Ned said first, shaking Murtagh's hand warmly.

"May the fair winds be at your back, me friend!" Murtagh grabbed Ned and hugged him. Margaret watched as her son brushed a tear from his cheek.

Then came the harder farewells.

Sean and Sara Boyd came up from below decks, bags in hand. Meera seemed strangely and sadly missing. During their fateful journey, the Boyds had decided to settle in Montreal, and the Hawkins would likely never see them again in this life. Sadness filled Margaret's throat and she could barely say goodbye to their friends, neighbors, and fellow passengers. Sean and Sara had become beloved friends, these poor Irish souls who lost their Meera on the journey to the New World.

"God be with ye both!" Margaret said as she tearfully

hugged Sara and Sean. The men solemnly shook hands, and one by one the children tenderly hugged them both. As the two families walked down the gangplank onto firm ground, Margaret wondered what the future might hold for them all as they went their separate ways in that strange and beautiful city.

Margaret felt as if she was herding cats and her heart beat wildly. "Children, stay close and hold on to one another! I don't want to lose a one of you in this throng." The people squeezed in tightly around them and Margaret feared she'd lose one of her brood. But shortly the swell of passengers and sailors and those greeting them lightened, and she breathed a sigh of relief.

Just a few yards from the gangway, Michael stopped and looked at his feet. "What be wrong with me legs?"

James smiled. "They be your sea legs, son. Fear not. They have learned to roll with the waves, and now that they be on solid sod, they don't know what to do."

"But how are we to walk?" Ned looked down at his shaky little limbs.

"They will find their way by and by," James said, "but first we must journey on the water a little longer."

"Oh, Mum, what a vast city this be!" Susan's eyes flashed with fear as she stayed close to her mum's skirts. Mary clung to Susan, popping her finger in her mouth for comfort, while James held John in his arms. Margaret held the baby close, and Ned clung to Uncle Robert's hand. Michael hung back a step and followed quietly.

Margaret's eyes widened as she took in the sights around them. The docks of Montreal seemed like another loud, scary, foreign world. The boisterous cacophony of the docks engulfed and overwhelmed her. Here everyone spoke French, and the noise and bustle and brashness overwhelmed her, casting fear and doubt for the days ahead.

What have we done? How will we get on to Wolfe Island? Will it, too, be this brash and noisy?

Fortunately for Margaret, the family had little time to

explore this new capital city of the United Canadas. Trailing behind two small carts containing all their earthly belongings, they were hurriedly led to the *bateau* docks to begin yet another arduous trek up the St. Lawrence before they would finally arrive at their new home on Wolfe Island.

CHAPTER 26
MAGGIE

"OH, BREE, YOU'RE COMING HOME? When?" Maggie did a little happy dance right there in the antique shop. "But are you strong enough to travel all this way?"

"One of the leaders is bringing me back and will help me. I'll be fine." Briana sounded weak but happy.

"I can't wait to see you, sweetie!" Maggie chatted with her daughter another few minutes, wishing she could keep her on the phone forever, but then she reluctantly said goodbye.

Maggie waited for Anna to finish turning the "Closed" sign over on the door. She couldn't keep from grinning or doing a little jig, ready to burst out the news.

"She's coming home, Anna! She'll be here in a few days!"

"I heard, and I see!" Anna laughed at Maggie still doing her happy dance.

"As a sort of celebration, why don't you join me for the next lecture at The Irish Shop tomorrow?"

"Oh, I'd love to!" Maggie grinned widely, thrilled to think of spending a casual Sunday afternoon with her friend and boss—and not be alone.

"I'm going to do a little paperwork before I leave. I'll meet you there tomorrow." Anna hugged her goodbye.

"You bet. Thanks, Anna. See you tomorrow."

That evening, Maggie made a quick dinner, called her mom to tell her about Bree's return, and daydreamed about having her daughter home again. She tidied and dusted Briana's room. Then she realized she hadn't done anything about finding her family's crazy quilt for two whole weeks.

She shrugged and reasoned, *I have had a bit of a crisis in my life!*

Yet Maggie still felt guilty, and she knew she would want to spend every spare moment with Bree when she got home. Since it was still early in the evening, she went to her computer and spent some time checking for clues online. She searched Craigslist and eBay, but she found nothing new, nothing even resembling her quilt. Then she did a Google search and found several crazy quilts for sale around the country, but none of them were her family's quilt.

I'll know it if I see it, I'm sure. But when can I look? And if I do find it, how can I afford to buy it back?

Maggie gulped in a deep breath to settle herself down. She moaned and made herself a cup of Sleepytime tea. "I'll just have to find the time—and the money!" She said aloud, determined not to fret.

Yet the next morning she woke up, worrying about Bree, wondering how she was doing, and fretting about how her girl would manage during the trip home. She felt anxious and fearful again and chided herself all the way to The Irish Shop, wondering when she would fully live a life of faith.

I'm working on it, but I have such a wee bit o' faith. Help it to grow, please, Lord!

Maggie smiled as she pulled into the parking lot. *A wee bit o' faith?* She giggled at her inward attempt to sound Irish.

She entered the shop, and Quinn met her at the door, a smile on his face. "Welcome! It's Maggie, right?"

"Yes, thanks for remembering." Maggie quickly realized she was the first one there. She and Quinn were alone.

"I'm glad you've come," Quinn said. "I had hoped you'd

come back. Tell me about yourself."

Maggie's thoughts soared and plummeted in a split second. *Tell about me? What can I say?* "Umm...well, I work part-time with Anna at Anna's Antiques and I really like it. Have you ever been to her shop?"

"Can't say as I have, but I should make a point to visit, if I ever get time away from here." Quinn waved his arm and chuckled. "Do you have a family?"

"My daughter is in Zimbabwe," she said, feeling as though a dark cloud now hovered over her. "She's recovering from malaria and should be home soon." Without warning, her eyes brimmed with tears.

Quinn's eyes grew wide with alarm. He took her hands in his, sending shock waves through her body. He drew her in closer, with obvious care and concern. "Dear God! How old is she?"

"Seventeen. But I'm trusting that God will take care of her." Maggie looked down, embarrassed by her obvious emotion. It was all she could say just then, even though her feelings didn't quite match her words.

"Oh, Maggie, I'm sorry." Compassion filled Quinn's words, and her heart melted. "I promise you I will pray for her, and for her mother, daily until I hear she is completely well. What's her name?"

"Briana. Thank you, Quinn. Really," she said as a couple and a teenage boy came through the door.

Maggie and Quinn were still standing close, and she realized that he was still holding her hands. She felt her face blush and she quickly pulled away, trying to discreetly wipe away her tears. A wave of adrenaline coursed through her and she could hardly compose herself.

Before long, Anna walked in and greeted Quinn, Maggie, and the couple. Then Anna turned to the boy. "It's nice to see young folk who care about their Irish heritage."

"I'm Sean, and I'm an Irishman first and last." Sean beamed.

Maggie smiled. The boy looked to be about sixteen and

had a full head of thick, curly, carrot-red hair. The freckles on his face were innumerable.

Maggie joined Anna and introduced herself to Sean. "What grade are you in, Sean?"

"I'm a senior," Sean said, grinning. "Yeah, I know I don't look it." The boy was confident beyond his years.

Sean's parents joined the conversation as more and more people came through the door. Quinn turned his attention to greeting each one of them. To her it appeared that many of them were regulars. Each person either introduced him- or herself or gave a hearty greeting and took a seat. Maggie and Anna joined them.

"Let's get started, shall we?" Quinn glanced at her and smiled. "Welcome. We have a fun topic today—and a special guest! Today we're going to talk about Irish music and have a concert by a professional tin-whistler."

The audience clapped. Maggie settled in to hear the special lecture and concert. "First, let me introduce Sean McKee, who will give us a live performance later on."

Sean stood, waved, and bowed slightly.

Confident and charming! How cool is this! Maggie loved Irish music, and she winked at Anna, glad she had invited her.

Quinn began. "Celtic music has a long and beautiful history, but it's also been fashioned in the furnace of tribulation. Who are the Celts?"

Sean's dad stood and spoke. "We probably all know that they are the native people of Ireland and Britain. But last spring we found out there was more to the story. My family took a trip to the northwestern part of Spain, the Galicia region to be exact, and we found out that there were Celts there and in a few areas in France, too. And there still are Celts in those places. We even heard Irish music on the streets of A Coruña, Spain."

"Thanks, Mr. McKee. That's really interesting, and quite true. The Celts are spread around the world more than many of us know," Quinn said. "The Irish and British languages are Celtic, and traditional Celtic music is the folk music of these people. Celtic music was one of the primary ways that the Celts transmitted the oral traditions, history, and stories of their lives."

Quinn paused and looked at the crowd.

"Before we get too far ahead of ourselves, Sean, would you please come up and play a couple of tunes that our audience might recognize?"

Sean nodded, went to the front, and removed the instrument from a beautiful leather case. "This is a John Sindt Brass Irish Tin Whistle in the key of D." Sean held up his whistle for the audience to see. "I'm going to play something that I'm sure all of you have heard."

Sean put the whistle to his lips and began the hauntingly beautiful introduction to Celine Dion's song, "My Heart Will Go On."

"That's from the movie *Titanic*!" Maggie said aloud, excited to recognize it.

"You're right, Maggie." Quinn smiled at her as Sean continued to play softly. "Many folks enjoy Celtic music today without recognizing it or knowing that one of the main instruments is the traditional Irish tin whistle."

Sean finished the tune and paused for a moment. And then he turned on his iPhone to play a song that he then accompanied.

A young woman in the back of the room spoke up. "That's from *The Lord of the Rings*!"

"Good ear," Quinn said, nodding to her. "The instruments accompanying our Master Sean are the guitar, the double bass, and the bodhrán—which is a traditional goat-skinned covered drum played with the bare hand or a piece of wood called a cipín, a tipper, or a beater. In fact, if you can remember the scene in the *Titanic* when Jack and Rose danced to the Irish band below decks, you'll see these instruments being played."

When Sean finished his song, Quinn said, "Thanks, Sean, for giving us a taste of Celtic music."

Everyone clapped as Sean bowed and took his seat. Then

Quinn continued. "The Irish tin whistle, often called the penny whistle because it cost a penny to buy in Ireland in the mid-1800s, is also called the tin whistler or simply a whistler. It usually carries the melody in a Celtic song, as you saw when Sean played just now."

Quinn smiled at Sean. "Around 1840, tin whistles were mass produced at a factory in Manchester, England, and thus began the widespread use of the instrument."

Anna spoke up. "I had to learn the whistle in music class at my Irish Catholic primary school. All the kids did."

Quinn nodded. "Yes, the penny whistle was often considered a child's toy and for the Irish, the first instrument a child may learn. But street musicians and the poor claimed it as a treasure. It was easy to carry, sturdy, and as common as the harmonica was in the earlier American culture."

An older man spoke up. "My folks came from Toronto, and it's easy to tell that the traditional music of Atlantic and Eastern Canada was influenced by the Irish and Celts as well," he said. "I grew up with music that sounded more like Irish music than Canadian, and I still enjoy it."

"You're right about that!" Quinn nodded. "In fact, much of the Irish music celebrates the sea, fishing, and seafaring of all kinds. Let's hear more from Sean."

Sean came up and stood next to Quinn. Maggie noticed he was a head or more smaller than Quinn, but his confident demeanor and winsome charisma warranted respect.

Sean's green eyes sparkled with delight. She liked that the young man seemed at home with an audience and with his instrument. "First, I'll show you a bit about how the whistle works. When I cover all the holes, I get the lowest tone, and when I open the holes from the bottom up, it gives me the rest of the notes. Simple." Sean played the scale forward and backward, fast and slow.

"You can even half hole the sound to produce other notes." Sean played the new notes.

This reminds me of the year that Bree took flute lessons.

Maggie sighed deeply and ached to be with Bree again.

Anna looked at her with concern, but she whispered, "I'm okay." Anna reached for her hand and held it as Sean continued.

"Now I'd like to show you a bit of tin-whistle 'ornamentation.'" Sean smiled widely. "These include cuts, strikes, and rolls."

Sean put the whistle to his mouth and began lifting his fingers so quickly that he didn't even interrupt the airflow. Then he tapped the instrument with his fingers quickly and made what he called strikes. Finally, he did both a cut and strike to make a roll.

Sean went on to show the audience tonguing, crans, slides, and vibrato. Then he showed them what he called his "tricks of the trade." He played several scales and created what he called "leading tones." After playing a couple of folk songs and even an Irish jig, Sean bowed to a standing ovation.

"Sean, thanks for that wonderful lesson and concert," Quinn said, grinning, as he patted Sean on the back. "It was splendid! The audience sure agrees."

The audience clapped again.

Quinn waited for the audience to quiet down, and he cleared his throat. "It would take an entire weekend to hear all the ballads, laments, and even drinking songs of the Irish. There is also the traditional dance music like the jigs and reels and even the polka! Later in the nineteenth century, the Celts even added set dancing to their musical diversity."

"But what I like most about Irish music is that the songs most often tell the history of their lives—of the famine and the hardships, yes, but also of the joys of being Irish!" Quinn paused. "Indeed, their music is truly their Irish story. I trust you've enjoyed our time together. I sure have."

Applause filled the air again as Maggie drifted into thoughts of Briana, and she turned to Anna. "Bree sure would have enjoyed this, Anna. We'll have to bring her here someday."

"Let's do that!" Anna squeezed her hand and stood to stretch. "These old bones get pretty stiff when I sit too long."

Maggie laughed. "That was a great lecture. Thanks for inviting me."

"You're welcome anytime, dearie."

As the meeting broke up, Maggie decided to buy a tin whistle. The store had a variety of whistles, but she chose a simple gold and green one. She waited behind several others who were buying items, and she watched as Quinn amiably and patiently worked with his customers and thanked each of them.

When it was her turn, she handed Quinn the tin whistle. "For Bree, as a homecoming gift. Since she's already learned to play the flute, I'm sure she'll pick this up easily. Besides, it will be something she can do in bed while she recuperates."

"What a great idea!" Quinn handed her the receipt. Then he leaned closer across the counter and whispered, "And I promise I won't forget to pray for the both of you, Maggie. Trust me."

Maggie smiled, said thanks, and said goodbye. As she drove home, she thought about what Quinn had said.

Can I trust again? Maybe, just maybe, I might be able to trust a man like Quinn. Maybe.

* * *

Once Maggie got home, she heated leftovers and called her mom. She told her about what she had learned about Celtic music, and she told her about Sean and the tin whistle concert. Elizabeth laughed.

"Your great-grandmother Susan loved to play the Irish whistle, Maggie," her mom said. "I guess it's in our blood more than we know. And I'm glad you got Briana a tin whistle. I'm sure she'll enjoy it."

"That's really cool, Mom!" she said. "You'll have to tell Bree about that when she gets home."

"I will, sweetie," Elizabeth said. "I sure will."

CHAPTER 27
MARGARET

WHEN MARGARET FIRST saw the *bateau,* she gasped in dismay. This was their "free" passage from Montreal to Kingston? The boat looked dangerously small and much less safe than she'd ever imagined, especially after being on a ship like the *Tom Bowline.* Yet taking this canoe-like contraption up the river was the only way to get to Uncle John and to their new home on Wolfe Island.

She grabbed James's arm and whispered in his ear. "Ten days on that horrible boat? With no shelter from the hot sun? What about the children?"

"Hold fast, lamb," James encouraged. "God be with us."

James held her close as the family's chest and crates and portmanteaus were loaded onto the *bateau* and secured in the middle of the boat. Then James guided her and the children as they boarded the forty-by-eight foot, rough-hewn *bateau.*

Margaret surveyed her surroundings before sitting down. The boat's bottom was planked and flat. That was good. And the *bateau* had a sail and gently sloping sides. But there was absolutely no shelter—and no railings—nothing to protect them. Nothing to hold them fast in the midst of a storm or in the deadly St. Lawrence rapids that she had heard fearsome tales about. And worst of all, there was no place for her children to safely stretch or move or even rest during the long days of travel up the great St. Lawrence River.

"This be worse than the ship!" Margaret whispered to James. She tried not to show her fear and concern, but she knew her eyes betrayed her dismay.

"Trust God, me lamb. We shall fare fine." James held her close and she felt a shiver from her husband. He was afraid, too. "Besides, this be the only way. Robert and I will do our best to keep thee all safe." She smiled weakly but said nothing.

As they pushed off from the dock and headed against the current, three other *bateau* joined in the journey. Across the water, the passengers greeted one another, glad to see a few familiar faces. "Godspeed to us all!" Robert bellowed in a cheery voice.

"You are a gift to us, Robert," James said, patting his brother on the back. "You always find a way to buoy our spirits, that you do."

Margaret nodded at her husband's comment and took in her surroundings. She could tell that the other *bateau* transported mostly Irish families—a few of the passengers she had seen on the *Tom Bowline*. But the others must have been from other ships for she knew none of them. They were strangers in a strange and fearful land—with strange and fearful boatmen.

She glanced at the French-Canadian boatmen. Each one of them was a mammoth man, muscular and brawny and stern looking. They spoke only French to each other, and when they did, their deep booming voices frightened her and the children.

She began to fret about enduring a week and a half with these men on the *bateau*. *Will we be safe with these wild-looking men?*

As they began their journey up the mighty St. Lawrence,

the crew began to sing in unison, all five of them. Margaret could hear the other crew members in the accompanying *bateau* singing as well.

The song was beautiful, enchanting, soothing. The pull of their oars became the beat of the music, and their loud, French voices filled the air. She assumed they were river songs and ballads made just for this mighty river. And even though she couldn't understand what the men were singing, the hauntingly beautiful sounds helped them all relax and even enjoy the moment—as much as they could.

"What are they singing about, Father?" Susan asked. "It sounds quite melancholy."

"I think they be songs about the river, lass," James answered. "'Tis beautiful, is it not?"

"Aye, Father," Susan said just as Uncle Robert added his tin whistle to the tune. The boatmen smiled and nodded, welcoming the addition. Robert played along, following the Quintet in a fine pairing.

"You be an artful musician, brother!" Margaret said.

"'Tis nothing," Robert said humbly. "I simply follow their lead and join the music."

"I want to play the whistle that well one day," Susan said.

"You have already mastered the basics, lassie," Robert encouraged. "Now you just keep practicing and you'll surpass me feeble skills."

"The boatmen are not as stern as they look, are they, Mum?" Ned asked.

"Nae, son," she assured him. "It just might be a fair journey after all."

* * *

After some time on the river, James found that one of the boatmen spoke English. James moved closer to him and started to converse with the man, but it was rather difficult given the sounds of the river and the boat, the children, and the singing boatmen. Yet eventually he learned that he was the commanding boatman, the headsman, and the brawny man assured him of their safety.

When they came to the famous Lachine Canal, the headsman told them that the canal had recently been enlarged and modernized. James and his lads watched with amazement as hydraulic power was used to work the canal.

"Oh, Father! What a splendor this be!" Michael said.

He and the lads were fascinated by the marvel of it, but Margaret and the others huddled in fear. The canal was a noisy, strange, and scary thing, but in the end, the canal provided safe and secure travel past the treacherous Lachine rapids.

But that was only the beginning of a long and dangerous passage.

James talked with the boatman and learned that, during their 177-mile journey, the boatmen had to navigate five sets of rapids between Montreal and Kingston, a full 230-foot climb above sea level! James cast a weary glance at his wife, glad Margaret was busy tending the children and had not heard this news. Had she heard, he feared she might have gotten off the boat and walked to Wolfe Island!

The tall, dark headsman continued. "A few years back they built the new Williamsburg Canal to by-pass an entire series of rapids for near thirty miles. Afore that, it was a more fearsome journey, I'll grant you that. Now the great St. Lawrence is open to seafaring ships of all kinds, and our work on the river has become much safer and surer."

James took wee John in his arms and held him tight. He looked beyond the *bateau* toward their destination. Indeed, the strong current, the rough waters, and the lack of shelter would surely make the travel formidable, especially with the wee ones aboard. But, if needed, he would give his very life for Margaret and each of his precious brood.

* * *

As the long days wore on, James, Margaret, and Robert

constantly tried to shield the children from the blistering sun as it beat down on their fair Irish skin. Yet all nine of them quickly became sunburned. Though they covered themselves with whatever they could, as best they could, each of them chaffed at the heat. James worried about his family more than ever before.

Then the wee ones broke out in heat rashes that made them all the more miserable. Baby Meg cried incessantly. John and Mary whimpered and whined. Ned and Susan fanned themselves continually. And Michael grumbled his way down the river. James was concerned that Margaret would want to give up, but he was proud that she stayed strong and tended to her children well.

Each night the family went ashore while the crew stayed with the *bateau*. The passengers took refuge wherever they could find a place to sleep—in people's homes or in their barns—along with the other passengers who were journeying with them in the other three *bateau*. No matter where they laid their weary bodies, they were crowded and miserable.

One evening, a man from another *bateau* passed around a flask of whiskey. "To ward off the burn of the day and the chill of the night," he told James, handing him the flask.

"Much obliged," James enjoyed a generous gulp while stealing a guilty glance as his wife looked on. Margaret shook her head in disappointment but quickly returned to a conversation she was having with Michael.

For all of them, the sunburns, along with the uncomfortably cool nights and incessant mosquitoes, gave little relief from their *bateau* ordeal. Even the overnights became difficult trials to endure.

"Oh, Father, this be worse than the ocean storms," Ned said one evening. "I weary of the sun."

"And I of the biting bugs," Susan said, scratching yet another bite.

"I know, children." James had tried to be strong, but the sight of his children's peeling faces and red bite marks hurt his heart. His own sunburn pained him, and his dry, cracked lips bled often. His head ached frequently from the blaring sun, yet he had gotten his family this far—thanks be to God—and he had to be strong for them a wee bit longer. "This will end before long, and then we will be on the island."

Just then, Margaret came up and joined them, slipping her arm in the crook of his arm. "We will get through this, family. We are close."

* * *

During one of the few cloudy days, James was grateful for the relief, but Margaret and he still had to work extra hard to occupy the children's minds, while hovering over the wee ones to ensure their safety. It was good to work as a team with her. It was even better to see the smile on her face as they talked and dreamed—about their homeland a little— more often than not about their new life on Wolfe Island.

"Will there be hedge schools on the island, Father?" Susan looked expectant and excited.

"I think there will be proper schools on the island, lass." He rubbed her braid.

"We'll have desks and seats?" Ned asked.

"And a roof over your heads, I believe," he smiled and looked at Margaret, encouraging her to join in the conversation.

"Shall we learn French in our school?" Susan asked, eyeing the boatmen and wiggling in her seat. "And Latin, too? I think I will love the Wolfe Island school beyond measure. I will!"

"Settle down, child!" Margaret laughed for the first time in days. "We have not all the answers to your many questions just yet."

When the children were still, James enjoyed taking in the views of the majestic St. Lawrence River. Its power and beauty were simply wondrous, nothing like he had ever seen in Ireland. The magnificence of the wide, expansive river, surrounded by massive forests, and on whose shore tiny villages dotted the landscape, caused him to praise God more than once, least wise, when they weren't trying to keep the wee ones safe! Indeed, Michael called it "nature's splendor" and Susan said it was "dazzling."

Yet when they came to the Long Sault rapids near Cornwall, James once again feared for their lives as the *bateau* shifted and writhed against the upcoming rapids. The whitewater seemed to engulf them, tossing them hither and yon, while they held their children close and prayed. Thankfully, the boatmen turned into another canal for a less treacherous detour, and they all sighed in relief.

"We nearly fell off the boat, Father," Mary said, tears rolling down her cheeks.

"There, there, child," he comforted. "We be fine, just you mind that." Little Mary sucked her thumb all that afternoon, and he held her on his lap until they tied up the boat to find lodging.

Each evening when they disembarked, the family was glad to be off the water and stretch their weary bodies a bit. But even though they were on firm ground, they still felt the rock and roll of the boat, and the discomfort of it was startling, especially to the children.

"Run it off, children," James would encourage. Uncle Robert would often take the lead and engage them in games of tag or leap frog or hide-n-seek—anything to exercise their little limbs and take their minds off the shaky feelings inside.

That evening James walked with Susan and Mary in the meadow instead, and the tall grass tickled their legs.

"I hate the water," Mary confessed. "It scares me. And that terrible boat."

"It will come to an end and we will be on firm earth for good," Susan encouraged. "We will meet Uncle John and settle into our new home. What a grand day that will be!"

James winked at Susan, nodding at her sisterly wisdom.

Yet the next day, a great storm arose and tested Susan's optimism, just as they were journeying through a rough section of the river. The *bateau* pitched and rocked as the mighty boatmen worked with all their might to keep it aright.

The headsman shouted orders in French to the boatmen, and the small crew yelled back and forth, but James and the others couldn't understand. They held each other tight as water sloshed into the floor of the boat.

As they worked to turn the boat against the waves to take the *bateau* to shore, the rope on the steamer trunk snapped. The trunk began to slide toward the edge of the boat, and Susan let out an ear-piercing scream.

* * *

"Save our trunk, James!" Margaret shouted over the storm. "Please!"

She grabbed wee John from James, and Robert joined him in saving the trunk. Robert held James's ankle while he cautiously worked his way to the edge of the *bateau* to try to save the trunk from falling overboard. Michael held on to Robert and they all heaved the trunk back to the center of the boat, sighing in relief as they tied her fast again.

"Thank you, men," Margaret said, tears mixing with the rain that soaked her through. "We would have lost the quilt and the portraits and the pictures. All our family memories and belongings would have been at the bottom of the river!"

Michael smiled, obviously proud to have helped, even a little. "'Tis our duty as men, Mum," Michael said. "We will keep it all safe."

Margaret looked at her eldest son with pride and amazement. *Me lad be growing into a fine young man. Through all the trials, he has fared well and grown.*

It took great effort for the boatmen to finally bring the *bateau* to land. When they did, all of them on board were weary and wet.

"We will rest until we can bid this storm to pass," the headsman said, wiping his brow.

"Shall we stay the night here?" James asked.

225

"We shall not, for this land is filled with wild Algonquin Indians and it is unsafe," the headsman said. "We shall journey on and stop at the regular meeting place when we can."

For nearly two hours Margaret, the family, and their crew sat in the drenching rain. The wind howled, and the thunder and lightning were fearsome. They had no shelter, no protection from the storm, so she silently prayed, cried, and begged for mercy. As she held baby Meg close, she shook with fear every time lightning struck, and she could see the others did, too.

Finally the storm ceased, and the sopping lot of them proceeded on to the appointed resting place. The relative calm after the storm was a relief, and as the sun came out and dried their hair, clothing, and covers until they were actually hot by the time they went ashore.

Margaret watched as the children ran and played for a long while once they came to a farmhouse and settled into the barn for the night. They laughed and caught fireflies and seemed to rejoice that they had lived through yet another storm.

"Look, Mum," Susan said. "Fireflies be plentiful here. Will they be on Wolfe Island too? I think I shall love it there."

"Me little sunshine," she said, pulling her in for a hug. "You even find rainbows in a storm."

* * *

Two days later, the headsman pointed to the city of Kingston. "O'er yonder is our port of entry!" he told them. "You shall disembark presently."

"Oh, Mum, I have butterflies in me innards," Ned said excitedly. "We be nearly home!"

"That we be, lad. That we be." Margaret ruffled his hair.

Kingston, the new capital of the province of Canada, was a growing port city on the edge of Lake Ontario. The headsman informed them that during 1847, a typhoid epidemic took the lives of over 1,400 Irish immigrants who were quarantined in the docks' fever sheds, and the Hawkins again held their breath as they prepared for their final inspection.

Margaret and James thanked the headsman and his crew for keeping them safe as they pulled up to the dock. An oarsman took her hand in his massive one and helped her up and out of the *bateau*. Robert hoisted the wee ones up to her, while Michael, Susan, and Ned scurried up onto the dock on their own. Then James handed Meg to Margaret, and the two brothers departed their boat, while the crew offloaded their belongings.

After they passed through the inspection station and had collected all their worldly goods, Margaret let out a nervous laugh. "Can it be that we are finally here?"

"We be free and our way!" James said with relief after the inspectors waved them past. "Now we must find the ferry to Wolfe Island."

Robert stepped up and took charge. "James, why don't you wire Uncle that we are coming? I will take Michael, and the two of us will find the ferry. Margaret, you and the children rest and watch the belongings until we return."

Margaret smiled. "Thank you, Robert. That sounds like a fine idea." She and the children settled under a wide oak tree just beyond the bustling docks. There she changed her children into their Sunday best, pulled out the men's best, and waited as the children played nearby.

In less than an hour, James, Robert, and Michael returned. They loaded their things onto a rented wagon and headed to the ferry terminal.

"'Tis a mere half-mile ferry journey to the island, family!" Michael said excitedly. "I hope Uncle got the wire. We will be home in the shake of a lamb's tail."

"Wonderful!" Margaret said, her voice cracking with emotion. "Wonderful!"

CHAPTER 28
MAGGIE

MAGGIE STOOD at the airport gate, anxious to see her daughter walk through the jet way door. She had talked with Bree just three days earlier and was thrilled that she was scheduled to finally come home.

The plane finally drew up to the gate. Maggie craned her neck to see the passengers deplane, but Briana wasn't there. Panicked, she went to the desk and asked about her.

"Briana Dolan?" the airline attendant asked. "She's on the list."

"But she didn't get off!" she said.

Just then, a flight attendant came through the jet way with Briana—in a wheelchair!

"Oh, Bree! I was so worried." Maggie bent down to hug her daughter. Then she looked at Bree—pale, tired, several pounds thinner, and terribly frail.

"Hi, Mom," Briana said weakly. "I'm glad to be back."

"Let's get your bags and get you home." Maggie was overwhelmed with relief but brokenhearted to see Bree that incapacitated. An attendant pushed Briana through the airport toward the exit and she walked beside them. Maggie and Bree chatted for a few minutes, but she sensed that her daughter needed to rest. She reasoned that her girl was just exhausted from the 30-plus hour travel. *I can't imagine how grueling the trip must be when you're well; poor Bree had to endure it like this?*

Bree dozed off during the hour-long drive home from the airport, and Maggie used that time to pray for her daughter. *She's so weak and sick, Lord. Please heal her.* Tears ran down Maggie's cheeks as she thought about seeing Bree in a wheelchair, helpless and debilitated. Her thoughts drifted to meeting Lily in Anna's shop.

That memory sent her into a near panic. *What if Bree doesn't recover? What if...?*

What if...Abraham...

"I trust You, Lord," Maggie whispered aloud as she pulled into their driveway. Briana awakened and smiled.

"There's no place like home," Bree said wistfully. "Thanks, Mom."

Maggie helped Bree get into the house and to her room. Then she put on the kettle and retrieved Bree's bags from the car. After making a pot of tea, she took a cup to Briana and found her fast asleep on top of her bedspread.

Maggie sighed as she covered her with an afghan. *So much for catching up and reconnecting!*

It was nearly dinnertime when Bree finally awakened and came into the living room. "Sorry, Mom." Bree sounded a little more chipper than before. "That trip took it out of me."

"I understand, babe," Maggie said, glad to see her doing somewhat better. "What would you like to eat?"

"Anything but airplane food!" Bree said. "Actually, soup would be great."

Maggie smiled and before long the two were sitting down to a meal of homemade chicken soup and sandwiches. *Glad I made that soup yesterday, just in case.*

"How did you know I'd want this?" Bree asked, puzzled.

"I just knew." Maggie patted Bree's hand. "It's good to

have you home, honey. Do you want to talk about it?"

"A little maybe," Briana said, looking down at her bowl. "But be patient with me, Mom, because that sure was a rough time."

"I can't imagine, Bree," Maggie said, her tone soft. "I wish I had been there to help you."

"That clinic was filthy." Bree crinkled up her nose. "There was blood on the walls and floor."

"Goodness, I'm so sorry. Tell me about the girl who stayed with you at the hospital. Wasn't her name Reagan?" Maggie tried to change a more positive topic.

"Yes. She was great." Bree folded her arms as though she felt a chill. "She had just graduated from college and works for the mission there. She stayed with me all the time and made sure they did things right. She wants to come and visit us sometime."

"That'd be just wonderful, Bree. She's welcome anytime."

Briana went back to bed shortly after dinner and slept the entire night. Maggie peeked in on her several times, just like she used to do when Bree was little.

Maggie's company had let her use her sick days, and she had taken the rest of the week off to be with Bree. She was glad she did. Briana awakened the next morning with a high fever and chills.

Maggie scheduled a doctor's appointment for that afternoon. But getting Bree to the doctor wasn't easy—the poor girl was weak and feverish and she could hardly walk.

"She just needs rest," the doctor said, unconcerned. "This is a lot like mono—let her rest and give her lots of fluids."

Sheesh! That sure wasn't helpful, Maggie thought as she got Bree back into the car.

"Would you like a smoothie, hon?"

"That'd be great, Mom. Thanks." Bree closed her eyes and rested her head back against the seat. "I took my meds. I just don't get it. Why? Why did I get malaria?"

Maggie didn't know how to respond. She just squeezed Briana's arm gently and drove. They picked up smoothies and headed home, and Bree went straight to bed again. Since the doctor had not been helpful, Maggie decided to do some research about malaria and how to treat it.

Maggie knew that a parasite caused the disease, but as she read further, she learned that there were different species of the parasite. Worse yet, they could mutate and become resistant to the medicines. *That must have been what happened to Bree!*

Then she read about the life-threatening complications that could come with a certain form of malaria, and she became more and more alarmed. Infection, fluid in the lungs, kidney failure, anemia, and even the deadly blackwater fever. She stopped reading and started praying. She had to.

After checking to see that Bree was still resting, Maggie called her mom. "Mom, what should I do? It says that malaria can mess up her immune system and that it can make her red blood cells stick together and block the blood vessels! I'm scared for her."

"Do you know what they did for her in Zimbabwe?" Elizabeth asked.

"I have no idea. But our doctor didn't seem to know anything about malaria. And I'm not surprised. It's not like we have this disease here in Colorado."

"True," her mom said, indignant, "but he can research it, for goodness' sake!"

"Well, I'll find a doctor here who will treat her if I have to call every clinic in town!"

"Hey, why don't you check with your boss Anna?" she said. "Since she was a missionary, she might know of someone."

"Great idea, Mom! You always seem to have good ideas. Thanks!"

After a little more chitchat, the two women said goodbye and hung up. Maggie called Anna and asked her for advice, and Anna said she'd make a few calls. An hour later, her phone rang.

"Hi, Maggie," Anna said. "I talked with a missionary

friend of mine who gave me the number of a semi-retired missionary doctor who is here in Colorado Springs. He worked in Africa and should be able to help."

"Thanks, Anna. You don't know how much I appreciate it."

"Oh, yes, I do, dearie! You just take all the time you need to get your daughter back on her feet. Your job will be waiting for you—when you're ready."

What a godsend that woman is—and the job, too! She thought as she hung up the phone.

Bree came out of her room looking more fragile and feverish than ever. Maggie gave her a cold cloth and warm broth, and she made up the sofa for Bree could be close to her. But Maggie knew Bree needed more than that. She needed healing.

"Tell me about your new job and what's happening with the quilt, Mom," Briana asked. "I want to hear all about it, even if my eyes are closed and I don't respond much. Please."

First Maggie told Bree about the missionary doctor who might be able to help her get well, and then she started at the beginning, telling Bree about how her search for the quilt led her to Anna's Antiques and what that had meant to her since then. She told her about the trip with Nana to Wolfe Island and learning about their Irish history.

Most of the time Briana seemed to be sleeping, though Maggie knew she wasn't. Maggie could see her twitch in pain, and beads of sweat gathered on her forehead. Intermittently, Maggie would stop her story and get Bree a fresh cold cloth, and then Briana would mumble, "Thank you." Maggie sensed that Bree just needed to hear her mother's voice, no matter what she was saying, so she droned on and on for over an hour. When she had finished, Bree smiled.

"Thanks, Mom. I needed that." Bree opened her eyes and reached out for her mother's hand. Maggie went over and sat on the floor next to her daughter, holding her hand, until Briana fell into a restful sleep.

When Bree awoke, it was dark, but she looked less

flushed. "I need a shower, Mom. Can you please hang close?"

"Of course, honey," Maggie said, guiding Briana to the shower. She sat outside the bathroom, praying for her daughter, trying not to cry but failing miserably. It was simply agonizing, seeing her girl this sick. When Briana came out of the shower exhausted, Maggie helped her get pajamas on and into bed.

Maggie made her another bowl of soup and brought it to her, but Briana was barely able to eat. "What am I going to do, Mom?" Briana asked, tears running down her cheeks. "My senior year starts in two weeks!"

"Honey, let's take it one day at a time," Maggie said, trying to comfort her daughter. "I'm hoping you'll be well by then, and ready to go to school."

"I doubt it. I can't live like this! Why, Mom, why?"

"Oh, baby, I can't begin to answer that question, but God has some kind of plan in all this." Maggie sat on the edge of the bed. "Anna shared a Bible verse with me and I memorized it because it meant so much to me. Jeremiah 29:11 says, ' "For I know the plans I have for you," declares the Lord, "plans to prosper you and not to harm you, plans to give you hope and a future." ' I think the Scripture verse can help you, too, Bree."

Maggie paused and let it sink in a bit, and then she continued. "He has plans for you, Bree, good plans. He has a future for you. He will not harm you! That's a promise."

"I know, Mom. I know," Briana acknowledged. "It's just hard going through this. I'm scared. It was scary being there, all alone, without you, and being so helpless." Briana broke down and wept for a long time, spilling out all her fears about then and now and the future. Maggie knew Bree needed to release those tears. She needed to share her fear and her brokenness.

Maggie cried with her, prayed with her, and held her close until she fell asleep. After she closed the door, Maggie went to her own bed and wept for her daughter.

She thought about all she'd been through during the past

several weeks—how her family's missing quilt had consumed her thoughts, her time, and her emotions. Then Maggie thought about seeing her daughter sitting in a wheelchair, looking like an invalid, and how sick and weak she was now. Maggie bowed her head and prayed.

I thought that finding the quilt was important. But it's just a thing, a thing, and it pales in importance to this! Lord, please help Bree get well. Please!

CHAPTER 29
MARGARET

"Look! There be Wolfe Island!" Margaret said, pointing as the ferry approached land.

"God be praised!" James exclaimed. "He got my telegram. There be Uncle John himself!"

As the ferry pulled up to the dock, excitement filled the air. Margaret's heart pounded with anticipation as she held Meg on her hip and looked at her other children. Michael appeared to be a little reticent, but Susan and Ned wiggled and giggled and talked together, obviously excited. Mary clung to Susan and seemed to play off her excitement, for just then Mary popped her thumb out of her mouth and joined in the laughter. John seemed oblivious as he lay his head on Robert's shoulder.

The hot, humid, midday sun beat down on them, but they didn't care. They were home.

Home. Our new home.

Margaret and the wee ones disembarked while James, Robert, Michael, and even Susan helped to carry their belongings off the ferry. It took a moment for Uncle John to recognize her, but when he did, a big toothy grin crossed his weathered face. Before long, Margaret was swept up into a big bear hug until baby Meg cried in protest. She laughed while the rest of her brood looked on.

"This cannot be Michael?" Uncle John said to her. "Why he was the wee babe's size when I left the Emerald Isle!" Then Uncle addressed Michael. "You be near manhood." That brought an immediate smile from her eldest son.

Then their aging uncle turned to the others. "Welcome to our island, young 'uns. Tell me your names, please."

As usual, Susan stepped up and presented each of her siblings. "I am Susan, and this is Ned. He can read already." She went on to introduce Mary and John as well. "Mary is learning to read, too. Is the school good, Uncle?"

"Hold your tongue, sweet lassie," Margaret said, kissing the top of her head. "They're will be time for questions later."

Uncle turned to the men. "My nephews! God be praised you all arrived in one piece." James and Robert took turns shaking Uncle John's hand and slapping his back. But Uncle drew them into a bear hug as well. When he stepped away from his nephews, tears glistened in his eyes. "How I have prayed for thee all!"

Margaret joined Uncle John in shedding a few tears of joy, and the children did too. Then James and Robert finished out the teary, dockside reunion. Only wee Meg was oblivious to the relief that filled all of their hearts. The long and arduous journey was over. Their new life was about to begin.

"I brought my big farm wagon, and I believe your goods and your persons will fit in one load." Uncle James bellowed a laugh that startled Margaret.

"Thank you, Uncle," Margaret said, taking his arm as he led them to the wagon.

After loading the family and their goods into it, they journeyed to his farm. On the way, they drove through the only town on the island, Marysville.

Margaret pointed here and there, showing her wee ones their new world. Susan clapped her hands. "That be a store, a real store! And there be a blacksmith. And that sign says, 'doctor'—a real doctor! Imagine that." Susan's excitement grew at each new discovery. "We will have a proper life here!"

Margaret laughed and let her daughter do the commentating as they passed a hotel, a tavern, and other buildings. Margaret was glad to be near a town, but more than anything, she was simply happy they were finally on dry land and with their kin—all alive and well. After nearly six weeks of water travel, to her that was the best of all.

Margaret had thought about this arrival day so often. Dreamed about it. Pictured it. Wondered about it. Yet there were no golden streets or affluent mansions. Marysville was small, rural, and simple. But people were laughing, and they didn't look scared or hungry or dirty. That was enough.

"'Tis good to be here, Uncle," Margaret said, a lilt in her voice. "Thank you for giving us a new start."

"Glad to have you here, all of you," Uncle John said, smiling widely and turning to wink at the children. His salt-and-pepper hair sparkled in the sunlight, and his toothy grin made him a likable chap from the start. He was short and stocky but quite muscular, and his rough skin exposed the wear of hard farming.

Michael and Ned grinned and laughed as the wagon drove through town. "I could apprentice there," Michael said, pointing to the wheelwright, "or maybe learn the blacksmith trade. But afore ye know it, I be taking up with the railroad."

Ned nodded. "And I be a following you."

Margaret heard the two lads and readied a reply, but then Uncle John drove up to what was surely his property. Her heart sank.

'Tisn't much more than a few shanties.

Margaret was used to seeing the solid Irish cottages of stone and thatch, but these buildings were strange to her eyes—wood-framed, unpainted, and weatherworn.

As she looked around she saw five structures—the main house, an outhouse, a small barn, a chicken coop, and another building.

Where will we abide?

"'Tisn't much to start, I'll grant you that," Uncle John said, driving up to the fifth building. "But it is yours, and it will keep you warm and dry until you can add to it. And Robert, you can stay with me in the main house."

"We be obliged to you, Uncle," James said. "Much obliged."

Uncle John explained that the cabin had been his son's place until he had bought his own land and moved down the road a few years earlier. Then Uncle gave each of them a hug and left them to get settled.

* * *

As they entered their new home, Margaret took in her surroundings, pleased at what she saw. The inside of the cabin was much nicer than the outside, and it was surprisingly clean. The walls were planked and limestone pasted. It would make a sturdy home after all. The living room, kitchen, and dining area were all one room, but at the far end were two doors, side by side.

Bedrooms! Margaret fairly ran to the two doors and looked in. *James and I can be alone? Glory!* One bed and dresser filled the room, but there appeared to be room for a cradle as well. The children were already in the other room, arguing about who would reside there.

There was but one bed with bedding. Margaret spoke decisively. "Susan and Mary, you will share the bed. Me laddies, you will bunk on the floor until we make another bedstead for you."

After looking further, Margaret was pleased that the kitchen was more than workable—complete with a table and four chairs, and a large stone fireplace for heating and cooking. Several shelves on the wall would store their wares, and the sideboard would be just perfect for the family mementos. It was obvious that Uncle John had planned for their arrival. And the house even had a window with real glass in it!

"Look, Mum," Susan said, "Uncle John even has eggs and bread and other food here! He be a kind man, is he not?"

"Truly kind, me lassie. Now help me prepare a meal, and then we'll start to unpack."

After a simple supper of eggs and bread, Margaret couldn't wait to see that all was well with her family treasures. Everyone helped her unpack the things they had brought from Ireland.

Margaret pulled the items out of the steamer trunk, one by one, and inspected them. "The portraits fared the voyage as did the crazy quilt! It has a small water stain on it, but I reckon I can wash it clean. Thank you, God."

"Thank you, God!" they all repeated, almost in unison. They all looked at one another and laughed—relieved to be safe, to be well, to be home. And together.

"This sideboard will hold our family remembrances," Margaret said. She took the quilt and folded it carefully as her family watched in silence. She placed the quilt on the sideboard. Then she took the tiny portraits of the Earl and her parents and set them next to the quilt. "There. Now take care, children, and be careful with our treasures." She set the sewing basket on the sideboard as well, along with the fabric that would one day be sewn onto the quilt.

The lantern was set on the table, and the iron bake kettle, skillet, frying pan, and teakettle were unpacked. Then came Father's ax heads.

"Just what I need for making a bedstead for you lads," James said, holding his prize tool carefully. "And we'll make stools, too."

That evening, Margaret and James sat on the porch while the children caught fireflies in the yard. "'Tis a fine start to our new life, don't you think?" James asked, stroking her cheek.

Margaret leaned her head on James's shoulder and whispered, "Yes, it most certainly is."

* * *

For several days after arriving on Wolfe Island, the ground still seemed to sway like the ocean waves beneath Margaret's feet. It took time to acclimate to their new island life. She and the lassies worked on making their house a home while James and the lads made a crude bedstead and stools.

Whenever Uncle John needed their help around the farm, they were glad to lend a hand. It was a busy farm, and they all knew they must do their part to earn their keep.

Uncle John raised cows and chickens, and he often sold the extra milk, butter, cheese, and eggs at the Baker's General Store in Marysville. Susan especially enjoyed going with him or with Uncle Robert to town. Michael and Ned enjoyed helping both of their uncles with the several crops that had been planted.

"They all be faring quite well, and I be glad of it," Margaret said to James as they sat on the porch that evening.

"I be pleased, lamb, mighty pleased." James kissed her temple.

The next day the sod stopped moving and settled firm beneath her feet, so Margaret rejoiced. No longer was she reminded of the challenges of the sea with each step she took. She could now put the trials of the voyage in the past and move forward.

"I don't feel the ship any more, Mum," Mary said, looking at her feet, "and I be glad."

Margaret agreed and they celebrated with a sup of warm milk and a piece of her soda bread. Though it took a few weeks to settle into the rhythm of farm life, when they finally adjusted, it felt good and right.

"Wolfe Island feels like home!" Ned said one evening as they ate supper around the table.

"Indeed it does," James said, smiling at his family's quick adjustment. Margaret's heart swelled. If only her father could see them now, she knew he'd be pleased.

* * *

The warm summer days on the island helped the children quickly regain the strength they had lost on the voyage. Margaret and James did, too. She was happy that Uncle John's church community soon became a weekly part of their lives. Indeed, they truly had freedom and faith there.

The constant river breeze kept the bugs at bay, and the warm wind refreshed her as she worked. The cool comfortable evenings made the busy days a delight, and the abundance of fireflies gave the children hours of entertainment. Many a night Margaret allowed the children to stay up a little past their bedtime. She would sit in the cool night air and watch her children chase fireflies and bring them to baby Meg, who delighted in their twinkle.

Margaret sometimes sent the older children to find wild berries and nuts, and they always enjoyed the adventure of it. When they returned from their forages, they told her about the abundance of wildlife they saw on and near the farm— deer, rabbit, squirrel, and birds. And Uncle John had told them that further out around the island, they could see beaver and muskrat.

"I love it here," Michael said one evening. "Thank you for bringing us."

Margaret smiled at Michael. And then she looked at James and mouthed the words, "Thank you," not just to her husband but to God. He was forging their future, step by step.

By and by, each one of them took on regular jobs that would help the farm run more smoothly. Margaret, of course, kept the house and cared for the wee ones. Susan and Mary assumed the chores of fetching the water, feeding the chickens, and collecting the eggs. Michael and Ned fed and milked the cows and helped the menfolk whenever needed. James and Robert worked with Uncle John around the farm and spent many warm summer evenings on Uncle John's porch, making plans for the harvest and then for the winter to come, and, now and then, enjoying a guilty pint together.

* * *

One Sunday afternoon following a fine church service, Margaret and Susan stayed with the napping wee ones and took the time to cut patches of their sailing clothes to one day sew onto the quilt. James, Robert, Michael, and Ned went fishing on the river's edge, overlooking Simcoe Island.

"Remember, Mum, how scared we were when Ned fell overboard?" Susan said, hugging the patch of cloth she had cut from the shirt Ned wore that day. Then she picked up another piece of fabric her mum had just cut. "And remember how kind Uncle Robert was to clean up the cabins after the terrible storm? How truly blessed we are, Mum!"

"These are the memories you can tell your children and your children's children one day, Susan," Margaret affirmed, "and aye, God has blessed us. He took us through storms and dangers and many challenges on our way here. And I believe He will take us through whatever our futures hold as we trust Him."

Susan hugged her mum, and Mary, still awake, joined the two. Just then, little John and baby Meg woke up, and she went to tend to their needs.

"I be looking forward to proper school, Mum," Susan said as she changed the baby's cloth diaper.

"And I, too!" Mary said. "I be big enough now."

"That you be," Margaret replied. "I expect, with Susan's help, you will be following fast in Ned's shoes."

Mary smiled and clapped her hands. Susan smiled too. "And to think we'll have desks and slate boards! We will be scholars!"

Margaret threw back her head and laughed a hearty and free laugh.

"'Tis been awhile since I've heard that beautiful sound," James said, entering the cabin with his string of fish. "'Tis music to me ears. I think we be having a fish feast tonight to celebrate." James hugged her and danced around the cabin with her in a surprising display of affection.

"We will find our way in this new world, together, that we will," Margaret said, looking deep into her husband's eyes.

"God has given us a hope and a future!" James said, touching his wife's cheek.

Michael and Ned came through the door just then and stopped in their tracks. They looked at their parents and then at each other and all the children began to giggle.

That night they invited Uncle John to join them for dinner. The abundance of food, fish, fowl, and wildlife was amazing to these Irish who had suffered the lack of it for so long.

They were grateful. None more than Margaret.

CHAPTER 30
MAGGIE

MAGGIE AND BRIANA left Dr. Van Leer's office much encouraged. He knew just what to do to treat malaria. The specialized antibiotic regimen wouldn't be easy, and it would take a while to finally rid Briana's body of the parasite, but they were confident that it would work.

"At least we have a solution to this nightmare," Bree said as they drove home.

"There's an answer." Maggie's eyes glistened with tears.

"Thank God! School starts next week...then I'll have my SAT's and finals, and then I have to get ready for college next year." Briana got more anxious with each word she spoke. Maggie chuckled.

"Slow down, Bree. The doctor warned us to keep your stress levels low, and although that may be a challenge, we need to do as he says."

"I know, Mom, but you know me. I like to plan things out!" Despite her tiredness, Bree's eyes finally brightened a bit.

In the weeks that followed, Briana had many ups and downs, and the progress was slower than they expected. School began and Maggie could see Bree's frustration. With Bree's low energy, schoolwork and studying, along with the hours she spent in class every day, became more difficult. Bree rarely had the strength to engage in social activities. The fevers continued at random times and sometimes at the most inopportune times.

At one point, Briana's fever shot up to 104 degrees, and Maggie called Dr. Van Leer for help.

"This is an insidious disease and we have to work through it. It must get out of her system for good," Dr. Van Leer encouraged. "I'm sorry there are no simple solutions. Keep her cool and make her rest."

Briana recovered from that particular fever, but she remained weak and weary of the struggle. After having been in school for several weeks, Briana sat at their kitchen table with her head in her hands. "I can't take this anymore, Mom. I've got to get ready for college. My grade point average will start slipping if I can't study like I usually do. I feel like I'm wasting my senior year. I'm too tired to hang out with friends."

"You will get well, Bree. Be patient with yourself and with your treatment."

That evening, Maggie and Briana were invited to have dinner with Anna. Briana told her mom how excited she was to finally meet her boss and friend.

"Welcome!" Anna said as the two entered her humble abode. The tiny, turn-of-the-century home in the downtown area looked quaint and charming.

Maggie glanced at the living room. Just like her shop, Anna's home was neat as a pin, with lots of lovely antiques. Anna had family photos proudly displayed on the mantle, and the smell that wafted from the kitchen made Maggie's mouth water. "Something smells good, Anna." Then turning to her daughter she said, "Anna's a wonderful cook. I should know."

Briana nodded and shook Anna's hand. "It's nice to finally meet you, Mrs. Kelley."

Anna pulled Briana into a warm and grandmotherly embrace and held her there for a long time. "I've wanted to meet you for a long time, Briana," Anna said, loosening her hold and looking straight into Briana's eyes. "I hear you and I are kindred spirits."

Briana looked at Anna, and Maggie had a feeling that she wasn't sure what Anna meant. Anna continued, "We both have a heart for missions and for God's plan for the world, and that brings me great joy! I'm too old to go overseas now, but it's good to know God is raising up a new generation to serve Him around the globe. Now, let's sit and enjoy a nice dinner together, shall we?"

Anna led her and Bree to the table set with antique china, candlelight, and several dishes of steaming food. "I think I may have gone a little overboard," Anna admitted with a shy smile. "I don't have company over much, and it's easy to forget how much to cook."

The table looked like a Thanksgiving feast, only with roasted chicken instead of turkey. Maggie guessed there was enough to feed a dozen people or more!

"You'll have leftovers all month, Anna." Maggie laughed.

"But most of this will freeze, and *we'll* have lunches for a long time. I'll bring double portions for the both of us on Friday," Anna added.

The conversation quickly turned to Briana's trip to Zimbabwe, her struggles with malaria, and her plans for the future. Bree was animated and energized just talking about her desire to serve others overseas. "I'm not sure where I'll end up, and I really don't care. I just know that mission work is what I'm supposed to do."

"Would you go back to Zimbabwe?" Anna asked.

"I doubt it," Briana replied slowly. "Too many memories there." She went on to explain how terrible the medical care had been and how frightening it had been to be sick without her mother near.

"I know what you mean." Anna leaned back in her chair and sighed. "When my husband died in Kenya, handling everything alone was the hardest part. But somehow the Lord helped me through it all, and I learned a lot about trusting Him during that time. It wasn't easy for my children and me, and I know I failed to trust Him many times. But the twists and turns of those hard circumstances—all the little miracles we experienced and the lessons we learned—became the stitches and threads that created the fabric of hope in our lives."

"That's an interesting way to put it, Anna," Briana said. "It's been quite a journey for you, just as it has been for Mom and me."

Anna nodded and then turned to Maggie. "You both have had quite the struggles of late. Your family changes, your illness, Briana, and the issue of finding that quilt! But the promise is that God does have good plans for both of you, and He weaves all our challenges and changes together to make us more like Him and to give us a bright and beautiful future."

"It'll be interesting to see what that future holds," Maggie said.

"And what about your family's crazy quilt? I haven't asked you lately," Anna questioned.

"Nothing yet, and frankly, I'm tired of searching," Maggie confessed.

"Don't give up just yet," Anna suggested. "You never know where it might turn up."

"Yeah, Mom, don't give up, please!" Briana begged. "It's part of our family story."

After insisting that she and Briana stay seated, rather than get up to help clear the dishes, Anna got up from the table and went into the kitchen. They sat there, silently looking around and enjoying the quiet.

"I like her a lot, Mom. She's great!" Briana whispered. "She's like a grandma."

SUSAN G MATHIS

"I knew you two would get along divinely!" Maggie whispered back, thankful that she could share Anna's friendship with Briana. She'd enjoyed seeing Bree connect with Anna over faith and a love for missions.

Anna returned with a silver tray, which held a pot of tea, as well as three dainty little tarts on tiny china plates. Maggie looked around the table and saw that there were no teacups.

"Can I help you with anything?" Maggie said.

"No, I'm fine," Anna said, grinning and sitting in her place. Then she bent over and picked up two green gift bags with sparkling gold tissue paper sticking out of them.

"These are for you!" Anna handed a bag to each of them. "Just a little welcome-home-get-well-soon-nice-to-meet-you surprise."

"Well then, I certainly don't deserve a gift," Maggie replied.

"Then that's a friendship gift for you," Anna countered. "Open them, please."

Maggie and Briana looked at one another and smiled. They carefully opened the gifts in unison, and oohed and ahhed at the same time. Both were Irish china teacups, but each one was different. Maggie's teacup was fluted and dainty with a claddagh symbol painted on it. The cup's rim was gold, as was the handle and the bottom of the cup. The rim of the saucer was gold-rimmed, too. Briana's teacup was sturdier and had a broader cup with just three large shamrocks, and it had a gold rim as well.

"Oh my!" Maggie exclaimed. "This is lovely!"

"Mine is too," Briana agreed. "Thanks a lot!"

"I saw them at the Irish Shop last week when I was there," Anna explained. "And they just called out your names. Though they will never replace your family's Irish crazy quilt, these teacups can make beautiful family memories for you both in the days to come, and you can pass them on, just as you might have passed on the quilt."

Maggie's eyes welled up with tears, and so did Briana's. *This woman is such a giver. How can I ever repay her?*

"I thought you could use them tonight with our dessert," Anna suggested as she lifted a teacup for herself from the chair seat next to her.

"A little sneaky, are we?" Maggie teased.

"All in good fun," Anna said.

They enjoyed their dessert and tea, but before long it was time to leave.

"What a great time we've had tonight, Anna, thank you!" Maggie hugged her.

"It's been fantastic!" Briana agreed, hugging Anna tightly, and it surprised both Anna and her. "I wish you were my grandma!"

"Well now, I'd be honored, Briana," Anna replied, startled and pleased. "Call me Grandma Anna, will you?"

"You betcha! Thanks!"

As Briana gathered her things, Anna pulled Maggie aside and handed her a sealed linen envelope. "Quinn asked me to give this to you."

What in the world? Maggie blinked, startled at the unopened letter. "Thanks," was all she could say.

On the way home, Briana couldn't stop talking about how much she'd enjoyed the evening, the conversation, and especially Anna's wisdom and kind gift.

"I can't believe she just went out and bought us teacups," Briana said. " I want an employer like her one day."

"Well, looks like you got a 'grandma' in the deal," Maggie said, laughing.

"I guess that's even better! Hey, I was thinking that I could help you search online for the quilt. If I follow the doctor's orders and rest more, I just can't sit in front of the TV. I can do my part."

"How thoughtful of you, Bree. That'd be great. But do you remember it well enough to know the quilt when you see it?"

"I've got a good idea and Nana's photo of Aunt Mabel with it will help. I can always collect the links online, and we can look at the pictures together if we need to."

"Awesome, girl! Great idea," Maggie said.

That evening, after Briana had gone to bed, she opened the strange envelope from Quinn. It was a letter, in handsome, fine handwriting.

Dear Maggie,

Ever since the last time we met and you told me of your trauma, I have prayed daily for your daughter and for you. I know it must be very hard to see her sick. Anna has kept me up-to-date on her progress of healing, and I'm sorry that it has been slow.

Please don't think me bold or read anything into my offer, but I would like to help you in some way. Since my mother raised me on her own, and I saw the needs she had that were never met, I have a deep compassion for the challenges that a single mother faces. If you ever need anything, anything, please call me at the store. Though I am a master of none, I have become a jack-of-all-trades, so to speak, and could help if you need a handyman, help with your car, or whatever you might need.

God has kept you on my heart, and though we don't yet know each other well, I know you are His child and He has good plans for you and your daughter. As you seek Him, I trust He will give you hope for the future.

All the best,
Quinn

Maggie sat on her bed, stunned. *Who is this man, and why does he care a whit about Bree and me? He seems sincere and kind, but does he have ulterior motives? And what of the mention of hope for the future? People sure keep mentioning that Jeremiah 29 thing.*

She turned her concerns into prayer—prayer for Bree, for herself, for Anna, and even for Quinn. She thanked God for these newfound friends who seemed to continually bless her and speak wisdom into her life, and she asked for healing. Healing for Bree's body and soul, healing for her own heart, and healing for the past hurts that continued to haunt her.

As she finished her prayer time and got into bed, Maggie had one last thought. *Maybe, just maybe, God really does have a wonderful future for me after all.*

CHAPTER 31
MARGARET

AUGUST SECOND DAWNED sunny and hot. Margaret woke early, knowing the day was to be one of celebration, for it was Meg's first birthday. As she prepared breakfast for the family, she thought of how fast Meg's first year had passed. It was filled with many adventures she would ne'er remember. Just a wee thing and she'd already traveled over the ocean!

"Uncle John is lending us his wagon. We can go and enjoy a day at Big Sandy Bay," James announced at breakfast. The children cheered and could barely sit still enough to eat.

"We've ne'er been there, Father!" Mary said.

"And there be a beach there, aye?" Susan asked.

"Settle down, children," Margaret replied, laughing at their joy. "Eat your porridge and do your chores, and we'll be gone presently."

James smiled and kissed her hand. "I believe we will have a fine, fine day, me wife!"

When all the chores were done, Susan and Mary helped pack a picnic lunch and gather an extra set of clothes for each of them. They loaded the wagon and were off.

It was a far piece to the sheltered bay southwest of them, and it was the first time they had been anywhere, save Marysville, since they'd reached the island. The six-mile trip took them on a rugged dirt road, not unlike those in Ireland. Memories flooded Margaret's mind, nearly pulling her into melancholy. She let herself remember the good and the bad of the past, but she quickly shook herself to the present.

"The crops look fine," James mentioned to no one in particular, his gaze on the rows of corn to the left of them. "I would like to meet these neighbors someday."

"I hear Marysville has a great harvest celebration," Margaret replied. "Perhaps we will make their acquaintance then."

At Big Sandy Bay, they all helped to carry the picnic to the beach. And, oh, what a beach it was! She just knew her children would be thrilled to climb and play on the glorious sand dunes, and the sandy beach surely called their names. The wetlands and grassy area surrounding the bay would be fun for the children to explore. Margaret sighed, knowing she'd need to gather them before they dispersed to play.

"Let us eat first, children, and then you can wander and play," Margaret directed them. "And later, you can venture into the river."

The eight of them enjoyed a fine picnic lunch of fried chicken, potato salad, berries, and her soda bread. Then she pulled out a small cake and they all sang, "Happy Birthday" to baby Meg. The family enjoyed a piece of the sweet treat, and the children were quickly off to explore their new surroundings. Baby Meg napped in the shade, while she and James enjoyed some rare time alone.

"I ne'er thought we'd settle as well and quick like," James said, holding his wife close. "It be quite beautiful and bountiful here."

"'Tis true, James," she agreed, "and Michael seems as content to be here as the others."

James kissed her. "As do you, me lamb. And that makes me happiest of all."

"Thank you, James, for being patient with me and for all your loving care when I was so forlorn on the journey and even before. You be a strong and godly husband and father. That you be!"

James smiled and hugged her tightly.

Just then, John and Mary came running, with Michael, Susan, and Ned following close behind.

"Shamrocks, Mum!" Mary announced excitedly. "Our island has shamrocks, just like Ireland."

"Lots of them!" John said, handing his mum a bouquet of the clover.

"Thank you, lad," she said, with tears filling her eyes.

"How I love them!" Mary said, caressing her own bouquet of shamrocks. Then she gave each of her siblings, and her father, a small clump of the clover.

James smiled. "Ah, 'tis a gift from the good Lord, that it is, and a fine remembrance of our Irish homeland. We must ne'er forget her, our beloved Ireland. She be our birthplace, and she must be treasured in our hearts forever."

The children all sat down on the blanket, hoping to hear more.

"Remember how St. Patrick used the shamrock to teach about the Trinity?" Margaret asked.

"I know!" Susan said. "May I tell the wee ones? Please, Mum?"

"Go on, lassie."

"See these three leaves?" Susan began, addressing Mary and John and pointing to the three heart-shaped leaves. "They show us the Holy Trinity—the Father, the Son, and the Holy Spirit. St. Patrick traveled all over Ireland and taught people about God by using a shamrock. When was that, Father?"

"The fifth century, a thousand and more years ago. And the shamrock is still a symbol of the great work he did."

"And why we like to wear green!" Susan added.

"We tried to find a four-leaf shamrock, but we couldn't," Ned said. "But I be glad we found clover here on the island."

"We are blessed, laddie," Margaret said, smiling, "and I've heard it said that the three leaves also teach us about the faith, hope, and love that St. Paul wrote about in 1 Corinthians 13."

"And the fourth leaf symbolizes man's redemption," James added. "And because three is Ireland's special number, it can represent the past, present, and future."

James took one of the shamrocks and held it out for his family to see. Then, one by one, he plucked off the leaves.

"This be our past, our life in Ireland, the place of our birth," James said, handing the leaf to Margaret who passed it around.

"And this be our present, right here on baby Meg's first birthday, celebrated on Big Sandy Bay," James continued, passing around another small leaf.

"And this be our future, held in the palm of God's hand, safe and secure, full of promise, for His plans be good." He took the last leaf and held it gently in the palm of his big hand, showing them but not passing it around.

"We will trust God, Father," Susan said solemnly, and all the others nodded in agreement, even little John.

"Enough for now," James said, handing Margaret his leaf. "Let's take a dip, shall we?"

James and the children got up, ran to the water's edge, and dipped their feet in the river. Margaret watched, quite sure it was cold but refreshing. James splashed and chased his children like he was a teenager again. The children squealed with glee.

Margaret enjoyed seeing the fun. *James was right all along. We are family, and that's what matters most. Our beautiful and ever growing family crazy quilt is just one way to pass on the past, not an excuse to hang on to the past.* She smiled and thanked God for her past, her present, and for what the future might hold.

Soon clouds began to gather over the mighty St. Lawrence. The family changed their clothes, packed up their belongings, and headed home. By the time they arrived back at the farm, rain had begun to sprinkle, but they didn't care. On such a day, a little rain couldn't dampen their spirits a bit.

* * *

For the next two days it rained on and off, keeping the family inside most of the time. Susan didn't mind, though. Uncle Robert had bought a new tin whistle at the general store and he gave Susan his old one. With it, she happily entertained the family with the few songs she had learned.

"I must get more lessons from Uncle," Susan said after she finished playing all the songs she knew. "May I go up to the big house, Mum?"

"It has stopped raining. Aye, you may go," her mum said. "But stop by the chicken coop and check on the eggs, please."

"Can I go, too, Mum?" Mary asked.

"You may, and help your sister."

Susan and Mary put on their boots, for it was muddy and wet. After gathering three eggs, they took them up to Uncle's house, knocking on the door.

"We gathered these eggs for you, Uncle," Susan said, handing them to Uncle John.

"Did you now? Thank you." Uncle John hugged the little girls as they entered. "Why do we have the pleasure of your company, little lassies?"

Susan waved as Uncle Robert came out from the kitchen. "I came to see if Uncle Robert can teach me a new whistle song,"

"Well, nieces, 'tis a sweet treat to see you both," Uncle Robert said, picking up Mary and twirling her around. Mary giggled and hugged her uncle.

"I miss you, Uncle," Mary said, squeezing his neck.

"I'm just steps away," Robert replied. "Visit me anytime."

"And you, sweet Susan, want another tune?" Robert asked, setting Mary down. "On such a stormy day, it would be a joy to learn you a new tune."

"Uncle John," Susan said hesitantly. "We wanted to ask if you had any scraps of fabric that Mum and I can add to our family quilt? Pieces of your clothes and your wife's, God rest her soul. And your sons' too."

"And something from you, too, Uncle Robert," Mary added, turning to Robert.

"Well, now, I am much honored at your request," John said, "and it happens that I have the time to fetch you some. Mary, would you care to come and help your old Uncle?"

"Oh, I would, Uncle," Mary said, delighted to be his helper.

Uncle John and Mary disappeared into the back bedroom, while Uncle Robert and Susan settled by the fireplace with their whistles.

Robert explained. "This be a tune about the Irish coming to New York, America, but it can be sung by us just the same. I will learn you the tune and the words." For a long while, Uncle Robert taught her the song, "Paddy's Green Shamrock Shore" that he had learned in the Marysville pub.

When Robert was done singing the song and teaching the tune, she smiled. "Did you have a lassie back in Ireland, Uncle?"

"Nae, lassie," Robert said, "you and Mary are me lassies fair."

Robert finished writing down the words to the tune for her to take with her just as Mary and Uncle John came into the room.

"He has five pieces, Susan. Five!" Mary said, beaming as she showed her sister the patches of fabric. "One for Uncle, one for Auntie, and three for each of their sons."

Robert went into his bedroom and brought out the shirt he had worn on the ship. "And here is me contribution, lassie," Robert said, handing Susan the shirt. "There is but a few patches you'll get out of this one."

"Thank you, Uncles," she said joyfully. "You will be a part of the fabric of hope we are sewing into the quilt."

* * *

THE FABRIC OF HOPE

Throughout the summertime and into the fall, Margaret and Susan worked on the quilt, sewing pieces of their family story into it. One day, Susan had an idea.

"When the quilt is complete, shall we let it wear green, Mum?" Susan suggested. "We can buy a bit of Kelly green yarn from the store and make ties on the corners."

"Oh! It will look like shamrocks are all over it!" Mary added. "May I help, please, Mum? I'm big enough."

Margaret laughed at her growing daughters. "You may, Mary. And what a grand idea, Susan. 'Tis a fine way to remember Ireland's green shamrock shores."

CHAPTER 32
MAGGIE

BY DECEMBER, Maggie realized that her girl was finally past the worst of the illness. Bree rarely had malarial fevers anymore, but the headaches still lingered.

"I'm ready to have a nice, quiet Christmas break," Briana said at dinner one evening. "This semester has been a bear."

"I'm glad you're feeling better, though," Maggie said, "And I'm ready, too, for the Christmas season."

Briana frowned. "Sorry you never found the quilt, Mom."

"Me too. I guess it wasn't meant to be." She sighed deeply.

Briana excused herself to do her homework as she started to clear the dishes. *Wish she hadn't brought up the quilt thing. It always makes me melancholy.*

Maggie shook herself free from the sad thoughts. She left the dishes, turned on Christmas music, switched on the Christmas tree lights, and glanced at the living room, decked with decorations, a manger, and their stockings on the mantle.

Maggie's eyes glistened with tears. *What will this Christmas be like, just Bree and me all alone?*

The holiday season had always been special for their

family, full of Christmas music and lots of Christmas cheer. Each year she had thrown a festive Christmas open house, despite a husband who was more of a Scrooge than not.

This year would be different. There would be no parties, no open houses, and with finances tight, there would be few gifts, except for the gifts her mom always sent.

Her heart ached at the thought of such a Christmas. *Bree might look forward to quiet, but I sure don't. And I wonder if her father will bother to connect with Bree? So many unknowns.* Just then, she had an idea. She grabbed her phone, punched in the speed dial, and waited for an answer.

"Hi Mom," Maggie said. "What are you doing for the holidays? Going to your brother's again this year?"

"I hadn't decided just yet," Elizabeth admitted. "I've been too busy volunteering at the hospital."

"Why don't you come out here and have a Colorado Christmas with Bree and me?"

Maggie heard her mother laugh. "I was thinking about asking you if I could come this year, but you beat me to it. I'd love to spend Christmas with you two!"

"That's wonderful, Mom! We'd love for you to join us!"

The two women talked about their schedules and made tentative plans. After they hung up, she told Bree the news.

"That's very cool, Mom!" Briana grinned. "Honestly, I was a little worried about doing Christmas, just you and me. No offense, but I think it would have been a little lonely."

"No offense taken, believe me. I had the same concern." Maggie hugged her daughter.

A few days later, Elizabeth called to give her the flight information and make a few more plans.

"I want you to meet Anna and see the store, and I want to take you to the Irish Shop to meet Quinn," she told her mom. "I know you'll like them both."

"Isn't the owner of the Irish Shop the guy who offered to help you?"

"One and the same."

"Have you seen him lately?"

"Anna and I have been to a couple more lectures at the store, yes." She tucked the phone between her shoulder and her ear.

"And has he been over to help you with anything?"

"Not yet. There hasn't really been a need for him to," she said. "We spend a little time talking after each lecture, and I've come to really like him. He seems like a genuinely nice guy."

"That's good."

A few days after their conversation, Maggie got in her car and it wouldn't start. She tried everything and finally had to call a colleague to catch a ride to work. During her lunch break, she decided to call Quinn.

"Hi, Quinn. This is Maggie Dolan. How are you?"

"I'm great, Maggie. And you?" Quinn sounded surprised to hear her voice.

"I'm good, but my car isn't," she admitted. "It won't start, and I'm not sure what to do. Towing it to a repair shop is really expensive."

"I close the shop at five and could come take a look at it after that."

"That would be great, Quinn. Thanks! Hey, why don't you plan on having dinner with us? You can meet Briana!"

"A home-cooked meal? Can't say no to that!" Quinn chuckled. "Can I bring anything?"

She laughed. "Just your wisdom on what to do about my car."

"Don't know about wisdom, but I'll bring my elbow grease. See you around six."

She gave him their address and said goodbye. Butterflies filled her stomach. *It's not a date,* she reminded herself. *He's just a nice guy who is helping out a single mom. Get a grip!*

Maggie spent the rest of her lunch hour planning the evening. She made a menu and a list of "to do's" she needed to complete before Quinn came. She was relieved she had gotten groceries over the weekend, and the house was pretty neat. She had the ingredients for her favorite easy dish,

Moscato Chicken, and she had a brownie mix she could make quickly. She also had stuff for salad. Dinner would be quick and easy!

Yet all afternoon, Maggie struggled to work, she was too distracted. Her excitement grew at the thought of Quinn coming to her house, meeting her daughter, and having dinner with them. She texted Briana, hoping she wouldn't mind. Bree returned the text saying, "Can't wait!"

Maggie grabbed a ride home with her friend who left at four. When she got home from work, she rushed around, trying to prepare the meal and tidy the house. The more she prepared, the more anxious she got. *What will we talk about? Will he like what I make?*

Bree came home and helped too. "I haven't seen a smile like that in a long time, Mom," Bree said as she chopped the lettuce for the salad. "Do you like him?"

"He's a nice man, but I barely know him," Maggie said, dodging her feelings.

"It's okay if you do," Bree replied.

Maggie hugged her and retreated to the living room to tidy it. *What if Bree doesn't like him? What if it gets awkward?*

Quinn arrived right at six. "For you and Briana," Quinn said, handing her a large poinsettia plant as he came through the door.

"Oh, thanks, Quinn." Maggie hoped she wasn't blushing. "It's been a long time since we've had real flowers in this house. And this is so Christmas-y."

"My mom always loved to have a live poinsettia at Christmas."

Bree came into the room and greeted Quinn, and the three sat down to dinner. Quinn kept the conversation going so comfortably that both she was amazed.

"You've kept us jabbering about our lives, but we hardly know anything about you," Briana said boldly.

"Oh, sorry," Quinn said. "I guess I'm just a curious Irishman."

"Okay. You're Irish," Bree said, "and…"

Quinn chuckled. He took a sip of water and then began by sharing about his father dying when he was just a boy. He told them both of how he and his mother had struggled together, and how he had inherited the Irish Shop from his grandfather. As they listened to Quinn tell his story, Maggie learned that he loved to travel the world, explore new places, and experience new cultures. His wife had died of cancer and he had been a widower for several years, and he hadn't traveled since her death.

"We could talk all night, I know, but I need to get your car running," Quinn said. "Thank you for a fine dinner. And Briana, it was great to get to know you!"

"You, too, Quinn." Briana's head bobbed up and down. "We'll have to come by your shop. And maybe I'll join Mom for a lecture, although I get enough of those at school."

"I sure understand," Quinn said. "If you do come, you might meet Sean. He's a young man who attends the lectures now and then. I really like him. He's a musician and your age."

"Yeah, maybe." Briana didn't sound too interested in meeting a musician her age. Maggie quickly redirected the conversation back to the broken car. Briana excused herself while Maggie took Quinn to the garage.

Maggie flipped on the light and turned on the space heater she had ready for him. Quinn quickly checked the car over thoroughly and decided that the culprit was corroded spark plugs.

"This is an easy fix. I'm glad you didn't pay for towing and called me instead. I'll just head over to the auto parts store and be back in a flash."

In less than an hour, Quinn had returned, fixed the car, and had it running like a top. Quinn rubbed his dirty hands on a rag. "I replaced your filters, too. You should be good to go."

"Would you like a cup of tea before you go?" Maggie asked as they moved toward the dining area. "How can I ever repay you for tonight? I can't thank you enough, Quinn."

Quinn nodded and sat at the table. "No payment needed, but I would like to talk to you about something."

Maggie smiled and put on the kettle. After pouring the tea, the two sat face-to-face. Quinn took a sip of his tea and began. "I've been looking for an assistant for awhile now, but I just haven't found the right person. On the way to the parts store, I got to thinking that maybe you'd be interested in applying for the position."

Maggie sucked in her breath and tilted her ear toward him but said nothing. He continued. "I know you have another job besides the one at Anna's Antiques, and you might be happy where you are and not interested. But you're the kind of person I'm looking for—interested in Irish things, a believer, and, well, nice." Quinn lowered his eyes, seemingly lost for words.

After finding her tongue, Maggie thanked him for the offer and asked a lot of questions about the job. He, in turn, asked lots of questions about her. Before they knew it, the time was nearing 11 p.m., but she felt as though they'd been talking for mere minutes.

"I'll sure think about it, Quinn, and, more importantly, pray about it," Maggie said as he got ready to leave. "Thank you for the offer. This has been quite an evening!"

"For me, too!" Quinn smiled and then awkwardly shook her hand, holding it a little longer than normal. "It'll be interesting to see what happens."

After Quinn left, Maggie sat on her bed, pondering all that had transpired that night. *Another job offer without even seeking it, and a full-time one with benefits and comparable money to what I'm making now juggling two jobs? But what about the fact that I'd have to work Monday through Friday, and I'd only be able to work with Anna on Saturdays? Give me wisdom, please, Lord!*

She tossed and turned that night wondering what to do. The next day she talked with her mom, with Bree, and with Anna. All three had agreed that this was a move she should make, and she felt strongly that this was best for her and Briana.

Though she would miss her colleagues at her current job, she was ready for something different. Quinn and his interesting shop might just be the adventure she needed, and it would provide for her and Bree.

That evening, Maggie knew.

The following day she called Quinn and accepted the offer.

"That's great, Maggie!" Quinn's tone of voice and the speed of his words affirmed that he was pleased. "When would you like to start?"

She glanced at the wall calendar. "Would after the New Year be okay? I need to give the company time to find my replacement, and Mom is coming next week to be with us through the holiday season."

"That'd be just fine, and I'd love to meet your mom. Please stop by the store."

"Oh, we will. Thanks, Quinn." Maggie hung up the phone. She paced the floor, her mind racing. Bree was still sleeping. Maggie put on her tennis shoes, hat, gloves, and coat, smiling at the warm December Saturday and her plan to have a nice, long jog.

This is a Saturday I'll not soon forget. I used to hate change, but this one seems good, right. And working with Quinn? What will the future hold, I wonder? As she ran, she thought about the many possibilities for her future, and to be honest, she thought mostly about Quinn.

* * *

The week before Christmas, Maggie said final goodbyes to her colleagues and her job. Then she headed to the airport to pick up her mom and head home, knowing it was Briana's last day at school and she'd be waiting for them.

"I guess we're celebrating more than Christmas," Elizabeth said as Maggie drove, "with a new job to boot!"

"Yes, and I'm done with my old job. We can do whatever we want," she replied.

"No skiing, skating, or sledding, please," her mom teased.

"How about going to the Broadmoor and seeing the wonderful gingerbread house display? This year it's supposed to be famous international buildings."

Elizabeth nodded. "And how about Christmas movies, buttery popcorn, and hot cocoa?"

"Yes!" she agreed, then added, "I don't have money to shop, but how about window shopping? And there are several church nativity pageants and one is outside with real animals."

"And we must make our traditional Christmas cookies together with Bree. She always loves that and so I do, too."

"I do too, Mom. Count me in."

The two made plans all the way home, bantering back and forth, laughing, and enjoying each other's company. When they got home, Briana greeted them at the door, helped with the bags, and hugged her grandmother tightly. "I'm glad you're here, Nana! I love you! I finished my exams and can hang with you two—most of the time."

Maggie and her mom laughed, and Maggie added, "Be sure to spend a little time with your friends, too, Bree."

Over dinner that night, Maggie got out the calendar and filled it with fun holiday plans as her mother and daughter rattled them off. It would be a happy holiday after all.

The next day, Maggie took Briana and her mom to both Anna's Antiques and The Irish Shop. She had already made plans for them all to have lunch with Anna and then go to Quinn's.

At the antique shop, there were so many shoppers that she and Bree both jumped in to help while Elizabeth happily browsed the store. Finally the crowd dispersed, Anna locked the shop for her lunch reprieve, and the four women enjoyed a Christmas-y visit. Anna, of course, had a table in the back set with Christmas dishes.

"I thought the table was just for display," Elizabeth said.

Anna shook her head. "It's for our Christmas luncheon. Now if you three would help me carry out the lunch, it's just in the back. I've made Irish stew with all the fixin's and fig pudding for dessert."

After a wonderful lunch and nice visit, the three hugged Anna and wished her a safe trip to her son's. Then Anna gave each of them a Christmas gift bag. "To put under your tree. No peeking until December twenty-fifth!"

Maggie thanked her and the others did too. After another round of goodbye hugs, the three headed to the Irish Shop.

Upon opening the Irish Shop door, Maggie immediately smelled hot cider and cinnamon. Soft Irish Christmas music played, but the sound of several customers told her Quinn was busy.

But Quinn made sure to greet them and Maggie introduced her mother. Then she showed Elizabeth and Bree around the store. Over in the corner where the lectures were held, a table with hot cider and Christmas cookies drew Bree to taste and enjoy. "These aren't packaged cookies; they're homemade. Does Quinn cook, too?" Briana winked at her mother and smiled. "Nice!"

Maggie ignored her daughter's comment and poured a cup of cider for her mom and herself as Bree handed them each a cookie. While Quinn waited on customers, the three browsed the store, enjoyed the ambiance, and talked about the displays and interesting Irish items.

When the other customers left, Quinn approached them. "I'm sorry you've waited so long. Thanks for coming." Quinn turned to Elizabeth. "Especially you, Mrs. Graham. Would you three be interested in coming to dinner next week at my house? I'd love to cook an Irish holiday dinner for you."

Maggie looked at Bree, who bobbed her head up and down and smiled broadly. Then she looked at her mom, who winked impishly, and said, "Sure. We'd love to!"

Just then, four more customers came into the shop and Quinn apologetically shrugged his shoulders. "So sorry. I'll call you to schedule a time, okay, Maggie?"

She nodded, the three said goodbye, and left the store.

"They're both great places—and great people," Elizabeth

said. "I'm happy for you, Maggie."

"Me, too!" Briana agreed. "Those two places suit you much more than the grey cubicle you've been in."

"I agree." She laughed. *Family! What a gift they are!*

As Christmas approached, mother, daughter, and granddaughter spent lots of time together laughing and enjoying the Christmas season. They went to the Broadmoor, a five-star hotel, to see their annual display of gingerbread houses. They visited three Christmas concerts at local churches. The three ladies even went to the Cheyenne Mountain Zoo at night to enjoy the million-plus Christmas lights on display around the zoo.

But on the day before Christmas, Maggie knew something was up. For two days she had seen her mother and daughter whispering and giggling together, embarrassed whenever she caught them in the act.

"What's going on, you two?" she asked over breakfast. "Are you scheming again?"

"Don't ask questions at Christmastime," her mother scolded with a smile. "If I've told you once, I've told you a hundred times."

Maggie smiled, shrugged, and went into the kitchen to do dishes, leaving the schemers to do their work.

On Christmas morning, she woke up to the smell of coffee. She assumed her mother had woken early. With a yawn, she made her way to the living room to turn on the Christmas tree lights. Her eyes rounded at the sight of an extra-large green gift bag sitting on the floor in front of the tree.

"Surprise!" said Elizabeth and Briana together, popping their heads out of the kitchen.

She jumped. "You startled me! Are you trying to give me a heart attack?"

"Open it, Mom! Merry Christmas!" Briana said, rubbing her hands together.

"Ah, this is what all those whispers were about?" Maggie picked up the bag.

"Yup, and I'll tell you, it hasn't been easy to wait for this one!" her mom said. "Open it!"

"Okay, okay! And Merry Christmas to you two, too!"

Maggie pulled out the red and white tissue papers, one by one, and let them float to the floor, as dramatically as she could. Slowly, excruciatingly slowly. *Hah! They held me in suspense. Now it's my turn.*

Finally she got to the bottom of the big bag and found something wrapped in layers and layers of white tissue paper. "You two are making me work for this, aren't you?"

"Open it, Mom!" Briana hollered, her patience long gone.

Maggie tore off the tissue paper in one big rip and burst into tears. She looked at her mom and her daughter and they, too, burst into tears. She held her family's crazy quilt to her chest and wept, caressing the quilt like a newborn baby.

"I found it online, Mom!" Briana said. "Just last week. The quilt was in Wyoming with an eBay salesman! Can you believe it? Nana and I bought it for you."

"God knew where it was, Maggie. He knew all the time!" Elizabeth said, hugging her daughter.

"Thanks, Mom! Thanks, Bree! This is the best gift ever—more than I could ever have dreamed," Maggie beamed and then the tears began to flow as she hugged her mother and daughter. She wiped away her tears, looked toward heaven, and smiled. "This has been a challenging journey, but God has been faithful. I guess this just shows that His plans for our future are, indeed, good."

ABOUT THE AUTHOR

SUSAN IS A VERSATILE WRITER OF FIVE BOOKS, creating both fiction and non-fiction for adults and children. Her husband encouraged her to write the story you just read upon hearing about her own family's crazy quilt. After many years writing non-fiction, Susan's personal experiences growing up Irish as well as extensive research into her own family's history gave her the vision to carry out his challenge.

Before Susan jumped into the fiction world, her first two books were nonfiction, co-authored with her husband, Dale. *Countdown for Couples: Preparing for the Adventure of Marriage* and *The ReMarriage Adventure: Preparing for a Life of Love and Happiness* have helped thousands of couples getting ready to marry. Susan is also the author of her first two indie-published picture books, *Lexie's Adventure in Kenya: Love is Patient* and *Princess Madison's Rainbow Adventure*.

Susan is the Founding Editor of *Thriving Family* magazine and the former Editor/Editorial Director of twelve Focus on the Family publications including the *Focus on the Family* magazine and the *Focus on Your Child* newsletters.

Moreover, Susan is an author in various book compilations including *Chicken Soup for the Soul: The Spirit of America, Ready to Wed, Supporting Families Through Meaningful Ministry, The Christian Leadership Experience,* and *Spiritual Mentoring of Teens.* Susan has also written hundreds of magazine and newsletter articles on a variety of topics.

Susan is vice president of Christian Authors Network (CAN) and a member of American Christian Fiction Writers (ACFW), and the Society of Children's Book Writers and Illustrators (SCBWI). She is a national and international speaker at multiple writers conferences, workshops, and teacher conventions and has been a guest on a score of radio shows.

Susan lives in Colorado Springs and loves doing life with her husband, Dale. Susan has two adult children, three adult stepsons, one teenage step-granddaughter, and four adorable granddaughters. You can discover more at her website: www.SusanGMathis.com or connect with her via Facebook, Goodreads, Pinterest, and Twitter @SusanGMathis.

If you enjoyed this book, would you consider sharing the message with others? Write a review on Amazon. Mention the book in a Facebook post, Tweet, blog post, or other social media outlet. Recommend it to your friends, family, book club, library, small group, or wherever. Thanks so much!

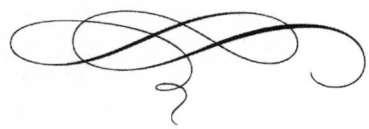

Made in the USA
Columbia, SC
06 August 2017